"Marti Green's look at the potential for abuse and corruption in the privatized, for-profit juvenile justice systems across America is taut, edifying, and, at times, terrifying. The thought that some of the terrible things described in this book really happened to youngsters charged with minor offenses made my skin crawl. This is an important novel as well as a top-notch thriller. I'd recommend it to anyone."

-Scott Pratt, bestselling author of *Justice Redeemed,*
on *First Offense*

Unintended Consequences is an engrossing, well-conceived legal thriller. Most enjoyable."

-Scott Turow, New York times best-selling author of
Presumed Innocent

"This one will grab you by the neck from the very first page."
-Steve Hamilton, Edgar Award-winning author of *Die a Stranger,* on *Unintended Consequences*

"A wonderfully clever plot, intriguing characters, and twists at every single turn—*The Good Twin* is better than good…it's a great read!"

—James Hankins, bestselling author of *The Prettiest One*
on *The Good Twin*

BURNING JUSTICE

OTHER TITLES BY MARTI GREEN

Help Innocent Prisoners Project Series

Unintended Consequences
Presumption of Guilt
The Price of Justice
First Offense
Justice Delayed

The Good Twin

BURNING JUSTICE

JUSTICE

MARTI GREEN

Yankee Clipper Press

Published by Yankee Clipper Press, Florida

ISBN –13: 978-0-9881980-4-3

ISBN – 13: 978-0-9881980-5-0

Cover design by Creativindie

Printed in the United States of America

Dedicated to my father, Simon Silverman
My mother, Ruth Silverman
And my sister, Judith Greenfield
You all have a place in my heart no one else can fill
You are dearly missed

1998

Becky Whitlaw sat in the old rocking chair, its white paint peeling, slowly moving back and forth. *The front porch needs painting, too*, she thought, staring down at the wide planks lit only by the full moon. The chirping of cicadas broke the silence surrounding her. Inside, her three children were fast asleep— four-year-old Benji, two-and-a-half-year-old Danny, and the baby, sweet Lacy, just ten months yesterday. Becky was twenty-three years old and felt like eighty. Once, the boys all thought she was the prettiest girl in school. Now, when she passed by a mirror, she was shocked to see how haggard she looked. Her formerly blond hair had turned a mousy brown and hung limply to her shoulders; her green eyes that once sparkled like emeralds when she flirted with a boy now looked lifeless.

She picked up a bottle of Real Ale's Devil's Backbone from the floor of the porch and took a swig. She frowned as it went down—despite the night chill, the beer was already starting to turn warm. She preferred it icy cold. Moments later, she saw the headlights of a car enter the long, gravel driveway to her house.

When it reached the end, the door opened, and a woman stepped out, dressed in a warm parka over flannel pajamas.

"Jesus," the woman said as she walked up the porch steps. "It's freezing out here. Can't we go inside?"

Becky shook her head, then handed her friend a beer as she sat down in the second rocker.

"What was so important that you dragged me out of bed?" Marci Brand asked.

"I just needed company, that's all."

Marci looked over at her. "You okay?"

Becky's eyes misted up, and soon tears began to roll down her cheeks. "Today's our anniversary." She paused, unable to speak. Finally, she said, "I just miss him so much."

Marci leaned over and picked up Becky's hand. "Of course you do, honey. It's only been nine months."

It still seemed impossible to Becky that Grady was dead. They'd been together since her sophomore year in high school and married as soon as she'd graduated. The accident was her fault. If she hadn't sent Grady to the all-night drugstore for baby aspirin, knowing how tired he was, knowing how exhausted they both were from sleep-deprived nights with a new baby, knowing how slippery the roads were from the drenching rain, he wouldn't have driven off the road and down the embankment. Instead, it would be Grady on the porch with her now, strumming his guitar and singing a country ballad, not Marci, looking at her with a face full of pity.

"The kids giving you a hard time?"

Becky shrugged. "They're kids. They can't help it." Becky knew that wasn't true. If she were a better mother, she would be able to control them. She wouldn't scream at their incessant whining, their battles with each other over the television and their toys. She wouldn't look at them and think how much easier her life would be if they hadn't been born. If she were free, she could go to college, have a career. Not be stuck in a dead-end waitress job, wishing it was she who had died.

"You want me to sleep over tonight?"

"No. Just stay with me a little longer."

And so, Marci did. She stayed until they'd finished the six-pack, and Becky sent her off. "I'll be fine now," Becky said as she walked Marci to her car.

After she watched the taillights recede, the car kicking up dust in its wake, a wave of loneliness washed over Becky, and once again, tears washed down her cheeks. She wiped them away as she walked back into the house, angry at herself for not being stronger. She stepped inside and looked around. The small ranch home was filled with secondhand furniture, once presentable but now falling apart from her children's abuse. Toys littered the living room floor, but she felt too tired to pick them up. *Tomorrow*, she thought. But she knew tomorrow, they'd just mess them up again. She hated her waitress job, working from five to midnight, but at least it got her out of the house, away from the constant noise. Some weeks, it paid barely enough to cover the babysitter.

She glanced down the hallway toward her bedroom. It was past two in the morning, and the baby would awake by six-thirty. She needed to get some sleep. Still, maybe one more beer would be okay. She was still too wound up. It would help her fall asleep.

She opened the refrigerator door and muttered, "Shit." No beer. She hesitated only a moment, then pulled out the freezer drawer and removed the bottle of vodka. She reached for a glass and poured an inch into it, stopped, then poured another two. She headed into the living room, then settled back into the couch and turned on the television.

The smell of smoke woke Jake Johnson. Even in winter, he always slept with the window open, at least a little, and his nostrils twitched from the odor. He glanced at the clock on his nightstand, saw it was six-eighteen, then lifted himself from the bed, careful not to wake Maddie, his wife going on forty-two years. He went to the front door, and when he opened it, saw clear through the dawn that Becky Whitlaw's house was on fire. He turned and ran back to his bedroom.

"Call 911!" he shouted to his sleeping wife as he slipped on his pants.

Maddie's eyes shot open. "What? What's happening?"

"Becky's house is on fire. I'm heading over there."

Johnson slipped on his shoes and bolted out of his house. There was a good three hundred feet between his home and his neighbor's, but he reached the front porch in seconds. Becky stood there, her face blank, her clothes covered with ash, her bare feet bleeding from cuts. Reddish-orange flames were visible through the windows.

Johnson took Becky by the shoulders and turned her to him. The roar of the flames forced him to shout. "Where are the children?"

Becky dropped to her knees, covered her face with her hands, and began wailing. "My babies! My babies . . . they're inside. My babies!"

Suddenly, she sprung up and ran toward the front door.

Johnson sprinted after her and pulled her back. The intense heat was almost suffocating. "You can't go in there. Maddie's called the fire department. They'll be here any minute."

Becky twisted away from him, ran down the steps to the yard, and picked up a rock. She ran to the end of the porch, then threw it into the bedroom her children shared. Instantly, flames burst through the window with a loud whoosh. Once again, she fell to the ground and sobbed.

The black smoke made it hard for Johnson to breathe. He lifted Becky from the ground and pulled her away, just as he heard the sirens blaring from fire engines. Moments later, two fire trucks pulled into her driveway. Three firefighters jumped out and began uncoiling the hoses while one firefighter, equipped with an air tank and a mask covering his face, heavy gloves on his hands, opened the front door, then disappeared into the black smoke. Minutes later, he exited, holding in his arms Lacy's lifeless body.

Johnson held Becky in his arms as she cried into his chest. "It's my fault. It's my fault," she repeated between sobs.

"What do you mean?"

She pulled away from him, looked over toward her dead daughter, then back at her burning house, and just stared.

Irving Howe and Sam Miner entered the burned remains of the Whitlaw house. Howe was the fire chief of Glen Brook, Texas, population 3,213, three less than it had been two days earlier, before Benjamin, Daniel and Lacy Whitlaw died in the fire that had barreled through their home. He'd spent more than twenty years battling fires. Miner, a fire captain in Fort Worth, was known as one of the best fire investigators in the state.

Together, the men moved through each room, collecting samples of burned objects and taking photographs. The lab results later confirmed what the two men already suspected: this fire had been deliberately set.

Sheriff Mike Duncan knocked on Sarabeth Travers's front door and waited patiently for his knock to be answered. Becky had been staying with her mother ever since the fire ten days earlier—that is, since she'd been released from the hospital. She was in shock, the doctors had said. The few burns on her weren't serious, but they worried over her mental state. Still, they gave her some pills and sent her packing after one night's stay. Duncan had already questioned Becky once, after the fire investigators had been to her house but before their report had been complete. Now, he was here for a different purpose.

The door opened, and Sarabeth gave him a thin smile. They'd known each other since grade school. Heck, everybody in Glen Brook knew everyone else. It was that kind of town.

Duncan bent his head and stepped inside. Despite his six-four frame, he didn't really need to stoop when going through a door; somehow, he'd just gotten in the habit and couldn't seem to break it. "Becky here?"

"She's in bed. Hasn't moved from there ever since she got here. Except when you came to question her. Got some more things to ask?"

"Something like that. Can you get her?"

Sarabeth disappeared down the hallway, then five minutes later came back with her daughter. Becky's long hair was disheveled, and she was dressed in sweatpants and a baggy sweatshirt.

Duncan reached into his back pocket and pulled out a set of handcuffs. "Rebecca Whitlaw, you're under arrest for arson and the murder of your three children. I've got to take you over to the jailhouse now."

Sarabeth reached over and touched Duncan's arm. "Mike, you don't mean that," she said, her eyes silently pleading with him.

"I'm afraid I do."

Becky stood still, silent, as tears streamed down her cheeks.

Duncan lifted her hands, snapped on the cuffs, then gently moved her toward the door. "You better call a lawyer," he said to Sarabeth as he left. "She's gonna need a good one."

Becky was alone in her cell, even though it was large enough to hold more people. Duncan had driven her to the county jail, not the one in town. The single holding pen behind the sheriff's office was used mostly to sober up drunks who'd gotten out of hand at one of the local bars, or someone who'd tried to drive home when he should have known better.

She stared down at her hands, still shaking, as they had ever since the fire. Sounds of her children's cries flooded her mind, despite her efforts to shut them out, to turn back the clock, to pretend that they all were still alive, clamoring for her to make chocolate chip pancakes for their breakfast. It didn't matter if she were in a jail or at home—her life was over. Not even Grady's death had compared to the crater-size stone lodged in her chest. Prison didn't matter. Nothing mattered anymore.

Tim Willoughby wasn't surprised when he received the call from Sarabeth Travers. After all, he was the only criminal defense attorney in Glen Brook. Becky's case, of course, would be tried in the county seat, and plenty of lawyers defended criminal cases there, but when your daughter was facing a murder charge, you wanted someone you could trust. And Willoughby had known Sarabeth for two decades. Even dated her a bit after her husband passed away, but they were better suited as friends.

"They think Becky set that fire on purpose," Sarabeth said. "She'd never do something like that. Can you get her out of jail?"

"I doubt any attorney can get her out before the trial. Judges tend not to grant bail when the charge is murder."

"Becky loved those kids! You know she's not capable of harming them."

"I agree with you, but they must have their reasons for thinking otherwise."

"Can you represent her, Tim? I don't have a lot of money, but I'll figure out a way to pay you."

"Are you sure you don't want bigger guns for Becky?"

"I want you. I want someone who knows her. Who knows she's innocent."

Willoughby hesitated. He felt fairly certain the prosecution would ask for the death penalty. After all, three children had died. He'd handled only one other death penalty case in his thirty years of practicing law, and that hadn't ended well for his client. Still, maybe he could work out a plea for Becky. Her husband so recently dead, trying to raise those kids all on her own, holding down a job. Surely, a jury would sympathize with her plight. The DA would know that. Get death off the table, then whittle down the number of years. Maybe top out at fifteen, she could be out in twelve. She'd still be young. Could start over.

"I'll do it," he said, then immediately hoped he wasn't making a mistake.

Two hours later, Tim Willoughby approached Becky's cell. She thought at first he was a detective, then slowly realized she'd seen his face before.

When the guard unlocked the door and let him inside, she asked, "Did my mother send you?"

"Yes. I'm an attorney. She asked me to represent you."

"I don't have any money."

"Your mother is taking care of that."

Becky hung her head. How had her life devolved to this—sitting in a jail cell, her husband and children dead, her mother paying her bills? Once, she'd dreamed big. Getting out of Glen Brook, going to college, becoming a nurse, maybe even a doctor. She'd always done well in school. Then, she got pregnant, and everything changed. She hadn't minded giving up her dreams, because she loved Grady with a fierceness she hadn't thought possible. Over time, though, the shiver that ran down her spine when Grady brushed his hand against her cheek slowly lost its spark, replaced by the dullness of every day. Waking up at the crack of dawn with the first cries of her children, changing diapers, cooking meals, picking up toys, dusting and vacuuming and scrubbing floors. Now and then, a darkness would descend over her, and she'd hate being home. Hate Grady for quashing her dreams. When she felt bleakest, one of her children—most often Danny, because he was never afraid to show his heart—would come over to her, wrap his arms around her neck, then whisper, "Don't be sad, Mommy. I love you." And always, at that moment, she felt like the luckiest woman in the world. Because, at that moment, she knew how much she loved Grady, how much she loved her children, how her dreams of college and whatever else would have happened meant nothing compared with her love for her family.

Now, they were all gone, and nothing mattered anymore.

"I have to be honest with you," Willoughby said. "It doesn't look good."

Becky stared at his kind face. She remembered him from when he took out her mother. She'd always thought him dashing, with the sprinkles of gray in his hair and the perfect posture of his trim body. He'd put on some pounds since then, and the hair was mostly gray, but his eyes still emanated warmth.

"It doesn't matter. Everything's gone." Her voice was a hollow shell, devoid of timbre.

"You don't understand. I've spoken to the DA. They're going to seek the death penalty."

Becky hung her head, then whispered, "Good. Then the pain will stop."

"Are you telling me you did this? That you set the fire on purpose?"

Slowly, Becky lifted her head, then spoke with a deliberateness in her voice. "I'm telling you I don't care if I die. At least then, I'll be with my family."

Willoughby took her hand in his. "You're depressed. It's understandable. I'll see if I can get some medication for you."

"No! I don't want medicine. I don't want a lawyer. I want to die. That's all. I want to die."

The trial was delayed for a year while Becky languished in a psychiatric facility, waiting for the medication and therapy to lift her depression, waiting for her to be able to take part in her defense. Once she emerged from the fog that had filled her head for so long, Willoughby told her that a plea bargain had been offered—twenty years to life, death taken off the table. With good behavior, she could be out in fifteen.

"I don't think anyone can get you a better deal," he told her. "I go back a long way with the DA. I know when he won't budge."

"Will I have to say I set the fire?" she asked. "That I meant to kill my children?"

"Yes."

"Then I want to go to trial."

"It doesn't matter if it's true or not. But the judge can't sentence you if you don't admit guilt. It . . . it's sort of like a game, and those are the rules."

Becky wrapped her arms tightly around her body. "Everyone will think I'm a monster."

"You'll be alive. You can leave Glen Brook. Go anywhere you want, and start over."

She shook her head. "My friends will know what I said."

"So, you'll tell them you had to. They'll understand."

Becky looked straight into Willoughby's eyes and straightened her back. She knew if she stood up in court and said, "I killed my children," people would always wonder if it was true, no matter what she said later. "No. I can't."

Every day for a week, Willoughby came by the hospital and tried to convince her to take the plea bargain. Every day for a week, she said, "No." Finally, Willoughby stopped asking.

Three weeks later, she was in court, facing twelve men and women who would decide her fate.

The trial lasted all of two days. Lindsey Hancock, the assistant district attorney assigned to prosecute Rebecca Whitlaw, wasted no time. As soon as the jury was picked and opening statements finished, she called Irving Howe, who described the fire at Becky's house and all he and his crew had done to put it out. While he was on the stand, she introduced pictures of Becky's home before the blaze and the devastation after it had been extinguished.

Next, she called Jared Miller, the county's medical examiner, to the stand. Dr. Miller's half-hour testimony boiled down to this: William, Daniel, and Lacy Whitlaw died of asphyxiation from the smoke that filled the bedroom they shared. The smoke came from the red-hot blaze that swept through the house. By the time the fire burned their small bodies, they were already dead. Willoughby asked no questions of him.

Next to the stand was Sam Miner. Hancock ran through his credentials, then asked, "Did there come a time when you investigated the fire that took place in the defendant's home?"

"Yes, two days after the blaze."

"And based on your investigation, did you determine the cause of the fire?"

"Yes. It was deliberately set."

"Based upon what factors did you reach that conclusion?"

"First, we made our way through the house. There was a distinct burn trail that started from the children's bedroom, into the corridor, and then directly to the front door. In the children's bedroom, we saw char patterns on the floor, what we call 'puddle configurations,' which occur only when a liquid accelerant is used. And the windows in that room had what's known as 'crazed glass,' kind of looks like a spiderweb, and that also is an indicator of an accelerant being used."

"Did you notice anything else in the children's bedroom?"

"Yes. Flames burn upward. But the floor there had the deepest burns, showing that it had been hotter than the ceiling, and that's not what a normal fire would show. That happens only when a combustible liquid is poured on the floor."

"Were there any other indications that the fire had been deliberately set?"

"We also found char patterns in the hallway, leading to the front door. We looked at the soot marks on the walls. We try to find marks that form a V, because that can point to where the fire began. In the defendant's house, we found three such marks—in the children's bedroom, the hallway outside it, and by the front door. When a fire has an origin in three different places, it can only mean that it didn't happen accidently. Add to that the intensity of the fire. It melted the aluminum around the windows. A fire needs to reach twelve hundred degrees Fahrenheit for aluminum to melt, and that just doesn't happen unless an accelerant was used."

"Did you have a lab test any of the burned items in the house?"

"I did."

"Any what were the findings?"

"There was a positive test for mineral spirits by the front door. A person had poured an accelerant there."

"Did the lab identify the type of mineral spirits?"

"No. They weren't able to distinguish what kind."

"Did you find anything in the Whitlaw house that could have been the accelerant used in the fire?"

"Yes. In the garage, we found a near-empty gallon jug of turpentine. That's a common accelerant used in cases of arson."

"Thank you. I have no further questions."

Willoughby's cross-examination lasted only a few minutes. "Did any of the laboratory tests identify turpentine specifically?"

Miner shifted in his seat. "No."

"Did the tests of burned objects anywhere else in the house positively identify a mineral spirit?"

"No. Probably because it was burned away."

"Isn't it true that you can't say with one hundred percent certainty that the fire was deliberately set?" he asked.

"I can say that in the over three hundred fires I've investigated, this was one of the clearest cases of arson."

"You didn't answer my question. Are you one hundred percent certain?"

Miner leaned forward in his seat. "Every fire tells a story. The fire doesn't lie. It tells me the truth about what happened. Everything about this fire told me it didn't happen by accident. Am I one hundred percent certain?" He turned toward the jury. "I am. A hundred percent."

"Were you one hundred percent certain when you testified at James Compton's trial that he deliberately set fire to his store?"

Miner shifted in his seat. "That was a long time ago. I don't really recall now what I thought then."

Willoughby walked back to the defendant's table and picked up several sheets of paper, then handed one page to Miner. "Maybe this can help you remember."

Hancock stood up. "What are you handing the witness?"

"It's Mr. Miner's testimony in Compton's trial." He handed a copy to Hancock and another to the judge, then turned back to Miner. "Would you read the highlighted portion, please?"

Miner glanced down at the page, and his cheeks reddened.

"Go ahead," Willoughby prompted.

"'Are you certain the fire was deliberately set? Yes, sir, I am. One hundred percent.'"

A faint smile appeared on Willoughby's face, then quickly disappeared. "Do you now remember you were one hundred percent certain that the Compton fire was the result of arson?"

"Yes," he answered, his head down and his voice low.

"Are you aware that Compton's conviction was overturned? That he was exonerated?"

Miner lifted his head. "I believe it was overturned for reasons unrelated to my conclusions. And fire science has improved considerably since then. I stand by my conclusion in this case. The fire that burned down the defendant's house was deliberately set."

Willoughby hesitated, as though thinking about whether to ask another question, but then just mumbled, "Nothing more," and returned to his seat.

The next person to take the stand was Susan Granger. Becky wondered who this thin woman with cropped, stringy hair and sunken eyes could be. When she began to testify that she'd shared a cell with Becky right after Becky's arrest, Becky had only a vague recollection of her.

"How many nights were you in the same cell as the defendant?" Hancock asked.

"About a week. The first night she didn't talk much, but the next day she didn't stop. Kept saying she'd started the fire 'cause she couldn't bear to go on any longer."

Becky grabbed Willoughby's arm and whispered, "She's lying. I never said any such thing."

When Hancock finished with Granger, Willoughby asked, "What were you in the jail for?"

"Selling drugs."

"Did the prosecutor promise he'd do anything for you if you said Ms. Whitlaw had confessed to you?"

"No, sir. Never promised me a thing."

"Were you convicted of selling drugs?"

"I'm still in jail, ain't I?"

"That doesn't answer my question."

She shifted in her seat, then said, "My trial's coming up soon."

"It's been over a year, and you haven't had a trial yet?"

"Yeah, well, my lawyer asked for some delays. You'll have to ask him why."

Willoughby asked her a few more questions, all designed to poke holes in her testimony, but she held fast to it.

Hancock next called Marci Brand, who told the jury that Becky had been drinking the night of the fire, that she'd seemed depressed, and that sometimes, not always, she'd seemed overwhelmed by her children. Tears rolled down Becky's cheeks as her best friend testified against her, even though she knew she shouldn't cry, not in front of the jury.

Hancock's last witness was Jake Johnson, Becky's neighbor. "Tell the jury what you saw when you got to the defendant's house," Hancock said.

"Becky was just standing there, staring at the flames. Stock still, not a tear in her eye. She didn't start crying until I stepped onto her porch."

"Would you say she looked upset?"

"No. It almost seemed like she'd waited for someone to show up before showing any emotion."

"Did the defendant say anything to you when she saw her daughter was dead?"

Willoughby called out, "Objection, hearsay."

Hancock turned to the judge. "Anything the defendant said at that time was clearly an excited utterance and so an exception to the rule."

"I'll allow it."

Hancock turned back to Johnson. "You may answer."

"She said, 'It's my fault.' Twice."

"Thank you." Hancock turned and walked back to her seat.

Willoughby stood and approached the witness. Becky heard him ask questions and heard Johnson answer, but their words just blurred together. She already knew how the jurors would decide. It's how she would rule if she'd been sitting in the jury box, listening to the testimony.

By the middle of the next day, her fears were confirmed. The jury was out for less than one hour. When they returned to the jury box, none would look in Becky's direction.

"Have you reached a unanimous verdict?" the judge asked.

"We have," answered the foreman.

The bailiff took a folded paper from the foreman's hand and brought it to the judge. He opened it, then asked Becky to stand. She stood, Willoughby standing at her side, as the foreman read off each charge: one for arson, and three for the death of each of her children.

"Guilty," he said four times.

The penalty phase began the next morning. Willoughby put on the stand Becky's mother, her employer, two teachers from high school. Even Marci, now testifying to save Becky's life. When there were no more witnesses, the jury retired once again. This time, it took two hours before they returned to the courtroom.

Again, Becky stood as the judge asked the foreman, "Is there a probability that Rebecca Whitlaw would commit criminal acts of violence that would constitute a continuing threat to society?"

"The answer is yes"

"Did Rebecca Whitlaw actually take the life of her children, intend to kill her children, or anticipate that a human life would be taken?"

"Yes."

"Taking into consideration all of the evidence and circumstances, the defendant's character and background, and the personal moral culpability of the defendant, are there sufficient mitigating circumstances to warrant that a sentence of life in prison without parole be imposed rather than a death sentence?"

The foreman looked over at Becky, then turned back to the judge. With a clear voice, he answered, "No."

Sarabeth's sobs almost drowned out the judge's next words. "Rebecca Whitlaw, I hereby sentence you to death by lethal injection."

2018

Dani Trumball looked over her living room one last time to ensure everything was in place. It was the first time she and Doug were entertaining since they'd moved to Stanford, California, two months ago.

After packing up two decades worth of furniture and memories, they'd decided to put some space between leaving their old home and moving into the new one. They had rented a thirty-four-foot-long Thor motor home and spent three weeks traveling across the country. Their cat, Gracie, wasn't too happy about it, but the rest of the family loved seeing America. Their first stop had been Cedar Point, the huge amusement park in Sandusky, Ohio. Doug and Jonah rode every roller coaster, even those that frightened Dani just looking at them from the sidelines. They spent a day in the water park and made sure to stop by the barnyard petting zoo, where Ruth Emma got close to camels, cows, emus, and alpacas. After two full days, they were back on the road, passing through Chicago for an evening, then continued nonstop to South Dakota. Dani had never seen Mount Rushmore, and as the family stood gaping at the giant stone carvings, Jonah gave a running commentary on each of the presidents profiled in stone. They camped in Custer State Park and spotted bison and buffalo, also a first for Dani. At Yellowstone, they joined the hordes and watched Old Faithful erupt. They took the scenic drives through Zion and Bryce Canyon national parks and viewed the Grand Canyon from the North Rim. It was an exhilarating trip and took a little bit of the sting out of leaving New York.

Their new home, a stately Colonial with large lawn and tall oak trees, was so different from the house they'd lived in for almost twenty years, back in Bronxville. She missed that home, even though it was smaller and older, with cracks that needed spackling constantly appearing in the walls and only a tiny backyard. Still, even though she'd balked when Doug had been offered the position of dean of Stanford Law School, it had been the right decision for him to accept the job. And it was right for the family to follow him there. He was so clearly happy in his new position.

Now that their first party was upon them, Dani wasn't sure she was quite as happy. *Just breathe*, she told herself, *and stay busy*. She'd tucked Jonah into bed and Ruthie into her crib just a few minutes earlier, after going through the ritual of reading each of them a book. Jonah, already fifteen, still asked to be read to occasionally. Maybe because of his Williams syndrome, or perhaps just because it was time he had her all to himself. Now, her guests were due to arrive in ten minutes.

She went into the kitchen, with its soapstone countertops and stainless-steel appliances, its rich mahogany-colored wood floors and track lighting. They never would have been able to afford this four-bedroom house were it not for a restrictive covenant that made it available only to faculty of the university. Even with that, it was still a stretch for them. Dani had wanted to hold on to their Bronxville home, just rent it out, in case the move didn't work out for the family. But Silicon Valley home prices, whether for sale or for rent, were astronomical, and they couldn't afford anything they liked without selling their old home. From the first time she'd seen this house, she'd loved it, and so she had agreed to cut her ties to New York. Not completely, though. She still was the senior attorney at the Help Innocent Prisoners Project, affectionately called HIPP, headquartered in the East Village area of Manhattan. Except now, she telecommuted.

"We all set?" Dani asked Elsa, as she surveyed the platters of hors d'oeuvres set out on the counter.

"Everything is good."

Dani's first task after settling on a house was finding a nanny for almost two-year-old Ruth. Back in New York, Katie had been the one to watch Jonah in the afternoons when he came home from school. After Ruth was born, Katie expanded her hours to full-time. Occasionally, Katie prepared a meal for Dani or Doug to pop in the oven when they got home. Over the years, she'd become like family, and Dani had had grave reservations that they'd ever find someone as good on the West Coast. She'd interviewed half a dozen women when Elsa walked in, and Dani immediately knew she was the one. Like Jenny Slenku, the nanny who'd cared for Dani when she was a child, Elsa had been born in Romania, coming to the United States when she was in her early twenties. Now, more than twenty years later, she still spoke with the vestiges of her Romanian accent. She even looked like Jenny. The same warm smile and twinkling eyes, her brown hair worn the same way, pulled back into a bun.

Elsa had agreed to work late that night to help Dani prepare for her first party. The kitchen was filled with the savory odors of appetizers she'd prepared—plum dumplings, bite-size

Romanian meatballs, a roasted eggplant-and-pepper spread. As Elsa bent over to pull a tray out from the oven, Dani said, "Mm, smells delicious. What is that?"

"*Langosi cu branza*—fried dough with feta cheese."

"Yummy."

Dani began to bring the trays of food into the living room while Doug set up a bar on top of the table in the L-shaped dining room. Just as they finished, the doorbell rang, and the guests began to arrive.

"What a lovely home," Ann Hutchins said as she entered the living room. Three other people followed her into the house. One handed Dani a bouquet of wildflowers, another a bottle of wine. Dani thanked them, then left them in the living room with Doug as she went to find a vase. As she filled it with water, the doorbell kept ringing as more guests arrived. Dani placed the flowers in the vase, set it in the center of the dining table, then rejoined her guests.

"How are you enjoying it here at Stanford?" one asked.

"I'm getting used to it. It's so different from Manhattan."

"In a good way, I hope. Personally, I can't stand the noise of Manhattan. And the rudeness of people there, always rushing with their heads down."

"I guess it's what you're used to," Dani said. "To me, Manhattan feels alive."

"And Stanford is dead?"

Dani blushed. "No, that's not what I mean. Stanford is lovely. Just different."

When Lauren and Gregory Stephens arrived fifteen minutes later, Dani felt relief. She'd been ill-at-ease at her own party, acting as hostess to Doug's colleagues, most of whom she'd met only briefly at a university cocktail party early in the fall semester. She'd met Lauren and Gregory at that same party and had immediately been drawn to Lauren when Doug introduced them. Despite Lauren being ten years Dani's junior, they'd gone out for lunch several times since then, and Dani considered Lauren her first friend in Stanford.

"This is my brother, Chuck Stanger," Lauren said as she stepped inside the house. "Thanks so much for including him."

"Happy to," Dani said as she shook his hand.

Dani led them into the living room, then pointed them to the drinks. "It's self-serve."

She moved from cluster to cluster of people, putting on a bright smile, trying to be a good hostess, hoping to get to know Doug's colleagues better, all the while silently waiting for enough time to pass so she could just plop down on the sofa and relax. The courtroom was her milieu, not parties. She was never at a loss for words arguing a motion, yet usually struggled to make small talk with acquaintances.

Finally, after an hour, she made her way to the den. Chuck's tall, slim body was scrunched up on the sofa, and he looked just as uncomfortable as Dani had been. She sat down next to him. "Lauren told me you're here on vacation."

He immediately brightened, seemingly relieved that someone had engaged him. "That's right. I live in Dallas and don't get away very often. I had a few days off and thought I'd visit my little sister."

"What do you do?"

"I'm a pediatric cardiac surgeon."

As stressful as Dani's job often was, his must be much worse, she thought. They had something in common, though—the lives of others were often dependent on their skills. "Had you always planned on that specialty?"

"From the time I was young, I was drawn to surgery. I don't know why, but the idea of it always fascinated me. It was when I was doing my internship that I turned to pediatric surgery."

Dani waited for him to continue.

"I was doing a rotation in obstetrics, attending a mother who was in her early forties. She'd had three previous miscarriages and two stillbirths. She'd been trying to have a child since she was in her twenties. When I delivered the baby, he was blue and breathing with difficulty. The two major arteries from his heart were transposed. A pediatric surgeon was called in and operated the next day, and the baby survived. I thought if I could save someone who had his whole life ahead of him—well, I couldn't imagine anything that would be more fulfilling. And it has been."

"How lucky for you. How lucky for the children you treat."

"I understand you work for an innocence project," Chuck said. "That it's a calling for you, like medicine is for me."

"Yes."

"Would you mind a little shop talk?"

Dani looked into the living room. Everyone seemed engaged, Elsa had kept the food refreshed, and a quick glance toward the dining room showed her the drinks hadn't run low. "Sure." She led him to the kitchen, empty except for Elsa, and they sat down.

"I belong to an anti-death-penalty advocacy group," Chuck began. "Citizens Against State Imposed Death. Mostly, I just contribute money, but I read the blogs on their website when I get a chance. About six years ago, someone who'd been exonerated after eighteen years on death row wrote a piece about what life is like there. I guess you're used to it, but it was devastating to read about."

Dani shook her head. "It's not something I ever get used to."

He nodded, then continued. "The guy finished by asking people to pick someone on death row and correspond with them. Whether they'd admitted their guilt or claimed they were innocent, they needed something to sustain them in their isolation. The website listed the names of people on death row in every state, the crime they'd been convicted of, and how long they'd been incarcerated. I decided to write to one in Texas. A woman."

"What was she convicted for?"

"Murder by arson. They say she purposely set her house on fire to kill her three children."

Dani felt her chest tighten. She'd taken other cases that had involved the death of a child, and inevitably, it tore her apart. Any murder was tragic, but the murder of a child, much less three children, was horrendous. "You think she's innocent?"

"I didn't at first. I picked her because of the children. I see mothers all the time who are devastated by their child's condition. They would give their own life if it would save their child's. I didn't understand a woman who would do what they said she did. Unless she was crazy, of course. But her attorney didn't even raise insanity as a defense. So, I wrote to her. Part of it was trying to help out someone on death row, and part was curiosity as to what drove her to do this."

"And did you find the answer?"

"We wrote a few times to each other. She was so grateful to receive my letters. After a while, I decided to visit her. I've seen her several times. And I'm convinced she didn't set that fire."

"Texas has a very fine innocence project. I can give you their phone number."

Chuck frowned. "I've already tried them. They turned her down."

"I'm sorry. It may be because their caseload is full, or it may be because they felt there was good reason to."

"I suspect it was the latter. At her trial, the fire experts were certain it was arson, and no one else was in the house."

"But you think otherwise?"

"I do."

"Why?"

"I wish I could give you a logical reason. Everything I do is scientifically based. I don't work on hunches; I work with facts. Proven facts. Yet there's something about this woman that makes me believe she's telling the truth when she says she didn't set the fire."

Dani understood gut feelings. Hers often guided her when choosing a client.

"Would you consider taking her case?" he asked.

She knew she should say no. One innocence project had already turned her down. Probability statistics pointed to her being guilty. She looked at Chuck, now completely slumped over. He was a nice-looking man, with sandy-brown hair that grazed his ears. His bushy eyebrows were knitted together, and he held his large hands tightly as he awaited Dani's answer. She thought he must be a good, decent man to take the time from his demanding practice to try to ease the suffering of a woman he initially thought guilty.

"No promises, but I'll take a look at it," Dani said. "What's her name?"

His face broke into a smile. "Becky. Rebecca Whitlaw."

The next morning, as soon as Jonah left for school, Dani entered her home office. It was a large room—much bigger than the office in her old Bronxville home, even bigger than her office at HIPP. The massive antique oak desk that she'd found at a flea market in Yonkers, which had overwhelmed her small room back home, now gleamed in its new surroundings. Two file cabinets lined one wall, and shelves filled with legal books were on another. She sat down in her high-backed leather chair and started where she always did—with a computer search for the newspaper stories surrounding the fire. Glen Brook, Texas, was too small for its own newspaper, but the *Star-Telegram* which served all of Tarrant County, carried the story from the outset.

"Fire Takes Lives of Three Children," was the first day's headline, followed ten days later by "Arson!" Dani read both articles and copied down the names of the fire investigators. She skimmed the stories about the trial, again jotting down names of Whitlaw's attorney and the people who had testified against her. When she finished, she turned to Lexis and began to read the appellate decisions. As was typical of the cases that came to

Dani, there was a long history of decisions, from both the state and federal courts. When she finished, she understood why the Texas innocence project had turned down the case. The fire expert testifying for the prosecution was considered the top arson investigator in the county at that time. Worse, the defense's own expert, Donald Hamburg, agreed the fire was arson.

She was meeting Lauren for lunch that afternoon and waited to tell her the bad news in person. As soon as they were settled in their seats at the restaurant, Dani said, "I want to let you know I'm not going to be able to help your brother's friend."

"You've checked out her case already?"

"Yes. Through Lexis."."

Lauren was silent for a minute. "My brother is the most perceptive person I know. There must be something about this woman that makes him think she's innocent."

"Prisoners become very adept at fooling others."

"Not Chuck."

"I wish I could help, but there are inmates with much stronger cases that need HIPP."

Lauren sighed. "All right, Dani. I appreciate your looking into it." She managed a ghost of a smile. "I imagine this never gets any easier for you, delivering hard news to people struggling to find hope."

"There are highs and lows," she allowed. "Sometimes the highs can seem awfully hard to come by."

"I can only imagine. I'm only tangentially involved, and it's heartbreaking. Chuck's going to be so disappointed."

"He seems like a wonderful guy, your brother."

Lauren nodded. "He's always led with his heart, even when we were little."

Tears had risen to Lauren's eyes. Seeing them, Dani's own vision blurred, so she didn't see Lauren reach out to her, just felt her friend grip her forearm.

"Dani, I know it's a lot to ask, I know it's a day out of your schedule, probably two. But is there *any* chance you could at least meet with her? If you come away unconvinced, then I'll drop it, I promise. So will Chuck."

Decisions about cases weren't supposed to be based on friendship. An unbiased review of the facts, an assessment of the likelihood of success, an evaluation of the cost. That's how it should work. But Dani knew other factors often crept in. Once, the need to raise money for HIPP forced their decision. Sometimes, the circumstances of the conviction hit a chord with her, and she'd choose that client. Just last year, she'd taken the case of an intellectually disabled man because of her own son's disability. Perhaps a quick trip to Texas to assuage a new friend would be okay. And, maybe she'd walk away agreeing with Chuck Stanger that this mother was innocent of the murder of her three children.

"Okay," Dani said. "Just one visit. That's all."

Three days later, Dani presented her attorney credentials at the Mountain View Unit prison, in Gatesville, Texas, where female prisoners on death row were housed. She'd flown into Dallas the day before, opting for the two-and-a-quarter-hour drive to the prison rather than flying to Waco, only forty-five minutes away but requiring a plane change.

She waited twenty minutes in the attorney interview room before a guard escorted Becky inside. Her hands were cuffed and her feet shackled. The newspaper clippings Dani had read that covered the trial had included a picture of the twenty-three-year-old mother of three—a pretty young woman, with light-brown, shoulder-length hair framing her high cheekbones, large round eyes, and full lips. The person who sat before Dani now bore little resemblance to that woman. Her hair was cut short, and although not overweight, her face and her body were fuller. Only her lips, which were held tightly together, looked thinner.

As soon as the guard left the room, Dani introduced herself. "Your friend, Chuck Stanger, asked me to look into your case."

Becky's body visibly relaxed when she heard his name. "He's been my lifeboat. Every time I get down on myself, I pull out one of his letters to reread and instantly feel better."

"He thinks you're innocent."

"I am."

Just a simple statement, Dani thought. Sometimes, inmates shouting their innocence went into detailed explanations of how the system had gotten it wrong, how they were railroaded, how they shouldn't be where they were. Not Becky. She'd made a simple declaration, then sat still, her face open, waiting for Dani's next question.

"Who do you think started the fire?"

"No one I know would do that. No one else was in the house."

"But the reports were clear. An accelerant was used."

Becky hung her head. "I was drinking the night before. A lot."

"Are you saying you could have done it?"

Becky looked up and shook her head vigorously. "Oh no! It's just—if I hadn't been so hungover, maybe I could have saved them."

Dani sat back in her chair. "Let's start from the beginning."

And so, Becky did. She told Dani about getting pregnant in her senior year of high school, about marrying Grady, his fatal accident almost five years later, about the depression that overtook her from time to time. About that night, when she thought of how different her life would be without her children, with no one to care about but herself.

"Is it possible," Dani asked, her voice soft, "that you started that fire but don't remember?"

Becky stared at her hands. "For a long time, I thought that's what happened. That I must have wanted to end my life and take the kids with me. That I had blocked it out. I thought that the whole time I was hospitalized. I wanted to die." She took a deep breath. "Gradually, I came to realize that no matter how much I'd drunk, I never would hurt my children. Never. They were my heart, my breath, my soul. I existed because of them."

Dani understood why Chuck wanted to believe Becky was innocent. Dani wanted to believe this mother could not have intentionally taken her children's lives. But the arson report was clear. Someone had committed murder, and no one else was in the house.

"Only a monster would do that to her children," Becky said, a quiet strength in her voice. "And I am not a monster."

⁓

Dani wasn't sure what to think of Becky Whitlaw. Although she'd professed her innocence, that was commonplace among prisoners, especially those sentenced to death. Dani hated the death penalty—it was absolute. Once meted out, it didn't matter if new evidence surfaced to exonerate the wrongfully convicted. Studies had shown that of the three thousand or so men and women currently on death row, about 4.1 percent were innocent. That meant 120 innocent people were at risk of being executed. Was Becky Whitlaw one of them? Dani didn't know. She wished her favorite investigator, Tommy Noorland, was with her. He was the yang to her yin. Dani wanted to believe everyone she interviewed was innocent. Tommy started out assuming they were guilty. Together, they worked to find the truth.

She'd flown out to meet with Becky as a favor. Now, she wanted to know more. She placed a call to HIPP's office and was put through to Tommy.

"I have a potential new client. Can you fly down to Dallas?"

"When?"

"Today. I'm already in Texas."

"Hold on." There was silence for a few minutes, then Tommy was back. "I just booked my flight. United. It gets in at 8:34."

"I'll pick you up. Thanks, Tommy."

"Anything for you, dollface."

Dani hung up with a smile.

⁓

Tommy couldn't stop grinning. Damn, he'd missed that woman. He worked with other lawyers at HIPP, liked them, too, but none were Dani. They'd started out as colleagues, then become close friends. The office wasn't the same without her. She'd pop into work with a coffee in hand and a look of fierce determination on her face, ready to fight windmills. Except, unlike Don Quixote, she wasn't loony; rather, the smartest attorney he'd ever worked with. And she used those smarts to win cases, to free men and women who didn't belong in prison. There were times he thought she'd gotten it wrong, that the client was pulling a fast one on her. But just about always, she'd prove him wrong. He was a hard-ass, and she was a soft touch, but together, they'd formed the perfect partnership.

He quickly telephoned his wife, Patty, and asked her to pack an overnight bag for him. He'd swing by his house in Riverdale and pick it up on the way to the airport. Then, he walked into the office of Bruce Kantor, the director of HIPP. "I'm flying out to Dallas in a bit to meet up with Dani. She's thinking about taking on a new client."

"Not another DNA case?" They both knew that since leaving New York, Dani's caseload had consisted solely of clients whose guilt or innocence turned on DNA found buried in old police files. Most times, Dani didn't need Tommy's investigative skills with those matters.

"Arson. Three children died; mother was convicted of setting fire on purpose."

"Interesting. I don't remember HIPP handling an arson case before."

"Not since I've been here."

"What time's your flight?"

Tommy glanced at his watch. "Five twenty. I better get going."

As Tommy stood up to leave, Bruce nodded. "This is good. The A-team is back together."

At 8:52 p.m., Tommy Noorland stepped out of the security area at Dallas–Fort Worth International Airport and into a hug from Dani. "I've missed you," she said when she finally stepped back. She looked him over. The same large frame, the same black hair, the same thick mustache. He was still Tommy.

"What did you miss most? My handsome face? My devilish charm? Or my killer body?"

Dani laughed. "I missed every damn thing about you." Although Tommy wasn't the only investigator at HIPP, he was the only one Dani used when she took on a tough case—one that couldn't be solved with DNA evidence.

As she walked with Tommy to her rental car, Dani filled him in on Becky Whitlaw's case. When she finished, she looked up and saw the scowl on his face. "You don't approve?"

"I'm surprised. You usually shy away from dead children cases. Especially since the prisoner isn't even sure she started the fire."

"You had to be there. She was certain she'd never purposely set a fire with her children in the house."

"Lots of drunks are sure they'd never do something during a blackout. Then you show them pictures doing the exact thing they swore they hadn't."

Dani slipped her arm through Tommy's. "That's why I need you here. To keep me from being too gullible. Because"—she stopped and smiled at Tommy—"I have to say, I really want to believe her."

By the time they checked into a Days Inn just outside Glen Brook, it was almost nine forty-five, local time. Dani knew that she should wait until 11 p.m. to call Doug. That would be nine o'clock in Stanford, when "honeymoon hour" would start. It was the time they set aside all other matters to spend with each other, even if it was only by phone. When one of them was traveling—almost always Dani—they'd long ago agreed to use the time wherever they were living. Now, that was California. She looked at her watch once more. She'd agreed to meet Tommy for a drink before they turned in. He was like family to her, and she hadn't seen him in months. She didn't want to cut it short to rush back for her phone call. Still, in the twenty-one years of their marriage, they'd missed "honeymoon hour" less than a dozen times. And always for a compelling reason. Would skipping it tonight start a dangerous precedent? They'd always held it sacrosanct to keep their marriage fresh, to reinforce that they were just as important to each other now as they'd been when first married.

I'm being silly, Dani thought. *Doug knows how much I love him. And he knows how much I've missed Tommy.* She picked up her phone to call Doug, and when he answered, let him know she was skipping "honeymoon hour."

"Just this once," she said, before hanging up.

⌐⌐⌐

"Fill me in on the kids," Dani said as she sipped her sauvignon blanc. Tommy had in front of him a scotch on the rocks, his standard drink.

"Tommy Jr. has actually settled into being a pretty good student. He's thinking law school after he graduates next year."

"I can't believe he's already a junior."

Tommy rolled his eyes. "He thinks he knows more than his old man now."

Despite his grumbling, Dani could tell Tommy was proud of his son.

"He really started doing well after Emily enrolled there. She's keeping eyes on him. She was always grounded, even when she was just a toddler." Emily was the second oldest of Tommy's five children and just a year younger than Tommy Jr.

"Brandon just started at Northwestern, right?"

Tommy nodded. "If it weren't for his football scholarship, I would have insisted he go to SUNY Montlake, like the other two. It makes Patty less nervous to have them together."

Just his playing football should be enough to make her nervous, Dani thought. What she'd learned about football concussions from representing a client last year should make every mother nervous. Still, Tommy learned the same things. She understood how hard it was to pull a child—no, he was a young man now— from a sport he loved. Especially when his talent for that sport won him free tuition at a university.

"And Lizzie and Tricia?"

Tommy groaned. "Driving me crazy, those two. You can't believe the outfits they think it's okay to wear. Skirts that barely cover their asses, tops so low-cut, they leave nothing to the imagination."

Dani would be surprised if she hadn't seen the same clothes on coeds walking around Stanford University. "Doesn't their high school have a dress code?"

"Oh, sure. But as soon as they get home, they change into something scanty, then head out with their friends."

"Can't Patty stop them?"

"She says I'm just being an overprotective dad. Claims I forgot how short her dresses were back when we were dating. All their friends dress that way, so I'm just supposed to go along with it."

Dani could practically see the fumes coming out of Tommy's ears. She thought back to her own teenage years, when she'd worn tiny shorts and strapless tops all summer long. She was glad Ruth had a long way to go before she turned thirteen, before Dani was forced to deal with those issues. Still, she knew Becky Whitlaw would welcome fretting over her daughter's clothes instead of mourning her death.

The next morning, Dani and Tommy drove to the office of Tim Willoughby. She still wasn't certain that she'd take on Becky's case, but the trial attorney was the best place to start. She usually had made up her mind about the prisoner's likelihood of innocence before traveling to meet a former attorney, but she hoped Willoughby would help with that decision.

The lawyer's office was the end unit in a one-story strip mall, anchored by a large hardware store in the center, with a Laundromat, dry cleaner, coffee shop, and barbershop filling in the rest of the space. Next to the cluster of shops was a gas station, surrounded by sagebrush on three sides.

Dani had called ahead, and as soon as they arrived, Willoughby's assistant ushered them into his office. He stood to shake their hands, and Dani was struck by his frailty. With his white hair and pasty complexion, he looked like a man in his eighties, although Dani knew from Martindale-Hubbell, the directory of attorneys in the United States, that he just turned seventy.

Willoughby must have read the expression on Dani's face. "Chemo," he said. "Can't keep a damn thing down."

"I'm sorry."

"Doctor wants me to stop working. Give my body a rest. But I'll go crazy if I don't come to the office every day."

"I appreciate your meeting with us."

"I'll do anything I can to help Becky. They're going to kill that poor girl for something she didn't do."

Dani leaned forward. "Why are you so certain she's innocent?"

"I knew that girl long before the fire. She wouldn't harm any living thing, much less her children."

"Still, the fire investigator's report was unequivocal about it being arson. Who else could have started the fire?"

Willoughby just shook his head and shrugged. "I had no business taking up her defense. She should have gone with a lawyer more experienced with death penalty cases."

"Why did you?" Dani asked.

"Her mother insisted. She wanted a lawyer who believed in her daughter. And I did. Still do. But I should have known being innocent's not enough."

"Can I get a copy of your files on her case? No disrespect to you, but maybe we can argue ineffective counsel and get a retrial with that."

"Already been tried. After she was convicted, and her appeals denied, I leaned on a friend to take over and make that claim." He took a deep breath. "Apparently, I wasn't bad enough to be considered ineffective."

Dani understood the ramifications. Without being able to claim ineffective assistance of counsel, they would have to find new evidence that hadn't been available at the time of her trial—something that was always difficult and time-consuming. She wasn't certain it warranted the time and expense when the client herself didn't know what had happened during those early morning hours. Still, there was something about Becky that touched her. She wasn't ready to give up just yet. "How long did the trial last?"

"Over and done in two days. I didn't have much to work with."

"Are Becky's files readily available?"

"All my old cases are stored in the back."

Dani smiled sweetly as she locked her eyes on Willoughby's. "I don't suppose your assistant could make me a copy of the trial transcript before we leave? Then send the rest up to my office?"

Willoughby picked up his phone and pressed the intercom button. "Margaret? Got some time now?" He nodded as she answered. "Pull Becky's trial transcript from the file, and make a copy for her new lawyer." As he hung up, he turned to Dani. "Should take about a half hour."

Dani thanked him, then she and Tommy took seats in the reception area and waited. They needed to start with the people who testified at Becky's trial—the people whose testimony endeavored to save her, and the people whose testimony sent her to death row. Before trying to find something new, they had to understand the old.

Twenty minutes later, they returned to the Days Inn so Dani could thumb through the transcript. "Poke around in town while I'm doing this," she told Tommy. "See if anything pops up."

Dani settled into the desk chair and began reading, making notes in the margins. She slowed as she read first the testimony of Sam Miner, the fire investigator who testified against Becky, then that of Donald Hamburg, Becky's expert.

"Do you agree with fire investigator Miner's conclusion that the fire that destroyed Rebecca Whitlaw's house and killed her children was deliberately set?" Willoughby had asked Hamburg.

"All the indicators for an accelerant were there."

"Would you say that there is no room for the possibility an accelerant wasn't present?"

"Of course, there's always a possibility. Maybe one percent?"

"If an accelerant was used, do you agree that it was turpentine?"

"There's no way to know that without lab confirmation, and those tests were inconclusive."

"What are some other common accelerants used for a fire?"

"Well, gasoline, of course. Then there's diesel fuel; Coleman fuel, like for camping; acetone; butane; kerosene."

"Do you know if any of those others were found in the Whitlaw house?"

"I don't. But I suspect if they were, it would have been in the investigator's report."

"So, it's possible that some other accelerant was used, one that Ms. Whitlaw didn't have in her possession?"

"Yes."

"And that would mean that someone else started the fire, right?"

Hancock called out, "Objection. Leading."

"Sustained."

"In your professional opinion, is it possible that someone else started the fire that killed Mrs. Whitlaw's children?"

"Absolutely."

Why wasn't that enough to create reasonable doubt? Dani wondered. She continued to read through the transcript. The jailhouse snitch was damaging, of course. Dani knew how tainted that kind of testimony was, but it had an outsize impact on jurors. Still, this was a capital case. Shouldn't jurors have wanted more? Guilt beyond a reasonable doubt was a high burden, as it should be before a decision to take a life. Sadly, all too often the decision was reserved for minorities—black and Hispanic men. But Becky was a white woman. Was it the neighbor, Jake Johnson, testifying that Becky said it was her fault? Is that what pushed the jury over the line to a guilty verdict? If Dani had tried the case, she would have brought in a psychologist to testify that Becky's behavior and her utterance were the result of shock, what people now understood as typical of post-traumatic stress syndrome. Willoughby hadn't done that, though, and now it was too late. She and Tommy would have to find new evidence, evidence that wasn't available at the time of Becky's trial, and that if known then, might have resulted in a different verdict. If they could do that, and get Becky a new trial, then Dani would have a shot at explaining Becky's so-called confession.

Either that, or find the person who really did set the fire.

When she finished going through the transcript, Dani called Tommy, and he swung around to pick her up at the hotel.

"Find out anything useful?" she asked.

"Just that everybody either knew Becky personally or knew of the fire."

"Those who knew her, what did they have to say about her?"

"That she didn't seem like the type to kill her kids, but they supposed everyone has a breaking point."

"So, not very helpful."

"Nope.

Dani plugged into Waze the address for Marci Farrady, and fifteen minutes later, they pulled up to her home. She had been Marci Brand back when she testified at Becky's trial, first against her, then for her at the penalty phase. A teenage girl, dressed in shorts and a cutoff top that showed off her flat midriff, answered their knock. Dani looked over at Tommy and saw him roll his eyes, as if to say, *See! This is what I'm talking about.*

"Whaddya want?" she asked, as she vigorously chewed a wad of gum.

"We're looking for Mrs. Farrady," Dani said.

"Not home. She's at work."

"Do you know what time she'll get home?"

"Six o'clock. Usually. Sometimes she has to work late."

"Thank you."

The girl closed the door, too uninterested to even ask who they were.

They walked down the front steps of the ranch home and back to the car.

"Where next?" Tommy asked.

"Let's try Becky's former neighbor. He should be retired by now."

As they drove down the driveway to Jake Johnson's home, Dani glanced at where Becky Whitlaw's house had once stood. The one-story home had been replaced with a sprawling, two-story Colonial, with a wraparound porch. Dani could just catch a glimpse of an elaborate wooden gym set in its rear yard. She wondered if the new occupants were aware of the history of that property. Although she normally dismissed supernatural stories, she knew that she wouldn't want to raise her own children in a home where a baby and two toddlers had perished.

"I see lights on inside."

Tommy's words pushed thoughts of ghosts away. After he parked in the driveway, they both walked up the porch steps and rang the doorbell. It was answered by a tall, hefty man with a full head of gray hair and a face filled with wrinkles.

"Jake Johnson?"

The man nodded.

"My name is Dani Trumball, and this is Tom Noorland. We work with the Help Innocent Prisoners Project, and we're looking into Becky's Whitlaw's conviction."

A frown quickly passed over Johnson's face before he composed himself and invited them inside. He escorted them into the living room, filled with knickknacks on every available surface.

"Terrible tragedy," he said after they were seated. "Those children were as sweet and pretty as any I'd ever known."

"How well did you know Becky?" Dani asked.

"Well enough."

"Do you think she was capable of setting that fire? Killing her children?"

"I think she struggled after her husband died. And maybe the amount she drank that night showed her a way to end that struggle."

Dani wasn't naive. She knew that people who'd imbibed too much did things they otherwise might not. But killing one's children? In such a cruel and painful way? No, she didn't think any mother would do that, no matter how drunk. Unless something was already off with her. "Had you ever seen Becky being harsh with her children? Neglectful, maybe?"

"She'd lose her temper once in a while."

"And then what? Hit them?"

"Can't say I ever saw her do that. Mostly yell at them."

"Did you ever wonder if Becky was strange? Like, she didn't respond to things the way most people would?"

"Can't say that, either. She was just too young to have so many kids. That's all I can say about her."

It didn't seem like Dani would get much more from Johnson, so she thanked him, then she and Tommy left. From Johnson's house, they drove to the home of Becky's mother. Although now close to seventy, Sarabeth Travers still lived alone in the Glen Brook home where she'd raised Becky. As soon as she answered the door, Dani could see the resemblance to her daughter. Both had large, green eyes and prominent cheekbones. Both had delicate noses and heart-shaped lips. Sarabeth's silver gray hair was worn in a short, layered cut, and she was slim, like her daughter.

She welcomed them warmly into her living room. "Becky told me about your visit. I'm so grateful," she said, then offered them refreshments. While she was in the kitchen getting them water, Dani looked over the room. Although the furniture was well worn and the style of the furnishings dated, everything looked like it was cared for meticulously. Sheer curtains hung over the windows, and a woven rug covered the floor.

When Sarabeth returned with their glasses, she also placed in front of them a plate of chocolate chip cookies that looked like they'd only recently been taken from the oven. "I was hoping you'd come by today. I baked these especially for you."

Dani had tried to swear off sugary sweets after Ruth was born but didn't want to insult her host. She picked one up and took a bite. It was every bit as delicious as she remembered home-baked chocolate chip cookies to be. "Thank you. They're scrumptious."

Sarabeth beamed.

"Now, Becky told me a bit about that night, and about what life was like for her after her husband died. I'd like to get your perspective."

Sarabeth sat upright in her chair. "She didn't kill those children. Never in a million years would she do such a thing."

"I wouldn't be here if I thought she had."

Sarabeth let out a sigh. "I loved my grandkids. I truly did. But she never should have married Grady. When she got pregnant, I begged her to give up the baby, find him a good home. She had her whole life ahead of her. She was smart as a whip, that girl. Could have become anything. I never went to college, but Becky could have. Would have, if she hadn't become pregnant. If she hadn't kept the baby."

"Did Becky ever tell you she regretted that decision?"

"No, of course not. She'd never admit her mother was right. But after Grady died, I knew how hard it was for her. I tried to help out as much as I could. But raising three kids under the age of five all by herself? It would have been a handful for anyone."

Tommy piped in. "Did Becky like to drink?"

Sarabeth began rubbing her arm, as she looked away toward the window.

"Mrs. Travers?"

She turned back to Tommy. "She wasn't an alcoholic, if that's what you're asking. She'd have a beer now and then. Ease the tension. Never when she was caring for the kids."

"Becky told me she'd had quite a lot to drink the night of the fire," Dani said.

"Yes, well, that was unusual."

"You'd never known her to get drunk before?"

"Once or twice in high school. I always grounded her if I caught wind of it."

"Do you know if she ever blacked out?" Tommy asked.

Her color drained from her face. "Of course not! And she didn't black out that night. Just fell asleep, is all. I keep telling you—she's not an alcoholic."

She's too defensive, Dani thought.

Tommy leaned forward in his seat. "Do you know of anyone who might have been angry at Becky? Maybe want to hurt her?"

Becky's mother seemed visibly relieved at the change of direction. The color returned to her face, and she smiled. "Oh, everybody loved Becky. She was always popular in high school, lots of friends."

"Is it possible that someone resented her popularity?" Tommy continued.

"I-I don't think so. I mean, Becky never complained to me about anyone."

"How about after she married?" Dani asked. "Maybe even after Grady died. Was there anyone hanging around her that made her uncomfortable?"

"A couple of men wanted to take her out after Grady was out of the picture. Even after three children, she still had her figure, you know. But she wasn't interested in anyone."

Dani stood up. "Thank you, Mrs. Travers. You've been help-ful. Is it all right if we come back to you another time if we have more questions?"

Her eyes misted up, and her lower lip quivered. "I'll do any-thing to help my daughter. She's all I have left."

As soon as they got into their car, Tommy asked, "What do you think?"

"I think she's hiding something."

"Me, too."

They headed toward the airport. It was hours before Marci Farrady would return from work, and even if they waited for her, they'd still have to come back and question her again if Dani agreed to represent Becky. She needed to review the remainder of the attorney's records. That's when she'd make her final deci-sion. After going through the documents, she would either take on Becky Whitlaw as a client, or bow out and let the State carry out its sentence of death.

Two days later, Dani sat in her home office and began going through the transcript of Becky Whitlaw's trial for the second time. She missed her office back at HIPP, where there was always a buzz of activity. She could close her door there if the noise distracted her, but that was rarely necessary. The quiet in her home office seemed more distracting somehow. Although her work was a solitary endeavor—pouring through transcripts, writing briefs, preparing for trial or oral arguments—she nevertheless missed the camaraderie of working in an office. She could pick up a phone and bounce ideas off Melanie Stanton, the lawyer at HIPP she'd trained, or Bruce Kantor, HIPP's director, but it wasn't the same as strolling into their offices and sitting across a desk from them.

She spent the entire day reading, first the files that Tim Willoughby had sent her, then those from Erica Slater, Becky's attorney after Willoughby's appeals failed. When she finished, a few things seemed clear—there was little dispute that the fire was arson, and Becky's attorneys, especially Slater, had done a decent job representing her. Dani knew this meant she should turn down the case, just as the Texas innocence project had done. She'd taken on hard cases before, though, and won her clients' release. If she believed her client innocent, she'd fight, even without a smoking gun in her arsenal.

After the fire investigator's testimony, the most troubling statements came from Susan Granger, the woman who had shared a cell with Becky and claimed that Becky had confessed that she'd intentionally set the fire. According to Willoughby's notes, Becky adamantly denied even talking to Granger, much less confessing to her. Dani picked up the phone and called Tommy. "I need you to prioritize locating Susan Granger. She was the one in the Tarrant County Jail with Becky."

"I've been working on it."

"No luck yet?"

"Nada."

Dani hung up, returned to the file. If Becky was innocent, and Dani tended to believe she was, then it meant someone else started the fire in her house. Someone who likely intended to harm Becky, not necessarily her children. Dani reached a decision. She wanted to take on this case. That meant she and Tommy had to find the true arsonist, more than twenty years after the fire had been set. It was a near-impossible task, yet somehow, she and Tommy had successfully done just that in previous cases. Could they do that once more?

At five to four, Dani exited her office. Jonah was due home any moment, and she always liked greeting him when he opened the front door and shouted, "I'm starving." At fifteen and a half, he was approaching Doug's six-foot height and seemed to have a perpetually ravenous appetite. Still, he wasn't overweight, and he gravitated toward healthy snacks, so Dani chalked up his food intake to the demands of a fast-growing body. She entered the den, empty now since Elsa had taken Ruth to the playground, and picked up a few of her scattered toys.

Five minutes later, Jonah bounded through the front door and straight into Dani's outstretched arms. "I'm expiring from hunger," he said once he pulled away. His unusual word choices, typical with Williams syndrome, always brought a smile to Dani's face.

She led him into the kitchen and rummaged through the refrigerator for a snack. His former nanny, the irreplaceable Katie, always had freshly baked treats for him. Elsa was more nutrition conscious, and for that, Dani was glad. Back in New York, after Jonah finished his refreshments, Dani always helped herself to a cookie or brownie. It was much easier to stay away from sugar when it wasn't staring her in the face. Earlier in the day, Elsa had made soft pretzels from scratch. Dani placed one on a plate, took hummus from the refrigerator, and placed both before Jonah. He scarfed the snack down in less than five minutes, then grabbed an apple and asked, "Can I go over to Keith's house?"

Keith, two years younger than Jonah, lived three houses away and had become fast friends with Jonah. He was a kind boy who knew Jonah was different but never made fun of him. Dani had been so worried about the impact on Jonah of their move across the country, but it had worked out better than she could have hoped, and Keith was a big reason why. Although Jonah had always had friends from his school—other children with various sorts of disabilities—Keith was his first neighborhood friend. Despite the short time they'd known each other, their friendship had grown quickly. They'd spend hours playing video games, and Keith had taught Jonah how to play soccer. Jonah had introduced Keith to classical music, and Keith had brought Jonah into the popular music world. They'd even attended a One Direction concert together.

"Don't you have homework?" Dani asked.

"Just a diminutive sum. I can finish it after dinner."

"Okay, then. Be back by six."

Jonah hugged her, then sprinted out the front door.

Dani returned to her office and put in another hour of work before Elsa returned with Ruth, her cheeks still rosy from running around in the sun. As soon as Ruth saw Dani, she rushed into her arms and planted kisses all over her face. She put aside all thoughts of Becky Whitlaw. For now, she just wanted to play with her daughter.

Just before seven, Doug returned home. He was putting in more hours than he had as a professor at Columbia Law School, but that was to be expected once he accepted the position at Stanford. If nothing else, it was a new job, and he needed to demonstrate his worth.

Dani had already fed the children, and they were each planted in front of a television—Ruth in the den and Jonah in the master bedroom. "Hungry?" she asked Doug after he'd checked in on the kids. "Or do you want to unwind first?"

"I'm famished. I didn't eat lunch today."

"How come?"

"Too many meetings."

Dani took the lasagna that had been kept warm in the oven and placed it on the kitchen table. "Come, sit down. Dinner's all ready." As Doug took his seat, Dani noted that his face looked peaked, the fine lines by his brown eyes seemed deeper than before, and his usual smile had disappeared. She hoped his new responsibilities hadn't placed too heavy a strain on him.

By the time they finished, the children's television shows were over, and it was time for bed. Ruth was first, and Dani went through their normal nighttime routine—bath first, then two books read with Ruth snuggled on her lap, then into the crib. Ruth was a good sleeper. She always went down easily and fell asleep quickly.

Jonah was old enough that he didn't need Dani's help any longer, but she still liked tucking him in when he was ready for sleep. The family rule was that he had to be in bed by nine, but he could continue to read in bed if he wanted.

At nine o'clock, Dani and Doug settled into the living room couch for "honeymoon hour." Although it wasn't cold outside, she picked up the remote for the gas fireplace and pushed the button to start a flame. Back in New York, they'd had a wood-burning fireplace, and on cold winter nights, they'd often light a fire. She'd thought it a chore, though, needing to keep a stack of wood outdoors, making certain the flue was open, and then closed after the fire was out, cleaning the ashes afterward. The ease of this gas fireplace tickled her, and the mesmerizing blue flames spread a feeling of warmth and tranquility through her.

"Are things going okay at the school?" Dani asked.

"I never appreciated how much bureaucracy went on in law schools. Or, at least, it was easier to ignore when I just taught."

"Welcome to my world. Nothing beats the bureaucracy of nonprofits."

"Oh, I'd say universities would give nonprofits a challenge."

Dani smiled. They both hated the nitty-gritty of their jobs, the nonlegal aspects that needed tending. For Dani, it had been most bothersome when she'd been forced to take on a case in exchange for a substantial donation to HIPP. In the academic world, Doug had always told her how grating it was to be forced to publish scholarly articles. Not that he minded writing. He just loathed being judged based on his publications rather than his effectiveness at teaching.

"Have you formed an opinion of your staff yet?" Dani asked.

"Oh, they're all top-notch. I knew they would be."

"I know they're all brilliant. But does that necessarily mean they're good teachers?"

"No, of course not. Some are better than others."

"Who? Who are you most impressed with?"

Doug seemed to mull over the question before he finally said, "Lauren Stephens. She's one of my favorites."

Dani picked up her wineglass and took a sip. "I'm glad to hear that. I really like Lauren myself."

"I like her husband, too."

New coast, new friends. Maybe Doug had been right—change was good for their family. At least, she no longer worried about it. Now, her worry focused on Becky Whitlaw.

After getting Jonah off to school and settling Ruth with Elsa, Dani grabbed a cup of coffee, then headed into her office and placed a call to the Mountain View Unit prison. It wasn't always easy to get an inmate on the phone. Usually, prisoners were allowed only to make outgoing calls, not receive them. An exception was made for the prisoner's attorney, and Dani had made sure that Becky had listed her with the prison administration before she'd left. "This doesn't mean I'm taking your case," Dani had cautioned her. "But if I do, it'll make it easier for me to reach you."

She had to wait fifteen minutes before Becky reached the phone. When she did, Dani said, "I'm in. I'm going to represent you." She could hear soft cries on the other end. She waited for them to subside, then said, "I'm going to try to overturn your conviction. It doesn't mean I'll succeed. We have an uphill battle. And I'm going to need your help."

"Anything."

"First, I want you to understand that anything you tell me is confidential. Even though you haven't signed a retainer agreement yet, I'm acting now as your attorney, and the privilege applies."

"I understand."

"Before the night of the fire, had you ever had an alcoholic blackout?"

"No."

"Are you certain?"

"Of course, I'm certain."

"I had the feeling that your mother was holding something back from me."

Dani heard a soft chuckle.

"That's Mom. She always warned me not to drink because I'd turn out like my dad. I guess part of her wonders if I did."

"Your father?"

"A falling-down drunk every Saturday night. Didn't touch a drop the other nights and was never mean. But toward the end, he'd black out almost each time. I think Mom's afraid that's what happened to me the night of the fire. But I never drank like my dad. Not even that night."

"You're probably smaller than your father and maybe tolerated less. The amount of alcohol that can lead to a blackout state is different for every person. It depends on their size, their metabolism, and frankly, how much they're accustomed to drinking. If you drank an amount that night that was unusual for you, then maybe—"

"No maybes. I didn't black out. I fell asleep. A deep sleep. Listen, in high school, drinking a six-pack was the norm. After the kids were born, I didn't do it often, but if we were at a party, I could do a six-pack on my own. Even if I included vodka in the mix, I never blacked out."

"Okay, Becky. I believe you didn't black out. And I believe you didn't set that fire, not deliberately, anyway. But if you didn't start the fire, then someone else did. Can you think of anyone who'd want to hurt you?"

"And my children, too? Nobody I knew could be that cruel."

"He or she might not have thought it would get out of hand. That you would wake up and get everyone out. Maybe the person just wanted to scare you. Can you think of anyone who would do that?"

"No one."

"Someone from work, perhaps? Or someone who was jealous of you?"

"Hah! No one wanted my life. They pitied me, getting pregnant so young and then my husband dying."

"Still, think back. It could even be someone from long before the fire."

Becky hesitated. "I . . . I'll try."

Dani spent a few more minutes grilling Becky for names of people from her past, then hung up and called Chuck Stanger. "I thought you'd like to know—HIPP is going to represent Becky Whitlaw."

Dani heard an intake of breath, then its release. "I'm so relieved. You see in her what I do, don't you?"

"Well, if you mean that I think she's innocent, I do, although I've been wrong before and no doubt will be again. But, like you'd said, there's something about her that makes me believe she wouldn't have wanted to kill her children."

"I'm so glad. Thank you."

"Going forward, I can't talk to you about the case. You know, attorney-client privilege. But you referred her, so I wanted to let you know how that turned out."

"I understand. Again, thank you."

Dani's last call was to Tommy. She shared with him the list of names Becky had given her and asked him to start tracking them down. "Early next week, let's go back to Texas. I want to start with Marci Farrady. She's the one who probably knows Becky best."

There wasn't much more to do with Becky's case while Tommy conducted his search, so Dani pulled out from the file cabinet in the corner of her office the folder of Rick Turner. Turner had been just twenty-two when he was convicted of the rape and murder of a young mother in her apartment while her infant daughter slept in the next room, then sentenced to life without parole. That was twenty-eight years ago. There had been little forensic evidence tying Turner to the crime. His conviction rested almost exclusively on the testimony of Ned Cheswick, who'd claimed he'd seen Turner run from the apartment, blood on his shirt, just about the time the crime occurred. Turner knew Cheswick. They'd gone to high school together, and both played on the football team. Six months earlier, Cheswick's girlfriend had dropped him and begun dating Turner. When the police obtained a warrant and searched Turner's residence, they discovered a knife with blood on it with a blade consistent with the woman's stab wounds. At trial, a forensic expert testified that a pubic hair found on the victim belonged to Turner.

From the outset, Turner maintained his innocence, insisting that Cheswick had lied. The blood on the knife, he said, was his own. The pubic hair couldn't possibly be his, since he'd never met the young mother. Turner was incarcerated in Reno, Nevada. Dani had met with him and believed his claims, then quickly discovered that the police kit had preserved the pubic hair found on the victim. When it was DNA tested, it excluded Turner. And, as Turner had insisted, the blood on the knife was his own. Over the years, hair analysis had been recognized as "junk science." An easy case, she'd mistakenly thought.

When Dani suggested to Paul Cohen, the prosecutor in Washoe County, Nevada, that they jointly move the court to reverse Turner's conviction, he practically laughed in her face. "Not a chance," he'd said. "We have enough to convict him." If Dani made the motion herself and his conviction was overturned, they'd retry him. "But," Cohen went on, "since he's already served twenty-eight years, I'm open to an Alford plea."

An Alford plea was based on a 1970 Supreme Court decision which ruled that a court could accept a guilty plea even if the defendant maintained his innocence, provided there were enough facts that a jury could return a verdict against the defendant. Since juries are notoriously unpredictable, there is great pressure on those charged with a heinous crime, facing life in prison or even death, to accept a plea offer of a lesser sentence. Even if that person is innocent.

Cohen's offer was certainly tempting—in exchange for the Alford plea, which despite the defendant asserting on record that he was innocent, was recorded as a guilty plea—Turner would immediately go free, with no retrial and no chance of being convicted once again. He would be fifty years old, set loose in a world that was now foreign to him, and branded as a rapist and murderer. When Dani presented the offer to him and explained the ramifications, he didn't hesitate. "I'm innocent," he'd said. "I won't ever say otherwise, and I won't have the world think otherwise. I'll take my chances at a new trial."

She'd proceeded with a motion and won a new trial for Turner. Once again, Cohen offered an Alford plea. Once again, Turner rejected it. A trial date was set, and Tommy and Dani began their investigation. They'd discovered that Cheswick had changed his story to the police and prosecuting attorney four different times, each new iteration altering the facts to make it easier for a jury to believe Turner was guilty. The prosecutor at that time was required to inform Turner's attorney of Cheswick's changed statements but hadn't. It was clear prosecutorial misconduct, but it would never blow back on the prosecutor—it rarely did. Armed with Cheswick's inconsistent statements and the DNA results, Dani was confident they'd succeed at Turner's retrial—except it had been nine months since a new trial was ordered. Nine months of Turner continuing to sit in prison. Each time the trial date approached, the prosecutor came in with an excuse for a delay.

The new date was three weeks away, and the judge had ruled it would go forward then, whether or not the prosecutor came up with a new excuse. Dani spent the rest of the morning reviewing his file, making notes for trial.

Dani timed her lunch break to coincide with Ruth's. Elsa had already started feeding her when Dani joined them in the kitchen. Ruth's face lit up when she saw her mother, and Dani beamed in return. She gave her a quick hug, then headed to the refrigerator to find something to eat. There was lots that Dani missed in New York, but she loved that she got to spend more time with Ruth and Jonah by telecommuting. When she lived in Bronxville and commuted to HIPP's office in Manhattan, she'd kiss the kids goodbye in the morning and wouldn't see them again until the evening. Supposedly, her hours in the office ended at three, enabling her to get home in time to greet Jonah as he got off the school bus. But more and more, as the years went by, that didn't always work out. Deadlines often pushed her to stay in the office hours later, and then she'd battle rush-hour traffic getting home. Now, there were no traffic jams between her office and her children. She could take a break whenever she wanted to spend time with them, then return to the task at hand.

Still, she missed her friends, many that she'd grown up with, gone to school with, and had bonds with that were precious to her. She missed her colleagues at HIPP, especially Bruce and Melanie. Even though she still worked with Tommy, she hadn't been out in the field with him since she'd moved to California until Becky's case. She used to see him every day. She missed the bustle of Manhattan, the plethora of museums and theaters, the diversity of the population. Sure, there was multiculturalism in Palo Alto, in Stanford, but real estate was so expensive that economic diversity was missing. Her home here was beautiful, all sleek lines and modern appliances, gleaming soapstone countertops and polished wood floors, but her old Bronxville house, with its worn floors and vintage stove, felt like home. She missed living in New York.

After she and Ruth had both finished lunch, Dani played with her for a half hour before Elsa brought Ruth upstairs for her nap. Then she retreated into her office for another afternoon of solitary work.

One week later, Dani and Tommy were back in Glen Brook. Tommy had determined that Susan Granger was no longer in any prison in the United States, but he hadn't yet been able to track down a current address for her. Dani knew that if she had any hope of getting a hearing for Becky, she'd need to knock out Granger's claim that she'd heard Becky confess. Jailhouse snitches were notoriously unreliable, and Dani thought Willoughby had done a poor job of attacking her credibility. But she couldn't do anything about it until she found her.

They'd made an appointment with Marci Farrady, and when they drove up to her house, the door was open, and she was waiting in the doorway.

"I hope you can help Becky," Marci said as she led them into the kitchen, where she had a pot of coffee ready and store-bought coffee cake on the table. As soon as Dani sat down, the scent of sweet cinnamon started her stomach rumbling, even though she and Tommy had eaten dinner. Sugar-filled sweets had always been her downfall during the years between Jonah's and Ruth's births, when she'd try over and over, each time unsuccessfully, to drop ten pounds. After Ruth's birth, she began jogging regularly, and between that and nursing her baby, she'd finally gotten down to her weight during college.

Once they were all settled around the kitchen table, Dani said, "You were the last person to talk to Becky before the fire. I understand she called you late at night and asked you to come over. Was that unusual?"

Marci brushed back strands of chestnut-brown hair that had fallen over her face. "Sometimes Becky just needed company. She knew I'd come no matter what time she called."

"Was there a particular reason why she needed company that night?"

Marci nodded. "It was her wedding anniversary. I mean, would have been if Grady was alive."

"So, she was thinking about him?"

"Yeah, I suppose."

"Did she talk to you that night about the children? Complain about them?"

Marci picked up her cup and took a sip of coffee. "Do you have kids?"

"Yes," Dani answered.

She turned to Tommy. "And you?"

"Five."

"So, you know how it can be when they're little. Always needing something. Becky was all alone. She had to work hard to support them, then come home to their demands. Sometimes she just needed to let loose."

"By drinking?"

Marci nodded. "She wasn't an alcoholic or anything. Most times, she didn't drink at all. Just, once in a while, she'd need to drink enough to stop the pain."

"Was the pain ever great enough that she thought about suicide?" After Dani's meeting with Becky, she didn't think that was the case, but she had to ask, anyway. Perhaps she hadn't wanted to harm her children, just herself. Still, fire was a painful way to kill oneself.

Marci shook her head vehemently. "Never." She stopped for a moment. "At least, not that she ever mentioned to me."

Tommy broke in. "Can you think of anyone who would want to hurt Becky?"

"And her kids, too?"

"Just Becky. Maybe someone who had a beef with her."

"Everyone liked Becky. And only a psychopath would want to kill her children. We didn't know anyone like that."

"Maybe someone didn't think they'd be killed," Dani said. "Maybe he or she just wanted to shake them up. Figured they'd get out in time."

"Or," Tommy added, "it was someone who wanted to play the hero. Rescue Becky and the kids, except got spooked when the neighbor showed up."

"Then it would have to be someone who liked Marci. Someone who she rejected. Right?"

Tommy nodded.

Marci dropped her chin into her hands and let her eyes drift closed. After a minute, she looked up. "There was a guy from back in high school. Billy Bingham. He'd had a crush on Becky but backed off when she hooked up with Grady. Becky told me he'd contacted her a few months after Grady died. Offered sympathies, then suggested they get together. Becky blew him off. Then, maybe a month or so before the fire, he stopped by the diner when she was at work. Asked her out again, and she told him no. But—he wouldn't hurt her. He liked her."

"Some people can do awful things when they're rejected," Dani said.

"Is he the kind of fellow that might?" asked Tommy. "You knew him, right?"

Marci shook her head slowly. "I don't know. He seemed a little off back in school, but start a fire? I just don't know. I mean, he didn't seem crazy or anything then. And I haven't seen him since we graduated."

"Does he still live in Glen Brook?" Dani asked.

"No. His family moved away shortly after graduation."

"Have any idea where?"

"No."

Dani wrote his name down in her notepad. When they finished up their interviews in Texas, she'd ask Tommy to try and find him. Billy Bingham was now a person of interest.

The next morning, Dani and Tommy drove to the Wilshire Woods development in nearby Brookville, where Irving Howe had moved after retiring from the Glen Brook Fire Department. Tommy had learned that Sam Miner, the fire investigator who testified against Becky, had died five years ago. Howe was the only one they could question about their findings.

Wilshire Woods was a retirement community, the kind they called "active adult," where people over fifty-five got to spend their post-work years acting like they were twenty all over again. The complex had a resort-style swimming pool, multiple tennis courts, a clubhouse, and a social director. They arrived at Howe's apartment shortly after 9:00 a.m., and when they sat down at his kitchen table, he offered them bagels. Dani would have demurred, anyway, since she and Tommy had both come over straight from their own breakfasts, but especially for bagels. In her view, any bagels made outside of New York City and its suburbs were unworthy of the calories. New Yorkers claimed the city water used in the dough made their bagels the best, and she believed that to be true.

"Your joint report—that it was arson—was pretty definitive," Dani said. "Did you ever entertain thoughts that you were mistaken?"

Howe sighed deeply. "Glen Brook is a small town. We don't have suspicious fires 'round here. That was the first one I ever investigated, and in all the years before I retired, there was only one other. That's why I called in Sam. Sam was the top fire investigator in our county. I've known Becky since she was a toddler. I didn't want to believe she'd set a fire, but Sam was certain. Said it was clear as a sunshiny day that fire was intentional."

As much as Dani had hoped otherwise, she'd expected Howe's answer. Becky's own fire expert hadn't been able to poke any real holes in Miner's conclusions. "Even if it was arson, couldn't it have been set by someone else?"

"I suppose so. That wasn't our job—to point a finger at Becky. We just said it wasn't an accident. Sheriff is the one who decided it had to be Becky. And the jury agreed with him."

"You said you'd known her most of her life. Did you ever think she was capable of killing her own children?"

Howe gave Dani a hard stare. "Anyone's capable of doing the unthinkable if they feel desperate enough. And that poor girl had enough burdens weighing her down that it didn't seem outlandish she'd be feeling desperate." He shook his head, then murmured, "Three babies and a dead husband. Hard not to feel overwhelmed."

Dani and Tommy spent another hour going over each detail of Miner and Howe's report. He was unshakeable. Someone had purposefully set Becky Whitlaw's house ablaze.

Next stop was the Tarrant County Sheriff's Office. The office was housed in a single-story brick building, standing alone on a lot surrounded by dead brush. Mike Duncan was still there, a year past when he should have retired, Tommy had learned. They pulled up to his office shortly before noon and, once inside, were led to a conference room. A few minutes later, Duncan entered. He was a tall man, several inches more than Tommy's six feet, and with his trim body looked ten years younger than Dani knew his age to be. He still had a full head of hair, sprinkled with gray.

He shook their hands, then motioned for them to sit down.

Duncan was law enforcement, Tommy's bailiwick, and so Dani let him take the lead.

"We're looking into Becky Whitlaw's conviction."

Duncan nodded, and Dani was reminded that Glen Brook was a small town. After their visit to Tim Willoughby, Becky's first lawyer, and Jake Johnson, her former neighbor, enough time had passed for word to have gotten around.

"I understand you knew Becky," Tommy continued.

"Yep."

"You think she set the fire?"

"Who else could have done it? She was the only one there."

Tommy remained silent, his gaze never leaving Duncan's face.

Slowly, Duncan shook his head. "I never would have expected it from her. She loved those kids. But the evidence was clear."

"Clear that it was arson. Not that Becky started it."

"Even without the jailhouse snitch, she all but confessed."

Dani piped in. "She was in shock. Her children were inside, and she was powerless to do anything. Most mothers would feel a sense of responsibility in that circumstance."

"You have someone else in mind?"

"That's why we're here," Tommy said, "talking to you. You knew most of the folks in Glen Brook. Think anyone had a grudge against Becky?"

"Nope. Everyone liked her. Everyone felt sorry for her."

"Even Billy Bingham?"

Duncan's eyebrows knitted together. "Bingham? Name's not familiar."

"He moved away with his family more than twenty years ago."

Duncan scratched his head, then leaned back in his chair and closed his eyes. After a few moments, he sat back upright. "Wait—you talking about Frank and Helen's boy?"

Tommy shrugged. "Maybe. Don't know his parents' names."

"Must be them. They're the only Binghams I recall living around here. Their son was a real cutup. Always getting in some mess or another."

"Breaking the law?"

"Well, I wouldn't go that far. Never arrested him. Mostly just kid stuff. Egging houses on Halloween, cutting school more times than his parents could count. Once 'borrowed' his dad's car when he was just past thirteen. That kind of stuff. Why are you asking about him?"

"We understand he was sweet on Becky."

"I suspect lots of boys were. She was a beauty. But, as you point out, he'd been gone a long time before that fire."

"He'd come back. After Becky's husband died. Wanted to start things with her. She sent him away."

Duncan wrapped his long arms around the back of his head. "So, your theory is a spurned boyfriend wanted revenge?"

"We're considering that a possibility," Tommy answered.

"Seems a pretty extreme reaction, if you ask me. Somebody who'd do that, not care about harming those kids, would have to have a screw loose. And I don't remember that being the case with the Binghams' boy."

"Anyone in town back then who you thought did have a screw loose?"

The sheriff shook his head. "I wish I could help you. It doesn't feel good knowing that Becky's going to get the needle soon. But she changed after her husband died. And what she did—killing those poor babies? Well, she needs to pay for that. An eye for an eye, the bible says."

Dani knew they weren't going to get anything helpful from the sheriff, and so she signaled Tommy to wrap up his questions. They'd worked together for so many years that they didn't always need words between them. Just the slightest nod of her head was all it took to get her message across to Tommy.

"I guess that's about it," Tommy said as he stood up. He took out a business card and handed it to Duncan. "If you think of anything else, or hear of the whereabouts of Billy Bingham, give me a call."

Duncan took the card, then escorted Dani and Tommy to the front door. It was clear to Dani that they were getting nowhere. She'd interview Becky's appellate attorney before she returned home, but it looked like all they had was one fragile string to pull on. Once in the parking lot, she turned to Tommy. "Find Billy

Bingham for me. And anyone who might have seen him in Glen Brook the day of the fire."

A smile broke out on Becky's face when she saw who was waiting in the visitor's chair, a Plexiglas screen between them. She picked up the phone on her side of the barrier, and he did the same on his.

"What a nice surprise! I wasn't expecting you." She wished she could reach through the glass and touch his hand, stroke his cheek. Any touching was forbidden. After the soft, warm feel of her children's skin right after a bath, that's what she missed most—the touch of a man, caressing her.

"I was driving back from a conference in Austin. It was only a minor detour to swing by and see you. Hope that's all right?"

How could she ever express to this saint of a man how grateful she was for his visits, for his letters, for his friendship? For so many years after her conviction, she'd struggled to understand how the unthinkable had happened. Was it the smoke or her son's voice that woke her? Somehow, it had seemed important to know, but no matter how hard she endeavored to remember, the specifics eluded her. Finally, she gave up. Whichever it was, the ending was the same—her three children were dead, and she was on death row. There was nothing for her to do but wait for her own death. Then, she could join them. Then, she'd be reunited with Grady.

She'd gone through each day a zombie, curled up on the bed in her cell, not engaging with the other women on death row, eating her paltry meals and sleeping. Until she received the letter from Chuck Stanger. He wanted to understand her, but how could he when she didn't understand herself? Weeks passed, and then she wrote back to him. She told him she hadn't set the fire but felt responsible, anyway. She was supposed to protect her children and had failed. She accepted her sentence; she deserved to die.

He'd written back. "You don't deserve to die," he'd said, and for the first time, she allowed herself to believe in that possibility. After months of correspondence, he showed up at the prison, her only visitor in ten years, other than her mother. At first, Marci had visited, and so had her lawyer. But after the appeals had failed and there was no hope left, they had drifted away. When her mother visited, she always carried an aura of sadness. Her only child was sentenced to death, and the three grandchildren she'd adored were gone. Becky craved the visits with her, but always, afterward, she'd walk back to her cell with a raw ache in her chest.

Now, Chuck sat before her once again. He was a handsome man, with thick, wavy brown hair, almost delicate features, and eyes so blue, they looked like an island lagoon. He had broad shoulders atop an athletic body, and no ring on his long fingers. She checked each time she met him.

"What did you think of Ms. Trumball?" Chuck asked her.

Becky took in a slow breath. "I'm afraid to think about her."

"What do you mean?"

"I'm afraid to hope." Even as she said those words, she knew it wasn't completely true. Much as she tried to push it away, to tamp down the lightness that had filled her chest moments after hearing the lawyer say she would take Becky's case, she did feel hopeful. Still, she couldn't let that germ of hope, that thought of being saved, linger. She needed to accept her fate.

At least now there were two people who believed she hadn't set the fire. Two people who thought she wasn't a monster. Chuck and Dani Trumball. Her mother had always accepted her protestations of innocence, but that's what mothers were supposed to do. She was never certain her lawyer truly believed she was innocent. He said he did, but there were times she'd catch him looking at her in a way that suggested he was unsure. Even Marci, her best friend, had harbored doubts, Becky knew. She couldn't blame her. On her worst days, the ones she spent curled into a ball on the bed in her cell, unable to move, she fought the fear that she had been the one to set the fire. Set it, then blacked out all memory of doing so. When those fears overwhelmed her, she'd struggle to fight through the darkness, to remind herself how much she loved her children, how she'd never hurt them. Chuck's letters made it easier to do so.

Women on death row at Mountain View were given the option to work in the prison. Until Chuck had written her, she'd declined, preferring the isolation of her cell. But she'd allowed herself to open up in her letters to Chuck, to talk about her family and her loss, and it made her feel like a human being again, not the beast who everyone thought had murdered her children.

She'd started out crocheting blankets, the only work permitted for women on death row. After two years, an exception was made, and she was given the coveted job of converting textbooks into braille for local school districts. The work made her feel like she was doing something worthwhile. Before Chuck's letters, she usually passed up her allotted hours of recreation in the yard. Being outside just heightened her sense of what she'd lost. Now, she always took advantage of that small feeling of being free that the fresh air gave her.

"Hey," Chuck said, bringing her out of her reverie. "Don't think like that. She's done amazing things for people wrongfully convicted."

Becky knew Chuck was pleased that he'd gotten Dani to take her case. He wanted her to be happy as well. She pasted a smile on her face. "Maybe she'll be my miracle worker, too."

Becky hoped so. She wanted to live, to be free once more. There were still times, though, alone in her cell, awakened from a nightmare, when she wasn't certain she deserved to live.

"Coffee?" Dani asked.

Doug lifted his head from the newspaper, nodded, murmured, "Thanks," then buried his head once more in the story he was reading. It was one of the rare mornings when Jonah had already left for school, Elsa had taken Ruth for a walk, and the two were alone. Usually, Doug left for Stanford before Jonah boarded his school bus, but his early meeting had been postponed, and he'd decided to go in later.

"What's got you so absorbed?"

"Wildfires. Another one's started, over in Boulder Creek. That's less than forty miles from us."

Dani poured coffee into Doug's mug, then sat down at the kitchen table with him. "Are we in any danger?"

"I don't think so." He picked up his cup and gulped a swig of coffee, then buried his head in the paper once more. "Still, this is the eighteenth one this month, and we've got another week to go." He shook his head slowly. "Thirty-four people died in California fires so far this year."

"We never had to worry about this in New York."

"It's the drought. Preceded by a wet winter and spring, so there's a lot of new growth. With barely any rain over the summer, that growth turned to tinder. Throw careless people into the mix, and it becomes an inferno."

Dani picked up her smartphone, opened Google, typed in some letters, then began reading. With each article she scanned, she became more alarmed. "More than one million acres have burned in California just this year. It's the worst year on record."

"I know."

"You don't think a fire could start in Applewood Park, do you?" The city park was a nature lover's paradise, with miles of hiking trails, lots of trees, abundant wildlife, fields, streams, and a lake. It was barely two miles from their home and one of the places that Dani loved to visit. Their own street was filled with trees, and the homes in their neighborhood were all on one-acre lots, with a barrier of trees separating them on each side and the rear.

Doug shrugged. Dani could tell by his clenched jaw that despite his reassurance a moment ago, he was worried. They finished their coffee in silence, each absorbed in their readings about a state that seemed to be burning up.

⁓

Later that afternoon, Dani pushed aside her work to meet Jonah's school bus. When it pulled up at the corner, Jonah didn't exit with his usual unbridled enthusiasm. He normally bounded off the bus with a wide grin on his face whenever he saw his mother waiting for him. Before they'd moved to California, when Dani worked in Manhattan and lived in Bronxville, a Westchester suburb, she'd greet Jonah at the bus stop if she arrived home in time. That happened less and less as Jonah got older. When she was knee-deep in a case where a death sentence was ready to be carried out and multiple last-ditch appeals needed to be made, she'd work in her office into the early morning hours, returning home for a quick few hours of sleep, a hot shower, and a change of clothes before heading back into Manhattan. Now, her office was in her home, so unless she was traveling to another state, she occasionally waited outside for Jonah, even though he was too old to need that. She held back from doing it too often, since she didn't want the other boys on the bus to make fun of a fifteen-year-old whose mother waited for him. She would stop altogether, but she knew Jonah enjoyed seeing her there.

"What's wrong?" Dani asked after she gave him a hug.

Jonah just shook his head and walked toward the house. Once inside, when they'd settled at the kitchen table, where Elsa had left a glass of milk and freshly baked oatmeal raisin cookies for Jonah, Dani asked again, "What's wrong? Did something happen at school?"

Jonah looked up at his mother with eyes that seemed on the verge of tears. "I'm not empowered to say."

"What do you mean? Who's saying that?"

"Matt. He says if I tell anyone, he'll hurt me more tomorrow."

Dani felt her body tense. She knew school bullying was rampant, despite the efforts of teachers and administrators to contain it. In Jonah's old school, back in New York, he'd never experienced it. To her knowledge, none of the other students there had, either. It was an environment that nurtured each child, and if anyone acted out, either toward a student or a teacher, he was helped to understand that behavior was wrong. It rarely happened a second time.

"What did Matt do?"

Jonah dropped his gaze down to the table and clutched his hands together.

"Jonah, tell me."

Quietly, he said, "He impaled me against the wall. He put his hand around my neck and squeezed. Then he took my lunch."

Dani willed herself to keep her voice calm. "I'm going to call your principal. She'll make sure this doesn't happen again."

Jonah jumped out of his seat. "No! You can't! He'll pummel me."

Dani hesitated. "Okay, Jonah. I won't do anything right now. But if he does anything to you again, promise you'll tell me."

Jonah nodded.

It was an age-old dilemma. Risk retaliation by reporting the abuse in the hope the school would handle it effectively, or wait and hope it didn't happen again. For now, she'd wait. But, for the first time since she'd moved to California, moved Jonah out of the school that had brought him so far, she wondered if she'd made the right decision.

That night, during "honeymoon hour," Dani told Doug what had happened to Jonah at school.

"What did his teacher say?" Doug asked.

"I didn't call her. Jonah begged me not to."

A scowl passed across Doug's face. She'd known he wouldn't be happy with her decision; it was the reason she'd waited until the children were asleep to talk to him about it. He'd been the target of bullies in elementary school, before he'd shot up in adolescence to tower over most of his classmates, before he'd discovered what working out in a gym could do for his strength.

Before then, he'd been taunted because he was a nerd, his head always buried in books, oblivious to the games his classmates enjoyed. Now, even knowing about the antibullying programs adopted by the more forward-thinking schools, he often questioned why school authorities didn't do more to stem that behavior. "They never do enough," he'd often said whenever the topic arose. "Bullying is increasing, not going the other way. And teachers too often ignore the obvious. Kids need to be taught from kindergarten that it's wrong, and to report it when it happens. Whether to their teacher or someone else."

Now, he just said, "You know you have to call her. Ignoring it won't make it stop."

"Maybe it's just a onetime incident."

"It might be. And if it is for Jonah, who's to say he won't move on to another child?"

Dani sighed. Doug was right, of course. Tomorrow she'd call Mrs. Gordon. Urge her to handle it with delicacy. Impress on her that Jonah didn't want it known he'd "tattled." She wondered for a moment why she was always the one who contacted the teacher when something was wrong. Doug was all for gender equality. He made dinner if he got home first and loaded the dishwasher after the meal was finished. If Ruth needed a diaper change and Elsa wasn't around, he changed it. He viewed Dani's job as just as important as his own, even though there was a great disparity in their salaries. When Jonah had a problem with homework, he'd often sit down and help him with it. Yet, when it came to handling problems at school, it was always Dani who spoke to the teacher, or the principal if a matter needed to be bumped up a level. *Why was that?* Did returning to school trigger memories of his own bullying? He attended teachers' conferences but stayed away when something unpleasant needed to be discussed.

Dani looked over at Doug. He always seemed so comfortable in his own skin. She'd often envied that. But perhaps she was mistaken. Perhaps even her strong, confident husband had demons that he kept buried. She leaned into his body, and he wrapped his long arms around her. "You're right. We shouldn't let it go. I'll take care of it. Tomorrow."

The next morning, Dani sent Jonah off to school with his lunch packed in his backpack, plus money to purchase food from the cafeteria in case Matt struck again. She didn't tell Jonah she planned to call his teacher and felt a twinge of guilt holding that back. She knew, though, that Jonah would be stressed all day if she'd let him know. As soon as the bus left, she dialed Mrs. Gordon's cell phone. When she answered, Dani first apologized for disturbing her at school. "Something happened yesterday that I think you should know."

"With Jonah?"

"Yes. Apparently, a boy named Matt in his class became physically intimidating with Jonah and took his lunch from him."

"I see. Did Matt actually strike him?"

A sense of unease began to grow in Dani. Although most teachers were sensitive to school bullying, Dani knew there were some who thought it was a rite of passage—a practice that had existed through the ages and would no doubt continue well into the future. "No. He pushed him up against the wall and had his hand around his neck."

There was a pause on the line before Mrs. Gordon spoke again. When she did, her voice was filled with concern. "I'm sorry that happened. Jonah is such a sweet boy. And Matt—well, his parents have been going through a divorce, and he's been acting out lately. I'll speak to him."

"If you do, it will come out that Jonah spoke up about it, and he's terrified of what Matt will do then. Do you think it's possible to just keep an eye on Matt? Maybe watch when they walk to the cafeteria?"

"Of course. I will speak to Matt, but without mentioning Jonah. I've been trying to get him to open up about his parents' situation, anyway, and his anger over it."

"Thank you. I really appreciate it." As Dani hung up, she felt her shoulders relax. Doug was right about notifying Jonah's teacher. She would handle it now, and Jonah would be safe.

Two days later, Dani sat in a courtroom of the Washoe County Courthouse, in Reno, Nevada. The building, built in 1910, in a neoclassical style, was noted for the large number of divorces it handled during the first half of the twentieth century, when Nevada's liberal residency laws made it a haven for quickie divorces. Her client, Rick Turner, dressed in a suit and tie instead of the prison jumpsuit he wore when escorted from prison earlier that morning, awaited his chance at freedom after almost twenty-nine years behind bars for a crime the evidence now showed he hadn't committed. She'd sat in that seat three times since winning him the right to a new trial, and each time Paul Cohen had stridden into court and given the judge an urgent reason for delaying the trial. It was a tactic designed to force Turner into accepting the Alford plea he'd offered. Finally, at the last request for a delay, the judge had put it over with an admonishment that no more delays would be forthcoming, no matter how "urgent" the prosecutor's reason.

It was now five minutes before the judge was scheduled to take the bench, and Cohen had yet to appear in the courtroom.

Dani began to get agitated, certain that Cohen was trying to pull a fast one to delay Turner's freedom even more. Three minutes later, a young woman dressed in a tailored suit and looking like she was barely out of college, much less law school, entered the courtroom. She walked down the aisle to the prosecutor's table and sat down. She glanced over at Dani and nodded, then quickly looked away. *Something's up,* Dani thought. She rose from her seat and started to walk over to her when the bailiff entered the courtroom and announced, "All rise." A moment later, Judge Maxwell Franklin entered and took his seat on the bench.

Once everyone was seated, he looked over at the young woman. "Where's Mr. Cohen? I hope you're not here to ask for another continuance."

The woman stood. "No, Your Honor. The people have decided that there's insufficient evidence to go to trial. We're dropping the charges."

Dani reached over and grabbed Turner's hand. In a flash, she realized that Paul Cohen had played a game with this man's life. He never intended to retry Turner. Instead, he'd hoped that by dragging out the trial date, Turner would grow frustrated and finally agree to the Alford plea. Knowing full well the unpredictability of jury verdicts, there were moments over the past nine months even she considered encouraging Turner to accept. But Turner had told her at the outset that he wanted his family to see him vindicated, and if remaining in prison was the price he had to pay, he was willing. So, she'd told him to remain strong, that he'd get his day in court. And now he had. The criminal charges were dropped, and he would go free, after serving twenty-nine years for a crime he didn't commit.

Dani saw that Judge Franklin's face was reddening. "I see," he said, through clenched teeth. "What's your name?"

"Kathy McIntyre."

"How long have you been working for the DA?"

"Three months."

"Your boss sent you here because he was too chicken to take the blows from me. Well, you go back and tell him I want him down here in one hour. He'd better have a good reason for keeping this man locked up a day longer than needed if the State knew they hadn't enough evidence."

"Y-Your Honor, I'm not sure Mr. Cohen is in the office today."

Dani almost felt sorry for the young woman. No doubt the judge was right. Cohen purposely sent a rookie in his place to take the brunt of the judge's annoyance.

"Then you'd better hope you can find him. Because if he's not here in one hour, I'm going to sanction him." He turned to Turner, who'd been slumped in his chair, his face buried in his hands, as soon as McIntyre had first spoken. "Sir, please look at me."

Turner looked up.

"Do you understand what just happened?"

"I think so. I think I'm going to be set free."

"That's right."

Tears began streaming down Turner's face. Dani took his hand. "It's over," she said softly. "You're going to go home."

"I think I found Billy Bingham's father," Tommy told Dani when she answered the telephone. Ten days had passed since they'd been together in Glen Brook.

"That's great. Where is he?"

"Still living in Texas, down in Houston."

"Have you spoken to him? Does he know where his son is living?"

"Tried to, but he hasn't answered the phone yet. Probably screening his calls, and I didn't want to leave a message before I spoke to you."

"Call him. Make up some reason why. We've got to find out if Billy was in Glen Brook when the fire started."

"Okay. I'll ring him tonight. More likely to be at home."

"How about Susan Granger? Any luck there?"

"Not yet."

"Keep on it. If we're able to get a new trial, we'll need to discredit her testimony."

Dani hung up, then returned to the files in front of her. She usually worked on several cases at a time, and having put to bed

Turner's case, it was time to find a new client. As part of the accommodation HIPP made for her work-from-home status, all letters that came to the office from prisoners seeking representation were now scanned into her assistant's computer and available for her to access through her home computer. She'd printed out ten that had seemed most promising and now read through the letters once again to narrow her choice to one. An hour later, she still had two battling for supremacy and finally decided to accept both as clients.

Dominic Webster had been convicted in Boulder County, Colorado, of the rape and murder of his girlfriend's three-year-old daughter. DNA testing on semen from the child's body was inconclusive, and so the primary evidence against him was the testimony of a forensic odontologist that the bite marks found on the child's body had "with absolute certainty" come from Webster's teeth. Dani had recently freed another prisoner whose conviction was based, in part, on bite-mark evidence, and had learned during her preparations that such evidence had no scientific basis. In fact, experts often couldn't distinguish between human and nonhuman bites.

After Webster spent eleven years on death row, a more sophisticated DNA test was performed, which excluded Webster as the perpetrator. Six months later, Webster's conviction was vacated. He hadn't been released from prison, though. The prosecutor announced his intention to retry Webster for the crime, and so he was moved from death row to pretrial detention. When his letter arrived at HIPP's office, he'd been there for five years awaiting his trial. Dani quickly typed a letter to Webster letting him know she'd take his case, then another to Samuel Xavier, the prosecutor who'd managed to delay Webster's trial for so many years. She advised Xavier that she was now Webster's attorney and would seek an immediate trial. In the meantime, she requested that he run the DNA sample through the database to see if it matched anyone else. That done, she turned to the second inmate.

Patton Swinton had been imprisoned for twenty-five years of a life sentence for a rape and burglary conviction. He insisted, as did all the inmates who wrote to HIPP, that he was innocent and had maintained his innocence consistently throughout his incarceration. According to Swinton, the crime had been unsolved for six months until a police informant with a criminal record claimed that Swinton confessed to him. Swinton denied ever doing that, but what caught Dani's attention was his assertion that the only other evidence against him was the testimony of a technician who'd been trained by the FBI in how to conduct hair analysis. He testified at the trial that a strand of hair found at the scene belonged to Swinton, with 99.9 percent certainty.

During Dani's previous research on bite-mark analysis, she'd discovered that the FBI had undertaken a post-conviction review of twenty-five hundred cases where its laboratory's microscopic hair comparison unit found a match between hair found at a crime scene and a defendant. The review was prompted after the exoneration of several men convicted primarily as a result of microscopic hair analysis testimony and a report in *The Washington Post*, which claimed that flawed forensic hair matches might have led to convictions of hundreds of innocent people since the 1970's.

The FBI's initial findings showed that nearly every examiner in that unit had given flawed testimony against criminal defendants, overstating the likelihood of a match between hair found at a crime scene and a defendant in 95 percent of the times they testified. The cases included thirty-two defendants sentenced to death, of which fourteen had already been executed.

Like bite-mark analysis, hair analysis was a pseudoscience, with no scientific support. It could rule out a suspect but had no reliability in identifying a perpetrator. Although the FBI notified each of the defendants in the cases reviewed they might have a basis for an appeal, it only reviewed cases where a member of the FBI had testified. However, almost one thousand state or local analysts had been trained by the FBI, using the same methods now known to lead to incorrect results. Swinton had been tried in a state court, so the FBI would not have reviewed the testimony given in his case. If the authorities had preserved the hair sample, DNA might now show whether in fact the hair came from Swinton.

Dani did a quick search on the internet and found the first appellate decision in Swinton's case. He was only seventeen when he'd been picked up for the crime. His entire adult life so far had been spent in prison. She dashed off a letter to him, then followed with another to the Osage County, Oklahoma, sheriff's office where Swinton had been arrested. She asked for a search to determine if the hair strands had been preserved, and if so, requested that they run a DNA test. She added to the letter documentation of the current state of microscopic hair analysis, in the hope that would spur their cooperation. If not, she'd have to make a motion with the court.

When finished, she sat back in her chair and fumed. Junk science had put too many innocent people behind bars.

It was almost time for Jonah's school bus to pull up when Tommy called. "I spoke to Frank Bingham."

"Did you get anything from him?" Dani asked.

"Yeah. Bad news. Billy died two years ago. Drug overdose."

Dani slumped in her chair. Billy Bingham had been the one name that had surfaced as the possible arsonist. If he'd started the fire, they'd never know. It was still possible that a stranger had started it. If so, finding that person twenty years later would be next to impossible. And, much as Dani hated to consider it, there remained the possibility Becky had started the fire while blacked out.

"We may still be able to get a new trial if we can find Susan Granger and she recants her testimony."

"I'm working on it."

Dani felt a heaviness in her chest when she hung up. Cases were so much easier when DNA, like a magic wand, could prove her clients' innocence. But DNA rarely had a place in an arson investigation.

This was the first one she'd handled. She'd pored over the arson reports that had been submitted into evidence, both the ones written by Miner for the prosecution, and the one written by Donald Hamburg for the defense. She'd reread their testimony multiple times. Miner had said he was 100 percent certain the fire was deliberately set. Becky's expert tried to put some wiggle room in that, saying there was a chance—a small chance, maybe 10 percent—it wasn't arson. On the prosecutor's cross-examination, when asked if, in his expect opinion, someone had intentionally used an accelerant and then struck a match to it, Hamburg had tried to hem and haw before finally saying, "Yes, I thought it was arson." Together, they'd both left no room for doubt—this fire had been deliberately set. The question was—by whom?

As she hung up, Dani heard the rumble of Jonah's school bus. She walked toward the front door, and when Jonah entered the house with his usual smile, Dani realized she'd been tense all day, worried that Jonah had been attacked again. It was clear by his cheeriness that hadn't occurred. As she felt the knots in her neck unwind, it struck her that all parents, whether rich or poor, regardless of race or religion or nationality, wanted their children to be happy. All parents would do whatever was in their arsenals to ensure that. A mother who would kill her children, who would do it in such a cruel and painful way, had to be psychologically damaged. And, even after a year in a psychiatric lock-up awaiting her trial, no one had reported that of Becky Whitlaw.

14

It had been almost three weeks since Dani had taken on Becky Whitlaw's case, and Dani had hit a dead end. No one had been able to point a finger at another possible suspect, other than one who was now dead, and Tommy had hit a brick wall in his efforts to locate Susan Granger. Sometimes that happened. Sometimes, she'd take on a case, convinced of her client's innocence, but be unsuccessful in finding enough new evidence to warrant a motion for a new trial. At those times, she'd reluctantly have to put the case aside and move on to someone else. She never closed out a matter completely. It went into her "On Hold" file, and every year she'd go back and give it another look—hoping that something new would pop out. Unless it was a client on death row. Then, she'd look anew at a file every three months, until the State carried out the sentence.

She had reluctantly just consigned Becky's case to the "On Hold" drawer and was steeling herself for the necessary call to update Becky when the telephone rang. Caller ID told her who it was. "Hi, Tommy."

"I finally found her," he said, a jubilant tone in his voice.

"Granger?"

"Yep. And she's in your home state."

"California?"

"LA, to be precise. Apparently moved out there after prison in the hopes of becoming a star. Changed her name to Candy. Candy Graham. How corny is that!"

Dani didn't care how corny it was. She now had a lead. "Did she do any acting?"

"Yeah, but I suspect it's not what she hoped for. She's a minor porn actress."

"And you have her address?"

"Got it from her agent. And her phone number. I pretended to be a producer."

Dani felt a rising excitement. Becky had insisted that she never told anyone she'd set the fire. If they could get Susan— or Candy, now—to confess, it could be grounds for a new trial. "What's your schedule? When can we meet her?"

"I'm jammed right now. At least a week before I'm free."

Dani didn't want to wait. "I'll go see her myself, then." Tommy gave Dani the address and phone number that Candy's agent had given him.

"You're the best," Dani told Tommy before hanging up. She opened the "On Hold" drawer and pulled Becky's file out. It wasn't over yet.

Two days later, Dani drove into LA. She could have traveled into San Francisco and taken a quick flight there, but between the travel time to and from both airports, and the need to arrive at least an hour in advance, she thought driving would be easier.

More relaxing, too, since she could listen to an audiobook on her phone for the six-hour drive. She'd taken the Pacific Coast Highway, hoping to see the spectacular views her friend Lauren had described to her, but instead had driven in fog much of the way. With the road's hairpin turns and a steep cliff on her right for what seemed like an eternity, she couldn't concentrate on a book. Instead, she clutched the wheel tightly and focused her attention on the road for hours. By the time she pulled into the Holiday Inn on North Highland Avenue, her nerves were frazzled. The hotel was officially called the Holiday Inn Express & Suites Hollywood Walk of Fame, and Dani figured that was a fitting place to stay, given that Tommy had called Granger claiming to be a Hollywood producer. He'd set up a breakfast meeting between Granger and Dani for the next morning.

Dani checked in and settled into her room, then left to explore the area. Despite her extensive travels with Doug before Jonah was born, and her traveling to other states for the clients she'd represented over the years, she'd never been to Los Angeles. It was approaching dusk by the time she left the hotel but still light enough to walk around. She headed over to Hollywood Boulevard and began walking along the sidewalks that comprised the Hollywood Walk of Fame. She joined the throng of tourists gaping at the five-pointed stars with names of celebrities inside.

One of Dani's college friends had hightailed it out to LA as soon as she'd taken her last final, not even waiting for graduation day, with the hope of breaking into movies. Dani had seen her perform in many college theater productions and marveled at her acting skills. Yet Dani had heard through the grapevine that her friend had returned five years later with nothing to show on her resume but waitressing jobs. She suspected Susan Granger had come to Tinseltown with the same hopes, but instead of heading home, she'd turned to performing in porn movies. Why? Dani wondered. Was it low self-esteem? An abusive childhood? Had she felt helpless from her years of incarceration? Or did it give her a thrill? It wasn't just idle speculation for Dani. She believed that Becky had never "confessed" to Granger. That meant Granger had lied at the trial. Few people were willing to admit to lying under oath. Dani needed to win Granger's trust, to get her to open up about her testimony at Becky's trial. And, to do that, she needed to understand Granger's life. At this point, she was the key to Becky getting a new trial.

Dani wandered around for another hour, enjoying the warm evening breeze, before popping into a coffee shop for dinner. By the time she returned to her hotel room, it was "honeymoon hour," and she called home to Doug. Whenever she traveled, hearing his voice, chatting about her day with him, brought her a comfort that was indescribable. Doug made her feel safe. When her emotions were ready to send her off the rails because of a bad court ruling, an insensitive system, an innocent person remaining behind bars, or worse, being executed, Doug calmed her down. He was the cocoon that wrapped her in love and washed away the ugliness in the world.

The next morning, Dani sauntered over to the Hollywood Roosevelt, where she was meeting Granger for breakfast. It was a more luxurious hotel than the Holiday Inn, and one that Tommy figured would be a more believable location for a producer to stay. She'd made a reservation at the poolside café and was immediately taken in by its décor, which harkened back to the sixties. A quick glance told her that Granger hadn't arrived yet, and so she took a seat at a window table and ordered a cup of coffee. Five minutes later, a woman she recognized from her Candy Graham website entered and looked around tentatively. Dani waved to her, and she walked toward her table.

She sat down and smiled tentatively at Dani. "My agent said you're doing a low-budget independent film? About a porn star? But not pornographic?"

She spoke in bursts, each sentence sounding like a question. Dani looked her over carefully. Her light-blonde hair was clearly bleached, and her unlined face had the mark of Botox injections. Not surprising, considering she had to be at least in her late thirties, and working in an industry that prized youthful good looks. Dani wondered if her full breasts almost bursting out of her low-cut V-neck sweater were real or something else she'd paid for.

Granger was looking at Dani with such hopefulness, Dani felt a twinge of guilt that she was about to dash those hopes. "Susan—"

Before Dani could continue, she was quickly interrupted. "Oh, didn't my agent tell you? I use the name Candy all the time. Saul gave it to me as a stage name, but you know, it's just easier to use just one name. Less confusing, you know?"

"Susan—Candy—I'm afraid Tommy Noorland got you here under false pretenses. I'm not a producer. I'm an attorney."

Granger looked at her quizzically. "Why? I haven't done anything wrong."

"I represent Becky Whitlaw. Do you remember her?"

Granger stared at Dani with a blank look in her eyes and shook her head slowly. "I don't think so. Is she another actress?"

"You testified at her trial for murder by arson twenty years ago. Do you remember now?"

Granger's eyes dropped down to the table, and she barely whispered, "Yes."

"You said that she confessed to setting the fire that killed her three children. Did she really tell you that?"

Granger looked up, and her face had hardened. "Look, it was a long time ago. If I said it, then it must have been true."

"Becky insists that she never spoke to you. That she never told anyone she purposely set that fire. That she's innocent."

"Yeah, well, I guess the jury believed me and didn't believe her." She started to get up. "Look, if this isn't about a job, then I'm leaving."

Dani reached out for her hand. "Please stay. Please hear me out."

Granger hesitated, then slowly retook her seat. "At least I should get a free breakfast out of this."

Dani looked around and motioned to a nearby waitress. They gave their orders—just a bowl of oatmeal for Dani, and a vegetable omelet with home fries for Granger. When the waitress left, Dani said, "Becky is going to be executed soon. If she's innocent, do you want that on your conscience?"

Granger squeezed her hands tightly together. "I don't want to get in trouble. I'm done with that."

"You won't."

"You don't care about me. No one ever has. As long as you get what you want, you'll tell me anything. If I lied—and I'm not saying I did—I could get arrested for that. I swore I was telling the truth, you know. So, lying when you do that is a crime."

"You testified twenty years ago. That's long past the statute of limitations for perjury."

"What's that mean?"

"It means you can't be charged with perjury. That's what they call it when someone lies under oath."

Granger scrunched up her face, as she seemed to think about that. Before she responded, the waitress approached their table with their meals.

"Anything else I can get you ladies?"

"No, thanks," they murmured in unison.

When the waitress walked away, Granger said, "My food's gonna get cold. Can we finish eating first?"

Dani nodded, and they turned to their meals. When Granger finished and they were on their second cup of coffee, Dani started in again. "I promise you won't get in trouble. Tell me why you said Becky had confessed to you."

Granger stuck her jaw out defiantly. "Because she did!" A second later, she said, "Oh, fuck it! I lied because the DA said I'd get out of jail earlier if I told the jury that woman said she set the fire on purpose." She pushed her chair back from the table and sat back in it with her arms folded in front.

There it was—the reason most jailhouse snitches fabricated confessions. Except this time, Tim Willoughby had asked Granger whether the prosecution had promised her anything in exchange for her testimony. "No, sir. Never promised me a thing," had been her answer. And the prosecutor had remained silent.

Dani had been certain Granger had lied decades ago. Had the jury known she'd lied, that she'd had a reason to lie, their verdict could have been different. Dani now had grounds to seek a new trial.

On the trip back home, Dani took the I-5. Now, without the stress of driving on curving roads next to the sheer drop of a cliff, she was able to relax and listen to the audiobook from the app on her iPhone through her car's speakers. She marveled to herself at how technology had evolved over the past twenty years. Between pocket-size phones, DVRs, iPads, and streaming video, it would be a foreign world for Becky if she were released from prison. *Not if,* Dani chastised herself. *When.*

As Dani listened to the honeyed voice of the narrator, her mind wandered briefly from the story to Susan Granger. Dani wasn't a neophyte attorney; she'd handled thousands of cases and dealt with an equal number of prosecutors. Most were honorable, but now and again, she ran across one who believed more in winning than in justice.

Withholding potentially exculpatory material was sufficient to warrant a new trial. Oftentimes, the prosecutor would argue whether the material was in fact exculpatory and the decision to withhold it the result of a reasonable, subjective difference in viewpoints. That wasn't the case here. The prosecutor had promised Granger a lighter sentence if she said Becky confessed to the crime, then remained silent while she testified there had been no deal for her. Dani felt her outrage festering. Becky Whitlaw had spent twenty years on death row because a prosecutor allowed a witness to lie. Not just allowed but gave her the words. Maybe the jury would have convicted Becky, anyway, but Dani thought not. There was no direct evidence tying her to the arson. A confession held a powerful sway over the jury. Powerful enough to send a possibly innocent woman to her death.

Dani arrived home just before Jonah's school bus dropped him off. She had just enough time to give Ruth a quick hug, then head out to the bus stop. Elsa had said she needed to tell her something, but Dani put her off. She wanted to be outside to greet Jonah. Although she didn't wait at Jonah's bus stop every afternoon, she made a point of doing so when she returned from travelling.

As soon as he stepped to the curb, Dani knew he'd been bullied again. His smile was gone, and worse, there was a purplish bruise under his eye.

"What happened? You okay?"

Jonah shook his head, a glum expression on his face.

"Was it Matt again?"

He nodded.

Dani put her arm around his shoulder and gave him a squeeze. "We'll figure this out." They walked together into the house, and as Jonah headed to the kitchen for a snack, Elsa pulled Dani aside.

"Jonah's teacher called. She said Jonah was in a fight. She wants you to call her."

A fight? That's not Jonah. Dani thanked Elsa, then joined Jonah in the kitchen. "Did you hit Matt?"

"He impaled me up to the wall again. Commanded I give him my lunch. But I wanted my lunch. Today was my favorite."

"So, what did you do?"

"I said no."

"Then what?"

"He tried to grab it, but I wouldn't let go. So, he socked my face. Then I socked his."

Dani worked hard to keep from smiling. She didn't believe in violence; neither did Doug. But she couldn't help feeling happy that Jonah had stuck up for himself. And maybe, just maybe, Matt would keep away from her son now.

"Jonah, you know fighting is wrong."

"I didn't start it."

"Maybe you could have just pushed him away, instead of hitting him."

Jonah was silent for a moment, as though he was thinking about Dani's suggestion. Finally, he said, "No. I think I did the correct thing. If I just pushed him away, he'd probably come back and sock me again. And I didn't like how that felt."

This time, Dani's smile broke through.

15

Twelve days later, Dani sat in the chamber of Tarrant County District Court Judge Marvin Gertner. With his black robes, straight posture, and grayed hair at his temples, he seemed to Dani indistinguishable from nearly all the other judges in whose courtrooms and chambers she'd sat throughout the country. Gertner's office was like nearly every other judge's office, with a large wooden desk, a leather high-backed chair, and walls lined with bookshelves filled with that state's statutes and case law. She wondered briefly if she were tiring of the practice of law. No, she realized. Not law itself, but of her particular area of law. The highs of freeing an innocent client balanced by the depths of despair when she failed to exonerate someone of whose innocence she was certain. Sometimes, it just seemed too much for her, especially since Ruth had been born. She'd stayed home for nine years with Jonah but had returned to work six weeks after Ruth's birth. Occasionally, guilt gnawed at her for leaving her daughter in the care of a nanny. Elsa was good, but she wasn't Katie, the woman who had cared for Jonah when Dani had returned to work, and then Ruth. Katie had become part of the family. Still, she had to admit that Ruth was thriving and seemed to be happy.

Five days ago, Dani had filed a motion for a new trial, pursuant to Texas Code of Criminal Procedure Article 40.001. Now, the judge had scheduled a conference with her and Jeremy Wilson, the assistant district attorney assigned to the case.

Gertner held Dani's motion in his hands, and his eyes fixed on her with a hard glint. "That's a very serious allegation by your witness."

"Yes."

"Especially when that prosecutor isn't around to defend herself. You know, she passed away two years ago."

"I understand. But if this witness is credible, and I believe she is, then ADA Hancock violated the law. She withheld from Ms. Whitlaw's attorney exculpatory information. And did so before, during, and after the trial."

"That's absurd," Wilson piped in. "Lindsey Hancock was one of the most respected attorneys in the district attorney's office. To say this about her is nothing short of blasphemous."

"Ms. Whitlaw is facing execution. Shouldn't this court be absolutely certain that the trial that led to that verdict was conducted fairly?"

Gertner glanced through Dani's motion papers, sighed, then turned to Wilson. "She's made out the necessary elements for a hearing." He looked back at Dani. "But you better have something more to back up this woman's claims."

Dani nodded.

"Okay, check your schedules. How does three weeks from tomorrow look?"

Three weeks later, Dani was back in the Tarrant County courthouse, sitting in the courtroom assigned to Judge Gertner. Tommy waited just outside with Susan Granger—or Candy Graham—making sure she didn't decide to bolt at the last minute. Jeremy Wilson sat at the prosecutor's table, dressed in the navy suit and starched white shirt that seemed de rigueur for trial attorneys everywhere. He was at least fifteen years Dani's junior, and with his hair trimmed close to his scalp and protruding ears, he looked like an eager Boy Scout poised to prove his mettle.

"Ready, Ms. Trumball?" the judge asked after he entered the courtroom and took his seat on the bench.

"I am."

"Call your first witness."

Dani wished she'd had a stronger case for a new trial. Everything hinged on Granger. She hoped it was enough. To succeed, she'd have to convince the judge that Lindsey Hancock had committed prosecutorial misconduct, and had it not been for that, a jury likely would have found Becky innocent. Dani hated that Hancock was a woman. Over the years, she'd run across a few prosecutors who'd skirted the line between what was legitimate behavior and what violated their obligations under the law. Never, though, had it been a woman. Tommy would argue that it was just coincidence, but Dani had wanted to believe that her gender had a stronger sense of fairness. Deep down, she'd known that was naive, even sexist thinking, but she'd embraced it, anyway. Now, with Susan Granger's accusations, she'd been proven wrong.

"I call Susan Granger."

The courtroom door was opened by a guard, and Granger entered. At Dani's urging, she'd dressed conservatively for the occasion in a black pencil skirt and a silk turquoise blouse buttoned so that no cleavage showed. A thin gold necklace hung around her neck, and large, gold loop earrings hung from her lobes.

Granger took her seat and the judge swore her in.

"State your name and address for the record."

"Susan Granger, 2609 Wilshire Boulevard, Los Angeles, California, 90057."

"Are you known by any other name?"

"Yes. My performing name is Candy Graham."

Dani heard a muted snicker from the few reporters seated in the gallery. Susan's work was going to come out. Better from Dani's questioning than from the prosecutor.

"And what is your profession, Ms. Granger?"

"I'm an actress. In adult entertainment."

"How long have you lived in Los Angeles?"

"Nineteen years."

"And before that, where did you live?"

"I grew up in Fort Worth."

"Before you moved to Los Angeles, were you ever arrested?"

Granger dropped her head and answered softly, "Yes."

"What were you charged with?"

"Selling crack cocaine." She looked up. "But it really wasn't fair. It was mostly my boyfriend's stash. It's just—we lived together in my apartment. And when he was busted, I was high. So, they charged us both."

"How much cocaine was found in your apartment?"

"My attorney said it was 540 grams."

"Did your attorney at that time tell you what the penalty could be if you were convicted of selling that amount of cocaine?"

Granger nodded. "He said I could get life imprisonment. Or a sentence with a ten-year minimum and up to ninety-nine years."

"While you were in jail awaiting trial, did there come a time when you met Becky Whitlaw?"

"Yes. She was arrested a week before me and was sent to the Tarrant County Jail. That's where I went first. They put me in her cell."

"How long were you together there?"

"Not long. They shipped her off to the loony bin after a couple of weeks."

"You testified at Ms. Whitlaw's trial that while you were together, she confessed to setting the fire that killed her children, right?"

"Well, right that I said that at her trial. Not right that she told me that."

"Just to be clear, are you now saying that Becky Whitlaw never told you she'd set the fire?"

"Yes."

"Did you understand that lying on the stand was perjury, which was a crime?"

"Now, see, I didn't come up with the plan to say that. It was the DA. So, I figured I couldn't be charged with lying if I said what she told me to say."

Dani returned to her table and took a sip of water. She wanted let Granger's testimony sink in. "Do you remember the name of the DA who asked you to lie?"

Granger nodded her head. "It was a woman. Ms. Hancock."

"How did it come about that Ms. Hancock asked you to lie about Ms. Whitlaw?"

"She came to the county jail one afternoon. They took me out of my cell and brought me into a room. It was just us; my lawyer wasn't there. She said that if Becky told me she set the fire, it would be helpful to me."

"And you agreed?"

"Well, sure. It meant I would get out of jail quicker."

"What happened next?"

"I went back to our cell. I kept asking Becky what happened, how the fire got started. I thought it would be better if she really did tell me."

"And did she?"

"She just kept saying she didn't know, and then she'd start crying. I figured she probably did start the fire, so I didn't think it was so terrible to say she'd told me that."

"What happened to the charges against you after you testified?"

"They were dropped, just like the DA promised."

"How much time had you spent in jail?"

"Just over a year. I got out a week after Becky's trial."

"Thank you, Ms. Granger. I have no further questions."

Wilson stood and walked over to the witness. "Did Ms. Hancock actually ask you to lie?"

Granger was quiet for a moment. "Not in those words. But she made it clear that all I had to say was Becky told me she started the fire. Then she'd reduce the charges against me."

"Isn't it possible she was just asking you to try to find out from your cellmate whether she started the fire? To get her talking?"

"That's not what she said."

"Isn't it possible that's what she meant, though?"

Granger smiled before answering, "No."

"How can you be sure?"

"Because the day I testified, that morning she asked me if I'd gotten Becky to talk. I told her no. She said our deal still stood."

Now, Dani smiled as well. The ADA had made a rookie mistake. Never ask a question to which you don't know the answer. She saw his face redden and watched as he returned to his table and fumbled with some papers. She knew he was stalling for time to regain his composure.

A minute later, Wilson returned to the witness. "When you were arrested for selling cocaine, that wasn't your first arrest, was it?"

"No."

"In fact, you'd been arrested for prostitution twice before, hadn't you?"

"Yes."

"And you served six months in jail each time, right?"

"Yeah, so what?"

"During your second incarceration, did you share a cell with Cindy Fergood?"

"Yes."

"Isn't it true that Ms. Fergood had her sentence reduced after she testified that another inmate had confessed to her?"

"I suppose so."

"So, when you were arrested and facing a long prison term, you knew that you could work a deal if you could testify against someone at their trial."

"Everyone knows that."

"Isn't it true that you approached Ms. Hancock and told her Becky Whitlaw had confessed to setting the fire?"

"No, it was the other way around."

"And I suppose we should believe you because you've led such a stellar life?"

"Objection," Dani called out.

"Sustained. Move on, Counselor."

"Was the judge in your case given a reason for the charges against you to be dropped?"

"Yeah. The DA said he couldn't find the cocaine they'd taken from my boyfriend's apartment. You know, in the evidence room. It was lost. So, they had to drop the charges."

"I'm finished with your questions." Wilson started to walk back to his table, then stopped and turned back to the witness. "Just so we're clear, you've claimed that back in 1998, you knowingly lied under oath."

"I explained why."

Wilson smirked. "Just so we're all clear that you have no problem with committing perjury."

"There's no jury here, Mr. Wilson," the judge said. "No need for theatrics."

"Sorry, Your Honor. Couldn't help myself." He sat down as Granger left the witness box.

"Any other witnesses?" Judge Gertner asked Dani.

"One more, Your Honor. I call Felix Kramer."

A bespectacled man with gray hair that fell in waves to his neck and a matching gray goatee entered the courtroom and walked to the witness box. He gave his name and address to the court reporter, then swore to tell the truth.

"Dr. Kramer, would you state your occupation?"

"I have a PhD in experimental psychology and am a full professor at the University of Texas at Austin. I teach three classes each semester in experimental psychology and conduct research at the university."

"In the course of your research, did you ever study secondary confessions?"

"I did."

"First, please tell the court what you mean by a secondary confession."

"A primary confession is one made by the defendant. A secondary confession is someone to whom the defendant confesses, who then reports that admission. It might be what is commonly called a 'jailhouse snitch,' an accomplice, or even a family member or other confidant of the defendant."

"Would you describe the nature of your studies in connection with secondary confessions?"

"Of course. It's well established that primary confessions have a powerful effect on jurors. We wanted to learn if secondary confessions had a similar impact. In one experiment, subjects were given a transcript of a murder trial in which there was eyewitness testimony, a secondary confession, and character witnesses. The secondary confession had the greatest impact on jurors and resulted in a higher conviction rate. In another experiment, we were able to determine that jurors were more likely to vote guilty when there was a confession, whether it was primary or secondary, over trials without a confession."

"One last question. Have you done any studies of the reliability of jailhouse confessions?"

"Not personally, but I've read published studies which show that in twenty-two percent of death row exonerations, a jailhouse informant had testified to a purported confession."

"Thank you." Dani turned to Wilson. "Your witness."

Wilson stood up at his table. "Dr. Kramer, are you familiar with research into whether a jailhouse informant having had an incentive to testify made a difference with jurors?"

"I am."

"And what did that research demonstrate?"

"Initially, it had no impact. But recent studies show jurors are more sensitive to the function of an incentive."

"To what do you attribute that change?"

"Probably the abundance of crime shows on television, both fictional and nonfictional."

"But in 1998, were jurors more likely to discount an informant's testimony if she'd received an incentive to testify?"

"No, not according to research at that time."

"Thank you. You may step down now."

Judge Gertner looked at Wilson. "Witnesses?"

"I call Herman Stolz."

The courtroom door was opened, and a stocky man, muscles bursting from his law enforcement uniform, walked briskly to the witness chair. After he took the oath and stated his name for the record, Wilson asked, "How long have you been with the Tarrant County Sheriff's Office?"

"Thirty-one years. This year's my last."

"And twenty years ago, what was your assignment?"

"I was coming off an injury to my back, and so there was a three-year period, from 1997 to 2000, that I worked the evidence room."

"And during those three years, did evidence ever get lost?"

"Unfortunately, yes. Especially when there's a long delay between arrest and trial."

"So, it wasn't particularly unusual for the cocaine found in Ms. Granger's apartment to be missing."

"It didn't happen a lot, but it did occasionally. Especially drugs. Back in 2002, a couple of bad cops were busted for stealing drugs from the evidence room."

"Thank you. No further questions."

Dani stood. "How many items are tagged in the evidence room?"

"Oh, probably thousands."

"And those times during your tenure when evidence was lost, how many were *before* the trial took place?"

Stolz hesitated. "I can't be sure. It was a long time ago."

Dani picked up a sheaf of papers from the defense table. "Maybe these can refresh your recollection."

As she started to walk back toward the witness, he cleared his throat and said, "Just once. With Graham."

"Thank you. I have no other questions."

Stolz left the witness box, and Wilson called Amy Barnett. After she was sworn in, Wilson asked, "Are you acquainted with Susan Granger?"

"Yeah, she was my cellmate back in '98."

"Was that before or after she shared a cell with Becky Whitlaw?"

"After. Becky got moved to the loony bin, and they moved me in with Susan."

"For how long did you share a cell?"

"Almost a year. Until she got out."

"During that year, did Ms. Granger ever tell you that Ms. Whitlaw had confided in her about the origin of the fire that killed her three children?"

"Yeah. Susan said Becky admitted she'd started it."

"Did Ms. Granger ever say that the prosecuting attorney had told her to lie about that?"

"Nah."

"Did Ms. Granger ever say she'd made a deal with the prosecuting attorney to get out of jail if she said Ms. Whitlaw confessed to her?"

"Nah."

"Thank you. I have no further questions."

Dani stood up. "Ms. Barnett, how many times have you been arrested?"

"A few."

"Can you be more precise?"

Barnett held her hand up and silently mouthed numbers as she counted. "Twelve."

"And what were you charged with each time?"

"Some were solicitation, some possession."

"Possession of drugs?"

"Yeah."

"Do you have a pending charge against you now?"

"Nah. I'm good."

"When was your last arrest?"

"Ten days ago, but they dropped the charge."

"Because you agreed to testify today?"

Barnett looked over at Wilson, then back at Dani. "Nah. It was a bad arrest. They didn't have the goods on me."

"I have no more questions." Dani glanced at Wilson, who shook his head. "You can step down now."

Wilson stood. "The State rests, your Honor."

Judge Gertner glanced up at the clock. "Let's break for lunch, and I'll hear wrap-up arguments when we return. Let's say one o'clock."

Dani gathered her belongings and headed out of the courtroom. She wished she'd had more to justify a new trial and hoped Granger's reversal was enough. She wasn't optimistic.

At one o'clock promptly, Judge Gertner returned to the bench. Dani and Wilson were both in attendance.

"Go ahead, Ms. Trumball."

Dani stood. "There are two issues present here. The first, whether the assistant district attorney improperly withheld important information from the defense counsel, in violation of

Ms. Whitlaw's constitutional rights, and the second is whether a jailhouse informant's false testimony unfairly swayed the jurors. With respect to the first issue, the Supreme Court has recognized that bartered testimony may be unreliable and prejudicial but has permitted it because the constitution requires that any incentive offered a witness in exchange for her testimony must be disclosed to the defense. That disclosure allows the defense to effectively cross-examine the witness's motivations and make it a factor for the jury to consider. Ms. Granger's testimony today is unequivocal that she was offered a break from the harsh penalties she faced in exchange for testifying that Becky Whitlaw said she'd purposely set the fire. The fact that her case was dismissed, allegedly because of lost evidence, supports her claim. And, the record of the trial is clear that no such incentive was disclosed to the defense. That failure by itself is sufficient to warrant a new trial.

"With respect to the second issue, Ms. Granger's reversal of her trial testimony is newly discovered evidence that warrants a new trial. Even with due diligence, the defense could not have discovered, before or during the trial, that the witness was lying. Her new statement is not cumulative, and the impact of her confession on jurors is such that had she not lied, it would likely have led to a different result. There was no direct evidence tying Becky Whitlaw to the arson, other than Susan Granger's lie that she'd confessed."

Dani stopped and took a sip of water. "Finally, Mr. Wilson has suggested during this hearing that Ms. Granger is now lying. But she has no incentive to change her story now, other than a desire to right a wrong. Her credibility is for a jury to decide. Becky Whitlaw deserves to have her case heard in a new trial, without the taint of prosecutorial misconduct and a lying witness. Thank you."

As Dani sat down, Wilson rose. "Your Honor, I will be succinct. It is not necessary to guess what Ms. Granger's motivation might be for changing her story twenty years later. It is enough to note that never, during the year leading up to the defendant's trial, or the twenty years thereafter, has she ever claimed to have made up the confession. Until now. The very suspiciousness of that change is enough to dismiss her testimony, and without that, there is no newly discovered evidence to warrant a new trial. Furthermore, even if there was the slightest chance that Ms. Granger is now being truthful, and had lied twenty years earlier, it still is not enough to warrant a new trial. Contrary to Ms. Trumball's claim, there was enough evidence without a confession for the jury to find the defendant guilty of this most heinous crime.

"With respect to the claim that the prosecutor withheld exculpatory evidence, namely, that an incentive was offered in exchange for Ms. Granger's testimony, there is simply *no* evidence to back up her claim. Ms. Hancock deservedly had a stellar reputation for integrity, and it should not be permitted to be sullied by a woman of questionable moral character."

Wilson retook his seat. Judge Gertner pushed back the glasses that had slid down his nose. "Okay, I'll take the motion under advisement. You can expect my decision by next week."

With that, Dani gathered up her papers. Once again, she hoped her argument had been enough. Once again, she feared it wasn't.

It was after eleven by the time Dani arrived home. She crept quietly up the stairs, tiptoed into Jonah's and Ruth's bedrooms, straightened their covers, then gently kissed their foreheads, and finally made it to her bedroom. She saw the light under the door and was secretly glad that Doug was still awake, even though she'd told him when the plane landed not to wait up for her.

She entered the bedroom and saw Doug propped up in bed, several pillows behind him, a book in his hand. She walked over to the bed and slid in next to him. Doug draped his arm around her, then pulled her in for a long kiss.

"I missed you."

"Me, too. I'm glad to be home."

"How did it go?"

Dani wasn't ready to talk about the hearing yet. During their brief phone call earlier, he'd also asked, and she'd put it off until she got home. "How were the kids tonight?" she asked, changing the topic.

"No problems. After Jonah finished his homework, he hung out at Keith's for a bit."

Once again, Dani appreciated how nice it was for Jonah to have a friend so close.

"Ruth was a bit cranky. I think another tooth is getting ready to pop through."

"I missed the kids, too."

"I know."

"I think the travel is wearing me down."

"You've always traveled a bit."

When Dani had first interviewed for the position at HIPP, Bruce had told her travel was part of the job. "Figure about two to six days a month," he'd said. She remembered thinking she would enjoy that, going to different cities, breaking up the time sitting behind a desk. And he was accurate, when averaged over a year. But some months she never left the office, and other months, she'd be gone ten to fifteen days. "When I started at

HIPP, Jonah was already in school. I didn't feel like I was missing out on key milestones."

"A new tooth is hardly a milestone for Ruth. She already has plenty." Doug turned his body to face Dani. "Is something else going on? Is that why you don't want to talk about your hearing?"

Dani felt her eyes get misty. "I'm afraid I'm going to lose. If that happens, I'll go through the appeals, but you know it's hard to overturn the trial judge's decision in a motion for a new trial. It will delay the inevitable, but when it's all done, I have nothing else for Becky."

Doug pulled Dani close once again. "You'll find something. You or Tommy. Together, you make magic happen."

Dani closed her eyes. If only that were true.

Tommy had had a hunch, and it had paid off big-time. After returning from Texas, he'd asked his hacker contact to do a search of suspicious or known arson fires in Texas for five years before and five years after the fire that destroyed Becky's life. He'd just gotten off the phone with him and learned that there had been three fires in Denton County before Becky's home burned down, all in abandoned or empty structures, and one in Tarrant County in a home while the inhabitants were away on vacation. On his own, Tommy's source had decided to check the roster of firefighters in each town's fire department on the dates of the fires, and one name popped up. Oscar White. Each of the towns where the suspicious fires occurred was staffed by volunteer firefighters, and White had served with each department when the fires occurred.

The hacker decided to go deeper, then discovered White had been arrested nine years ago for arson in Kensington, a small town in Tarrant County. Once again, the family had been away on vacation, and the house was believed empty—except it wasn't. Tucked away in a back bedroom was the homeowner's niece, who'd agreed to housesit the family's three cats while they were gone. She'd escaped with third-degree burns over one-third of her body, but she'd survived. The cats didn't. It was clear to the arson investigators that an accelerant had been used, but they quickly cleared the niece of suspicion.

His fellow firefighters were the ones who raised the specter of concern with White. At first, the sheriff dismissed those concerns. There was no evidence of forced entry, and White didn't have a key. It was only after the niece said she hadn't remembered locking the doors before she went to sleep—it was a small town, after all—that they brought him in for questioning. Five hours later, they had a confession. White was convicted of arson and sentenced to twenty years at the Eastham Unit of Texas Department of Criminal Justice prisons.

A hero complex, I bet, Tommy thought. *Set a fire, and then get accolades for putting it out. But it got out of hand at Becky's house. Burned too hot, too fast.* White was still in prison, and Tommy needed to speak to him. He could be the key to this whole case.

Becky sat in front of her computer, one in a bank of what looked to be a hundred set up in rows in an old room in the prison. A prison guard sat behind a desk in the front of the room, and two were located just outside. Five days a week, she left her cell on death row shortly before 5:30 a.m. and worked on transcribing textbooks into braille. She welcomed getting out of her claustrophobic cell. Transcribing braille had required training, and the prison officials had recognized she was smart. Becky had learned quickly and was now a top performer in the computer room.

They weren't supposed to talk while working, but the women did, anyway, in low whispers so as not to attract attention. "I heard you have a new lawyer," said Amy Dunkirk, sitting to Becky's right.

Becky nodded. "From an innocence project."

"I thought they turned you down."

"The one in Texas did. This woman is from one in New York."

"How does it look for you?"

"I don't know." Becky didn't want to let herself hope, to think there was a chance she could escape her fate. Even so, there were times she'd lie in bed at night, the lights out all along the corridor of cells, and wonder what life would be like if she were ever free. She had a skill now—transcribing braille. She doubted there would be a call for that in the small town of Glen Brook, but maybe in Dallas, or even Houston, they'd need people who could do that. Nothing was left for her in Glen Brook, anyway. Sure, her mother was still there, but so were her memories, bad memories, and she didn't want to return to that.

If she moved to Dallas, she already had a friend there—Chuck was the kindest man she'd ever known. She pictured him with the young children who needed his care, frightened at the thought of being cut open, of the problem in their bodies that he needed to repair. She carried an image of him soothing a young boy or girl, getting a laugh as he told a joke, erasing their fears with his soft voice. He'd been a godsend to Becky. Before, she hadn't wanted to die, but she accepted that in time her sentence would be carried out. Even as her lawyer went through her early appeals, she knew he wouldn't succeed and had been resigned to that failure. Now, though, she wanted to go free. She wanted to see how time had changed what she knew on the outside. She wanted to go to a movie or bowling, even to a bar and have a few drinks while listening to a local band hoping to make it big. She wanted to live.

"Do you think, maybe, they could help me?" Amy asked. "The lawyer from New York?"

Amy was an almost emaciated woman of thirty-eight who'd been convicted of murdering her husband eleven years ago. Over their years of working side by side on the computers, Amy had confided that her husband had beaten her so many times that she'd lost count. She'd suffered numerous concussions and broken bones and took it silently until the evening he threw their six-year-old son down a flight of stairs. As her son lay in a heap, sobbing in pain, Amy calmly went into her bedroom, opened her husband's closet, and from the top shelf removed the gun that he always kept loaded, then shot him once between his eyes. Her son, now living with Amy's parents and almost grown, visited her in prison every Sunday.

"I don't know," Becky answered. "I think they're only helping me because my friend knows the lawyer. She's doing him a favor." Becky saw Amy's face drop. "But I can ask. It can't hurt."

They worked silently at their computers for a bit. "What do you think you'd do first, if you got out?" Amy asked after a while.

"I don't know."

"I do. I'd go to Gramma's Ice Cream, on Main Street in my hometown, and I'd order a giant ice cream sundae. Five scoops, hot fudge, real whipped cream, chocolate sprinkles. I even know what flavors—black raspberry, pistachio, butter pecan, cherry vanilla, and coconut."

Becky laughed. "That's pretty specific."

"I've been dreaming about that sundae for a long time." She turned her head to look at Becky. "So, what about you? What do you dream about doing?"

"Don't laugh. I want to go to McDonald's. Buy a Big Mac and a chocolate milkshake."

"Jeez, you can get bad hamburgers in here."

It wasn't the food Becky yearned for. McDonald's was her kids' favorite place to eat. When she had the money to spare, that was their special treat. She wanted to return to that. That's what was impossible.

Becky's fingers few over the computer keys as she transcribed the history textbook propped on a book stand to her right. She was one of the fastest transcribers in the room and was often given the more advanced texts. The women surrounding her worked on books for kindergarten through college, and Becky had long ago requested and received college texts. She especially loved the science texts, even though they reminded her of her lost dreams. Although she'd given up her plans for college when she married Grady, she was now learning on her own. Sometimes, the guards would allow her to take a textbook back to her cell after she'd finished work for the day, and she'd tear through it, absorbing the knowledge contained on the pages.

The lunch bell rang, and one by one, the women finished the passages they were working on, stood, and headed out to the mess hall. All except Becky. Because she was on death row, she was required to take her meals in her cell, even on days she worked. She walked through the corridors, monitored with guards along the barren hallways, until she turned into the corridor for women sentenced to die. The guard standing outside smiled, asked her how the work was going, then opened the door into her cellblock. All the guards liked Becky. She never stirred up any trouble and always offered help when needed. She never got angry, nor moped or shouted or complained. For the entirety of her twenty years of incarceration, she'd been a model prisoner. If she'd received a sentence of twenty-five years to life, she'd have been up for parole, and likely had it granted. The guards would have put in a good word for her, and she'd have expressed remorse—always an imperative when appearing before the parole board—for the crime that had landed her in prison.

She did feel remorseful, every single day for the past two decades. Remorseful because her children were dead; remorseful because she'd been too drunk to wake up in time to save them; remorseful because that evening was a dark hole in her memory. She had no memory of turning off the television and falling asleep on the couch, and if she had no memory of that, she could never have absolute certainty over what else she might have done. She didn't believe she would have tried to wipe out her family, herself included, but that dark hole remained, and so yes, she could go before an appeal board, and show genuine remorse for setting a fire that killed her children.

She turned into her cell and sat down on the bed. She had no cellmates—women on death row were housed alone. A minute later, she heard the rolling clack of the meal cart's wheels coming down her aisle. When it reached her cell, the guard passed a tray of food through an opening, then reached underneath the cart and pulled out a package. "This came for you today," she said, as she handed it to Becky.

The brown wrapper had already been opened, then carelessly taped back up. All packages to prisoners were carefully inspected before they were delivered. Becky tore the wrapping open and saw a textbook. *Fundamentals of Nursing.* Inside the book cover was a letter from Chuck Stanger. *I saw this in a used bookstore and thought you might be interested. I remember you'd once thought of becoming a nurse. Perhaps this is something to consider when your conviction is overturned.*

Becky smiled. *When,* not *if,* he'd written. She wished she shared his optimism.

Dani spent the morning working on a complaint against the State of Nevada on behalf of Rick Turner, seeking compensation for his wrongful conviction. He'd been incarcerated almost thirty years, and although he no longer was in prison, his freedom came with challenges. Serious ones. Like all those in his position, he found his family and former friends were virtual strangers. His years of earning money from steadily improving work skills had been taken away; and he returned to a society that still viewed him with suspicion. Thirty-one states and the District of Columbia recognized that the wrongfully convicted prisoner's nightmare didn't end upon his release. With no money, housing, health insurance, job prospects, and often, education, their lives continued to be hellish. And so, those states enacted legislation that provided compensation when a prisoner was exonerated. It ranged from a low cap of $20,000 in New Hampshire, regardless of the number of years in prison, to a high in the District of Columbia of $70,000 for each year of incarceration, plus an additional $50,000 for each year on death row. Often, these states also provided health insurance and tuition waivers at state colleges.

None of this gave these men and women back the years they'd lost or make up for the hardships they'd endured while imprisoned, but it gave them a chance going forward.

Nevada was one of seventeen states that had no such statute. Rick Turner was released from prison penniless and jobless. Dani intended to make sure he didn't remain that way, and so she worked on a lawsuit to redress what that state had taken away from him.

Dani finished the complaint, then gathered up her purse and headed out the door. Whatever reservations she still had about the move from New York, it was lovely that she only needed a light sweater in early November. She drove to Chez Albert, where she was meeting Lauren for lunch, parked in their lot, then headed inside.

Since meeting Lauren at a law school faculty cocktail party, they had tried to meet up for lunch every other week, usually trying a different restaurant each time. Dani cherished those lunches—they were a break from the isolation of working from home. Her home office had everything she needed—a desk, computer, printer, file cabinets—everything but other people. She didn't have an assistant right outside her office—Carol was still back in New York, although she still sent Carol work from California. Dani typed her own motions and briefs, but she'd email them to Carol to format properly and submit to courts and opposing counsel.

When she entered the restaurant, Dani saw Lauren was already seated at a table. She headed over there and sat down. "Sorry I'm a bit late. Had to finish up something. Were you waiting long?"

"Five minutes, that's all."

Dani quickly scanned the menu, and when the waiter came to their table, ordered a Waldorf salad. They chatted easily as they waited for their food. Despite their difference in age, and home life—Lauren and Gregory had no children—Dani felt she'd found a kindred spirit in her new friend. They both loved the outdoors—especially skiing and hiking. Both loved to read, mostly fiction. Both loved live theater. Each time they met, Dani learned new things about Lauren, and each time it struck a chord in Dani.

As soon as their food was delivered, Lauren said, "I think Chuck has a bit of a crush on Becky."

Dani put her fork down. "My client Becky?"

Lauren nodded.

"All these years I kept pushing him to find someone, and he kept putting me off. 'Too busy,' he'd always say. And now he goes and finds someone completely unavailable. I guess she doesn't interfere with his busy schedule."

"She looks like someone who was pretty once, but I wouldn't say that now. I mean, she's not unattractive. Just worn down." Dani leaned forward. "He actually told you he has a crush on her?"

"Not in so many words. But I know my brother. I can tell by the way he talks about her. He's always been a sucker for the sad cases."

Dani leaned back in her seat. She'd had many clients on death row with families at home—spouses and children and parents—all who wanted their loved ones exonerated. But as much as Dani wanted the same thing for her clients, there was a distance between her and their families. If she was unsuccessful, she'd hold their hands at the execution and cry along with them, then go home to her family and never see them again. But Chuck was her friend's brother. He had been in her home. She would undoubtedly see him again from time to time when he visited his sister. She felt a weight start to press on her chest.

"Lauren, I don't know if I'll be able to save Becky. It's a really tough case."

"I know that. I just hope my brother does."

It took several days for Tommy to wrangle access to the prisoner. He was no longer law enforcement, and HIPP wasn't representing him. Visitors had to be on the prisoner's list. Fortunately, Tommy's ties to former colleagues ran wide, and those friends had friends who could help. Three days later, he arrived in Houston and drove to the Eastham Unit.

After going through the standard red tape, he was led to the visitor's room, filled with tables and chairs, some occupied and others empty. "Over there," the guard said, pointing to a table in the middle of the room. The man sitting there was pushing fifty, Tommy guessed, with male pattern baldness and pale eyes that looked weary. Tommy sat down. "Oscar White?"

"That's me. Who are you?"

Tommy introduced himself, then asked, "Do you remember the fire, back when you were working in Glen Brook, that burned down Becky Whitlaw's home and killed her three kids?"

"Of course I do. A real tragedy, that was."

Tommy gave him a hard stare. "You're sitting here because you set some fires yourself."

White glanced downward. "I'm not proud of that."

"Injured a woman pretty badly."

"It's no excuse, but she wasn't supposed to be there."

"Why'd you do it?"

White's eyes darted up, then back down, as he stared at his hands. "I like fires. Always have. I don't know why." His head jerked up. "But I never tried to hurt anyone. Never. I just—the flames are hypnotic, don't you think?"

Tommy ignored his question. "When you lived in Glen Brook, did you know Becky?"

"I knew who she was. I ate sometimes in the restaurant where she worked."

"Pretty lady."

White smiled. "About the prettiest one in Glen Brook. Probably in the whole county."

"Did you ever ask her out?"

White's cheeks reddened slightly. "Nah. She never even noticed me."

"Maybe she would have if her house was on fire and you rescued her children."

White looked up at Tommy. "What are you saying? That I started that fire?"

"You got to admit, you have a history of doing that."

"Not in occupied buildings!"

"Your prison sentence says otherwise."

"I told you, I didn't know anyone was home there."

"How did you know the homeowners were away?"

"I was visiting my friend who lived across the street and saw a few newspapers on their lawn. I asked him about it, and he told me they were on vacation."

Tommy leaned back in his seat. Was he telling the truth? Or had he started the fire in Becky's house, and because he'd been unable to prevent the deaths, become more careful about targeting empty homes? "Weren't you in the first fire truck that pulled up to Becky's house?"

For the first time, White's eyes hardened, and he stared at Tommy. "I did not start the fire in Becky's house. I would never have knowingly risked anyone's life. Never. I've done bad things in my life, but not that. Not ever."

On his way back to the airport Tommy phoned Dani. "I thought I had a live wire," he told her before filling her in on Oscar White.

"Do you believe him?" she asked when he finished.

"You know me. I'm always a skeptic."

"So, he's a possibility?"

"Yes. But I don't think we'll be able to prove it."

"Still. If I can get Becky a new trial, it may be enough to create reasonable doubt."

"I'll keep working on him."

"Do that, Tommy."

He promised he would, but he knew guys like White from his days at the FBI. If White had set the fire, Tommy doubted he'd admit it now. Maybe because what that would mean for another prison sentence. It could be planted on top of the one he was already serving. Or—and Tommy thought this was a possibility; the guy *had* seemed sincere—he simply couldn't admit to himself that he'd caused the death of three innocent children, and blocked it out so thoroughly that he believed his own lie. Either that, or the guy really hadn't started Becky's fire. Whatever the truth was, it wasn't going to help Becky. Tommy felt certain of that, no matter how hard he worked the guy.

J udge Gertner was true to his word—his decision arrived in Dani's email a week after she returned to California. She quickly opened the document and began to read.

> *Defendant has brought this motion for a new trial based on two pieces of evidence that she claims are newly discovered: first, that the prosecuting attorney willfully failed to disclose that she had offered a reduced sentence to Susan Granger. Ms. Granger was briefly a cellmate of the defendant. She testified at defendant's trial that the defendant confessed she'd deliberately set the fire that resulted in the deaths of her three children. Second, that Ms. Granger had been coached to give that testimony, which she now recants.*

> *To prevail on a motion seeking a new trial based on newly discovered evidence, the defendant must show that 1) the new evidence was discovered after*

the trial, 2) the failure to discover the new evidence prior to the trial was not as a result of lack of due diligence, 3) the evidence is not cumulative, and 4) the evidence is so material that it would likely produce a different verdict had it been known to the jury. Each one of these elements must be demonstrated to justify a new trial.

With respect to the fourth element, the defendant has failed to convince this court that if Ms. Granger had not testified, the result would have been different. There was substantial evidence that the fire was deliberately set by the defendant.

Defendant's second argument is that she is entitled to a new trial because the failure of the prosecutor to disclose that she had obtained the witness's testimony in exchange for a reduced sentence violated her constitutional rights. This claim also lacks merit. The defendant has failed to persuade me that such was the case. I find defendant's sole witness to that alleged misfeasance to be noncredible.

For these reasons, defendant's motion for a new trial is denied.

Although not terribly surprised, Dani was still disappointed. She'd wished she'd had more going into the motion. She would appeal Gertner's decision, but she knew that in these kinds of matters, appeals courts generally gave great deference to the trial judge's judgment. Failure of the prosecuting attorney to advise Becky's attorney that Granger had been offered a deal in exchange for her testimony was a clear violation of Becky's constitutional rights, but Gertner had determined that Granger wasn't believable—a ruling almost never overturned by an appeals court.

Dani pulled out Becky's file. She would start immediately on an appeal, one she felt certain she would lose. At least it would postpone what now seemed inevitable.

One week later, Dani was at HIPP's office in New York. Before she'd left for California, she and Bruce Kantor had agreed she should return to its East Village office every three or four months for a day of in-person meetings. This was her first time back since she'd moved to California in the beginning of August. The crisp mid-November air was colder than in Stanford, where it still felt like spring.

She'd arrived the night before, and although Bruce had offered to pay for a hotel room, she'd instead accepted Melanie Stanton's invitation to stay with her in her Flatbush brownstone. As soon as she'd gotten settled last night, Melanie had said, "I've got news."

Dani took one look at her slightly fuller face and rosy glow, and knew exactly what she was going to say.

"I'm pregnant."

Dani was thrilled for her. Melanie had started at HIPP four years ago and had been Dani's protégé. Three years ago, she'd married Brad Stanton, a Wall Street analyst whose income put him in the top 1 percent. Dani asked Melanie if this meant she would leave HIPP in favor of becoming a full-time mother.

"I'm not sure," Melanie answered, and Dani understood her conflicting emotions. She dealt with her own every day.

The next morning, she and Melanie arrived at the office together, after stopping at Dani's favorite corner deli and each picking up a steaming cup of coffee. Dani enviously eyed Melanie's blueberry muffin but refrained from indulging herself. As soon as they walked in HIPP's door, Carol, Dani's assistant, rushed over and gave her a hug, then stepped back and looked her up and down. "You look the same."

Dani chuckled. "Why wouldn't I?"

"Hmm. You sound the same, too. My cousin spent one summer at UC Berkeley and came back looking and sounding like she'd been a California girl all her life."

"It's still me, a New Yorker through and through."

Bruce must have heard her voice, for a moment later his office door opened, and he stepped out. "Good to have you back here," he said, a broad smile on his face.

"Feels good to be here."

He turned to his assistant. "Let's gather the attorneys and investigators into the large conference room. We can get started."

Dani and Melanie headed down the hall to the room, followed soon by Bruce, Tommy, and the four other attorneys and two other investigators working at HIPP. Before she began telecommuting from California, Dani always attended the once-weekly status update unless she was on the road. Since August, she'd called in for the meetings. It felt good to be back in HIPP's bare-bones office with colleagues she'd worked with for ages.

"First, some announcements," Bruce began, after he'd poured himself a cup of coffee from the urn at the end of the table. "It's just November, but we've already met our fundraising quota for this year and have a start on covering next year's budget."

Everyone clapped.

"Also, the New York County DA's office has just announced they're instituting a conviction integrity unit, beginning in January. We've agreed to work with them on identifying any cases we come across from that county that warrant them giving a second look."

Murmurs of, "Great," "Hooray," and "About time."

"That's it for announcements. Melanie, why don't you start us off?"

Melanie opened a folder in front of her.

"First, an update on my current cases. Marcus Desmond, if you remember, was convicted eighteen years ago of murdering his wife, in Guilford County, North Carolina. No forensic evidence tied him to the crime. Marcus's son, then three years old, was home when the murder occurred, said a monster killed his mother, and that his father wasn't home when it happened. Neighbors reported seeing a man hanging around their house and walking in the woods behind it. Despite the trial attorney's suspicion that the prosecution hadn't turned over all the exculpatory evidence, and the judge ordering them to do so, they in fact withheld significant evidence—some items found in the woods behind the house, including a bloody baseball cap. Three years ago, our office took him on, learned of the withheld evidence, and filed a motion for DNA testing of items at the crime scene. The judge allowed it but excluded the baseball cap. The DNA testing was inconclusive. I filed a new motion two weeks ago, and the court allowed the cap to be tested. Yesterday, it came back. His wife's DNA was on the cap, along with that of some other male. Not Marcus."

There was a round of applause at the table.

"Congratulations, Melanie," Bruce said. "I assume the prosecutor will join you in making a motion for his release?"

"He will. The original ADA is long retired, and the one now on Marcus's case is embarrassed by the history behind this. He's going to see if he can get it fast-tracked."

"Anything else?"

"Yes. I've made a motion for DNA testing for Clive Bunder, who was convicted twenty-three years ago, in Roanoke County, Virginia, for a rape and burglary, based on hairs found at the scene. Oral argument is scheduled for next Tuesday. And I'm taking on a new case. Milton Miller. He was convicted thirty-one years ago in New York for the rape and murder of a sixteen-year-old girl. He was convicted on sketchy evidence. Hair analysis, soil comparison, and—a new one for me—fabric print analysis. Oh, and throw into the mix a jailhouse informant."

There was a chorus of groans from those seated at the table.

"And you believe he's innocent?" Bruce asked.

"I do. There were a number of witnesses who placed him at a bar on the night of the murder."

"Okay. Rick, how about you go next."

One by one, the attorneys reported on their cases. Dani loved being in the room with them. Listening by phone three thousand miles away just wasn't the same. She loved hearing the noise from the street, horns honking, people shouting, muffled through the closed windows but still throbbing like a heartbeat that announced this city was alive. She loved strolling through streets and breathing in the smells from the food carts scattered throughout the borough—hot dogs, pretzels, or nuts. Even vegetarian crepes and lamb gyros and rice noodles and almost anything else she could imagine, the odors all blending together to make walking in Manhattan feel like an international journey. She'd been able to continue her work with HIPP, and her family was adapting to California. Jonah was doing well in his new school, Elsa was loving and reliable with Ruth, and Doug found his new job stimulating. Still, Stanford wasn't New York.

"Your turn, Dani," Bruce said when the others had finished their reports.

"Dominic Webster was sentenced to death for the murder of his girlfriend's three-year-old daughter. Five years ago, a DNA test excluded him, but the ADA on the case said he would retry him, anyway, and he's remained in prison ever since."

"How could that be?" Melanie piped in.

"Good question. Every time his case came up for trial, the prosecutor had a reason for delaying it. The ADA's name is Samuel Xavier. I've asked him to run the DNA through CODIS—see if it identifies anyone else—but so far, he's refused. I filed a motion last week to compel him to do that, and to set a firm date for the trial.

"I also took on the case of Patton Swinton. He was convicted twenty-five years ago, in Osage County, Oklahoma, for rape and burglary, and sentenced to life. The only evidence the DA really had was based on hair analysis."

Bruce shook his head. "It's shameful how many men and women were convicted on evidence that we now know has no scientific basis."

"He was only seventeen when they locked him up. He's been in prison for his entire adult life. I sent a request to the Osage County DA and asked for DNA testing on the hair. They've checked the files, and it's still there. He agreed, and we're now just waiting for the results."

"Anything else?"

"Yes. My motion for a new trial for Becky Whitlaw was denied. She's been in prison twenty years for the death by arson of her three children, in Glen Brook, Texas. I filed an appeal two day ago, but frankly, I don't hold out much hope. We didn't have much to work with. I'm not sure where to go with it now."

"I have something on that," Tommy said. "I've learned that Billy Bingham was in Glen Brook when the fire occurred."

Dani's mouth dropped open. "How do you know that?"

"His credit card was used at a few spots in town that week, including the night before the fire. In fact, one spot was the restaurant where Becky worked."

"That's twenty years ago. How did you find those records?"

A smile appeared on Tommy's face before he quickly wiped it away. "Let's just say I had some help."

Dani knew what that meant. He'd used his hacker source to troll through long-ago records.

"Who's Billy Bingham?" Melanie asked.

Dani turned toward Melanie. "Someone who had a crush on Becky back in high school. After her husband died, he tried to start something with her, and she blew him off. We wanted to question him as a possible suspect, but he died a few years ago."

"Now that we know he was in Glen Brook," Tommy said, "I thought I'd nose around and try to find his former friends. Maybe he told them something."

"That's a great idea, Tommy." Dani sat back in her seat. Tommy's discovery gave her a dash of hope—a slim dash, but at least it was something.

~

Dani arrived home the next day, shortly before Jonah's school bus dropped him off. It had been a brief trip back to New York, but it had imbued her once again with the passion she needed for her job. There were so many reasons to relish working from home—chief among them having Ruth so close at hand—but what she lost was being part of a larger group, all working together with a common goal.

As soon as she walked in, Ruth ran up to her, arms outstretched. Dani scooped her up and nuzzled her neck, eliciting squeals of delight from her daughter.

"She misses you when you're away," Elsa said.

"I miss her, too." Dani put Ruth down, then squatted to be level with her. "What did you do today, sweet pea?"

"Make cookies."

"Yummy. Did you leave any for Mommy?"

Ruth nodded, then ran into the kitchen, returning a moment later with a chocolate chip cookie in her hand. "For you."

Dani took a bite. "This is the best cookie I've ever had."

A big grin broke out on Ruth's face. "Elsa help."

Dani spent the next fifteen minutes playing with Ruth, until it was time to meet Jonah's bus.

"Guess what?" he said as soon as he got off. "There's going to be a talent show at Keith's school. I'm going to compose a new piece, and Keith is going to perform it."

"That's wonderful, but I didn't know Keith played an instrument. What is it? Piano? Violin?"

"No. Guitar."

Dani raised a brow. "You can compose for guitar?"

"Sure. For classical guitar. Keith is very masterly."

"I can't wait to hear it. When's the show?"

"In four weeks. Right before Christmas." Suddenly, Jonah's expression grew dark. "You'll be home, won't you?"

There it was, the familiar tug between work and motherhood. Especially with her job, where court calendars dictated her schedule and sent her all over the country. "Of course, Jonah. I wouldn't miss it." As she said the words, she silently made a wish that she wouldn't be forced to break that promise.

That night, during "honeymoon hour," Dani lay curled up in Doug's arms.

"Another wildfire broke out while you were away."

"Where?"

"North of San Francisco."

"Should we be worried?"

"I don't think so. Although some rain would help."

Dani never thought she'd rue sunny days. "Ever miss New York? We never had to worry about wildfires there."

"Of course I do."

"But you're happy here?"

"Aren't you?"

Was she? She was still working for HIPP, still hustling to free the wrongly convicted, free from the bitter cold of the winter months that were about to descend on the Northeast. She'd made a friend—Lauren—and found a good nanny. It would be selfish of her to complain. She turned to look at Doug, at his warm brown eyes that were always filled with love for her. "Sure. It's great here."

Sundays always seemed to drag on forever for Becky. On Saturdays, she volunteered to work crocheting blankets, her original prison job, but she didn't work on Sundays. It was still three weeks before her mother's monthly visit, which meant, except for a few hours of permitted recreation in the yard, and in the common room with other women on death row, she was confined to her cell from her 4:00 a.m. wake-up until lights out at 10:30 p.m. And so, on Sundays, she'd ruminate about her life, about what she had lost.

Becky put down the book she was reading and slid out a box from under her cot-size bed. She lifted the lid, then took out a group of pictures. Hers had been destroyed in the fire, but thankfully, her mother had given Becky some of her own. The first was of her and Grady, dressed for their high school prom, he in a tuxedo with a bright red bow tie, and Becky in a black chiffon floor-length gown, with a bodice-hugging, deep V-neck that showed off her bust, then flared out to hide the baby bump that had just begun to show. They'd already made the decision to get married at town hall, with the local justice of the peace presiding, two weeks after their graduation. She'd been accepted at the University of Texas at Austin, had sent in her deposit, and had spent hours poring over the course catalogue, dreaming of the classes she would take, of the parties she'd attend, of the new friends she'd make.

As soon as she'd told Grady she was pregnant, he'd proposed. Down on his knees and professing his love, not an "I guess we ought to" proposal, but one from his heart. She didn't hesitate before answering, "Yes." In an instant, her dream of college was gone, replaced with a fantasy of the American dream—a husband, children, someday a house with a picket fence, maybe even a dog. The next day, he'd taken her shopping for a ring. Not a diamond, an aquamarine stone—her birthstone—in a silver band, with two small diamond chips on the side. She hadn't thought about the money it would take to live the American dream; she didn't know how exhausted babies would make her. She was in love, and so she substituted one dream for the other.

She looked at the next picture, again of her and Grady but also Benji. It had been the picture they'd put on their first Christmas card as a family. Benji was only six weeks old, but he'd been a big baby at birth—9 pounds 2 ounces—and had a round face with big blue eyes that she'd thought girls would swoon over when he'd grown up. The lack of sleep showed in her face, but Grady beamed with happiness.

She continued looking at each picture, the remaining ones all of her children. Benji, at his one-year-old birthday party. Grady managed to capture his face as he had his first taste of something sugary—his birthday cake. His eyes had lit up, and his whole face seemed to explode with delight. She didn't have a picture of Danny until he was six months old, sitting in Benji's lap. She'd read about firstborn children who resented a new baby taking away their mother's attention, but Benji had adored Danny from the moment he'd been brought home from the hospital. By the time Danny could walk, he followed Benji around like a loyal puppy. Becky picked up the last picture. As always when she looked at it, she struggled to hold back tears. Lacy, clothed in a frilly pink dress, a pink bow in her soft brown curls, emerald green eyes that matched her own, smiling as she always did when posing for pictures. She hadn't yet learned to walk but still seemed destined to be the focus of attention.

Becky had been so happy when Lacy was born. Finally, she had a daughter, a little girl to dress up and pamper. She loved her sons, truly and deeply, but when she looked into Lacy's eyes, it was as though she was looking at herself. Lacy would do the things Becky missed. She would go to college, maybe even become a doctor. She wouldn't become pregnant while still in high school. No, Becky would make sure of that.

She was lost in the picture when a voice called out, "Whitlaw, you have a visitor." It startled her, and her head jerked up. A visitor? Could it be Chuck? She hoped it was, but he never visited her on Sundays. She stood up and waited for her cell door to open, then held out her hands for the inevitable cuffs.

The guard escorted her to the visitor's room, then directed her to the fourth chair along a row of Plexiglas. She sat down and stared at Marci. It had been years since she'd seen her, too many to even count. Marci had gained weight. Her face was fuller, and her hair was shorter, but she was still the woman Becky had once thought of as her best friend, her confidant. The trial had taught Becky that no one, even someone who'd known you since grade school, could ever be relied on to keep your secrets.

"Hi," Becky said.

As soon as Marci opened her mouth, words gushed out, like water that had broken through a dam. "Oh, Becky, I'm so, so sorry. Sorry I stopped coming to see you. Sorry I stopped writing.

Sorry I testified against you. And most of all, sorry a small part of me wondered if you really had set the fire."

Although Marci had visited Becky sporadically during her first few years of incarceration, she'd never said those words. "And now?"

"Now I know you'd never have done that to your children."

"What's changed your mind?"

"I think I always realized that. Even when the DA questioned me after the fire, I couldn't believe you'd do that. But he kept pressing me, and you'd seemed so down that night, the night of the fire. He made me question my own judgment. When your new attorney came to visit me, and I remembered Billy Bingham pestering you, it all made sense."

"Billy?"

"Don't you remember? He'd always been after you, from before you hooked up with Grady. After Grady died, he started up again."

Becky remembered him well. He'd stopped by the diner that night, the evening before the fire, and once again had asked her to join him for a drink after she got off work. Over the years, as she'd sat in her cell, she'd wondered if her family would still be alive if she'd said yes. She'd thought if she'd had a drink with him, maybe even two, the melancholy that had gripped her when she'd returned home from eight hours on her feet might have been kept at bay. She wouldn't have kept drinking to numb her unhappiness. She wouldn't have been passed out when the fire took hold and made it impossible to reach her children's bedrooms. So, yes, she remembered Billy Bingham, a passably attractive but at times overbearing boy with a crush on her. Annoying but harmless, she'd always thought. Could he have been a murderer? Could he have set fire to her house because she'd rejected him one too many times? She shook her head. No, it wasn't possible. Was it?

T ommy pulled off Route 35 onto North Flood Avenue, heading south into Norman, Oklahoma. He'd flown from Newark's airport into Will Rogers Airport in Oklahoma City and picked up his rental car twenty minutes earlier. Oscar White was still tucked away in Tommy's thoughts as the potential arsonist, but Bingham was worth checking out. He'd been successful in locating three men who'd been friends with Bingham over the years, two in Texas and one in Norman. He figured he'd start in the north and work his way south.

Bingham had met Jesse Gunner when both were incarcerated in the Joseph Harp Correctional Center. Both had been sentenced for selling drugs, mostly heroin, and mostly to support their own habits. Bingham hadn't survived his addiction; Tommy hoped Gunner had managed to kick his own.

Fifteen minutes later, Tommy passed a rectangular concrete block announcing, "Welcome to Norman. Established 1880." He followed the turns dictated by the Waze app on his phone, and soon pulled up to a small cottage-style house on a quiet street of similar houses. The house looked as though it had been carefully maintained, as did the others on the block. *A good sign,* Tommy thought. Gunner had been paroled two years before Bingham, but they'd spent six years as cellmates. Sometimes that proximity got inmates to open up, bare their souls, so to speak. In Tommy's experience, when someone got away with a crime that another person was doing time for, at some point down the road, the real perpetrator spilled it to someone. Maybe a spouse. Maybe a best friend. Maybe a fellow inmate. He hoped that was the case here.

He pulled into the driveway, walked up to the front door, rang the doorbell, then waited. And waited. After no response, he stepped off the front stoop and began to walk around. As he got closer to the garage, set back from the house, he detected an odor, familiar to him from his ten years with the FBI—a mixture of lighter fluid and rotten eggs. Someone inside was cooking crystal meth. He stopped. He didn't need to get involved with this. He wasn't law enforcement any longer, and he didn't carry a gun on him. As he turned to leave, he saw three men walk toward him. Each was slightly over six feet, Tommy's height. Tommy worked out regularly at the gym, but these three each carried at least thirty more pounds than Tommy, all of it muscle.

The center man held a sledgehammer in his right hand. He glared at Tommy as he asked, "You a cop?"

"Nope. Just a private citizen."

"Whatcha doing snooping around here?" He shifted the sledgehammer back and forth between his hands as he spoke.

Tommy steeled himself. It seemed he'd stumbled into an ongoing drug situation, and the men standing before him clearly weren't happy with his presence. His instincts told him to extricate himself as quickly as possible. He still had two other friends of Bingham to question; he didn't need Gunner. Maybe. Or maybe Gunner was the only person to whom Bingham had confessed. If he ever did confess. If he even set the fire.

Tommy hated this case, hated that three innocent children had died. If HIPP's client had been responsible, Tommy was fine with the state killing her. He wanted them to do that. But Dani was convinced she was innocent. And if that were true, Bingham was a possible perpetrator. If not him, they were at a dead end. Oscar White would never confess, even if he had set the fire. The tightness in his chest told Tommy to leave, but he knew he couldn't. Not yet. "I'm looking for Jesse Gunner."

The two men on the end clenched and unclenched their fists but stayed rooted in their spots. Tommy saw them glance toward the man in the center, as though waiting for his go-ahead to tear Tommy apart.

The center man gave a slight shake of his head. "What for?"

"He was friends with Billy Bingham. Back in the joint."

"So what?"

"Billy's dead now. And there's a woman who needs help. I'm hoping someone Billy talked to might be the one to give that help."

The guy with the sledgehammer stopped passing it between hands and just stared at Tommy.

Leave now, the voice in Tommy's head urged. Tommy thought he'd come out a winner in a one-on-one with any of the men, but not with all three on him. And not against a sledgehammer. *Get out,* his voice repeated. Instead, he stared back, his body tense, ready to act if needed.

Finally, the man's lips curled up in a smirk. "I'm Jesse Gunner. What do you need?"

Tommy felt his whole body unwind. "Can we go somewhere and talk?"

Gunner tipped his head toward the garage. "You know what's going on in there?"

"I don't care if you robbed the US Mint and have stacks of gold bars in there. I'm only trying to help get an innocent woman off death row."

Gunner nodded to the two men flanking him, and they turned and walked back into the house. "We can talk right here," Gunner said.

"Did Billy ever mention to you a gal named Becky Whitlaw?"

"She the one burned down her house with the kids inside?"

"That's her."

"Damn shame."

"Did he ever say anything to you about that night?"

"Just how bad he felt about it."

Tommy felt his pulse quicken. "Because he had something to do with it?"

Gunner spit onto the ground. "Hell, no. Why would you think such a thing?"

"You said he felt bad about it."

"Yeah. Because Billy had the sweets for her."

"Did you know he was in her town the night before the fire?"

"It don't make no difference where he was. He never would've hurt that woman. Or her kids. He'd talk all the time about how she was the prettiest girl in their high school, the sweetest, too."

"Is it possible he got angry that she didn't return his feelings?"

Gunner shook his head. "Not Billy. You got the wrong guy."

Maybe Gunner was holding back. Maybe he was telling the truth. Either way, Tommy knew he wasn't going to get more from him. He thanked him and left.

Just shy of three hours later, Tommy pulled into the home of Thorgood Banks, in Coppell, Texas, just north of Dallas. Tommy had learned that Banks and Bingham met after Bingham's family had moved from Glen Brook, and both ended up working for the same telemarketing company. *Banks must be doing pretty damn well,* Tommy thought, as he drove into the driveway of the stately Colonial-style home on a large plot of land, dotted with towering Southern live oak trees. As he got closer to the house, he spotted two magnolia trees flanking the sides and wished he'd gotten to see them when they were in bloom. Tommy loved studying plants and flowers. If he hadn't gone into law enforcement, he would have been happy as a horticulturist. Or even a landscaper.

It was Saturday, so he hoped he'd find Banks at home. His instincts were correct. A minute after he rang the bell, the front door was opened by a slim man, dressed in neatly pressed jeans and a Ralph Lauren short-sleeved polo shirt, with strands of hair beginning to gray combed over a balding top.

"Thorgood Banks?"

"That's me."

Tommy handed him his card. "My office is representing Becky Whitlaw. Your old friend, Billy Bingham, has passed away, and we were hoping before he died, he'd told you something about his relationship with Becky."

Banks just shook his head slowly.

"Would you mind if I come in, so we could talk?"

"You're welcome to, but I never heard Billy mention that name."

"She was a friend from high school. Someone he had a crush on. Ring a bell?"

"Sorry, no."

Tommy didn't bother to go inside. He thanked Banks and returned to his car. There was one more place to hit. Glen Brook,

Texas, where Bingham grew up. Where Jorge Martinez lived. Marci Farrady had identified him as Bingham's best friend, all through elementary and high school and even after the Bingham family moved away.

It was nearing 6:00 p.m. by the time Tommy arrived. He hoped that Martinez was at home, that he hadn't started his Saturday night activities early. If he wasn't home, Tommy would have to stay overnight at a local hotel, something he didn't want to do. He'd left the FBI more than ten years ago because his constant traveling had taken a toll on his marriage. With five children at home, his wife, Patty, was understandably annoyed that he never seemed around to help. Now, three of his children were away at college, but he still hated to be away from home. He guessed he was just getting old and appreciated the comfort of his own bed, his arms wrapped around his wife's warm body. If he finished this up quickly, he could make the 10:05 p.m. flight from Dallas back to Newark.

He was in luck. A teenage girl answered the door, and when he asked for Martinez, she called out, "Dad, it's for you." A moment later, a man came to the door dressed in sweatpants and a T-shirt. *Not going-out attire*, Tommy thought. After Tommy explained why he was there, Martinez opened the door and invited him in. He led him into the living room, and they both sat down.

"I knew Becky well, back in the day. We were all shocked by what happened."

"Did you think she'd set that fire?"

"Of course not. Not at first. But when the trial started, and the TV news reported on some of the testimony, well, I guess I wondered if she had."

"Did Billy ever talk to you about it?"

"Sure. We all talked about it, the ones who knew her."

"I'm told Billy had a crush on Becky."

"Back in high school. But she married someone else."

"What about after high school? After her husband died, I heard he came back, gave her another try."

Martinez chuckled. "Well, I suppose that's right. Billy was a sucker for punishment. Becky was never going to be interested in him."

"How'd he take that?"

Martinez paused, stared at Tommy. "What are you implying?"

"Just asking. I wondered if he might have felt rejected. Angry about being turned away." Tommy saw the hesitation in Martinez's eyes. It seemed clear he didn't want to betray his friend. "Did you know Billy was in Glen Brook the night before the fire?"

Martinez put his hands on his knees, then stood up. "I don't like where you're going with this."

"You knew Becky. She's going to be executed soon. Would you want that on your conscience if she didn't set that fire, and you knew something that could help her?"

Slowly, Martinez sat back in his chair, then buried his face in his hands. When he looked up, his jaw was clenched.

"Tell me," Tommy said.

"Billy always stayed with me when he came back to Glen Brook."

"Was he with you that night?"

"He started out here. He told me he was going to the restaurant where Becky worked. He planned on making another play for her."

"But she said no."

"Yeah. But I didn't learn that till the next morning."

"Why's that?"

"Because Billy stayed out all night. I woke up a little before he came in. About six thirty."

"Did you ask him where he'd been?"

Martinez nodded. "He said he'd picked up some woman at the bar in town and spent the night with her. He didn't even know her last name. Just a one-night stand for him."

The fire had started around 6:00 a.m. Early enough for Billy Bingham to have started it. "Did you ever see Billy do something that just seemed—off?"

"Off? What do you mean?"

"Like losing his temper too easily and hitting someone. Or, maybe, doing some vandalism? Maybe even setting little fires?"

As Tommy spoke, Martinez shook his head, more vigorously with each question. "Absolutely no. He wouldn't have set that fire. That just wasn't him. He'd never do anything to hurt Becky. If anything, he did things to try to impress her."

Tommy stopped for a moment. Was it possible? "Do you think Billy could have started a fire, planning to then rescue Becky and her kids? But it got out of control too quickly?"

Martinez's lips were squeezed together in a tight grimace, with his eyes glued to the floor. "I . . . I . . ." He stopped and looked up at Tommy. With his voice barely a whisper, he said, "I don't know."

Tommy waited a beat. "Do you know when Billy began using drugs? Was it before his family moved away?"

Martinez shook his head. "He stayed away from drugs in high school. He'd drink, get drunk plenty often, but never drugs."

"When did he start? Was it after the fire?"

Martinez hesitated. "I think so."

"How soon?"

"I didn't see him for six months after that. He'd already started."

Tommy held back a smile. "Maybe he was trying to block out feelings of guilt."

Although Martinez shook his head again, his voice said, "I just don't know."

⌒

Twenty-one years was a long time for anyone to remember whom a customer had been, but Tommy had to try, even though it meant missing the evening flight home. He grabbed a bite to eat at a local diner, then drove up to The Night Owl, the only bar in Glen Brook. He hoped against hope that someone behind the bar was old enough to have been there the night Becky's house burned down. It was after 8:00 p.m. on a Saturday, so the bar was full and the noise level loud. He quickly glanced at the man tending bar, saw his gray hair and wrinkled skin, and thought he had a chance to be lucky.

He walked up to the bar and grabbed a stool. It took a few minutes for the bartender to ask what he wanted. "Scotch, straight up."

When the bartender returned with his drink, Tommy asked, "How long have you been working here?"

"Since the day I bought it, thirty-four years ago."

"What's your name?"

"Mack."

Tommy took out his phone and brought up a picture of Billy Bingham from his high school yearbook. *Thank goodness for the internet,* he thought as he handed the phone over to Mack. "Do you know him? Billy Bingham?"

"Sure. It's a small town. I used to fish with his father. Heard he died."

"Yeah. Drug overdose."

"Shame. He was a good kid."

"Do you remember the fire that burned down Becky Whitlaw's house? Killed her three children?"

"Everyone in town remembers that fire. Worst thing that's ever happened here."

"Billy was in this bar the night before the fire. Went home with a woman. I don't suppose you'd remember who that might be?"

Mack laughed, a deep, hearty one. When he finally wound down, he wiped his brow. "Mister, I couldn't tell you who went home with who last week. I'm lucky if I remember what I need to stock up on, in the time it takes from checking my inventory to getting back to my office and writing it down."

Tommy gave a sheepish grin. "I know what you mean. And I figured you wouldn't, but I had to give it a try."

"Why do you need to know?"

Tommy shrugged. "I just wanted to check something with her."

Mack sauntered away, and Tommy stayed on the stool, nursing his drink. A few minutes later, he felt a tap on his shoulder. He turned and saw a middle-aged woman with frosted blond hair almost to her shoulders and heavy makeup. He thought she had probably been pretty in her time but now looked worn out.

"I was with Billy that night."

Tommy's pulse quickened. "How do you remember it was that night?"

She smiled at him. "How about buying me a drink?"

"Sure." Tommy called over Mack, and she ordered a vodka tonic. "So, how certain are you that it was that night?"

"As Mack said, that fire was memorable. It was the only time I ever slept with Billy, and when I woke up the next morning, it was all over the news."

"Do you remember what time Billy left your house?"

She took a sip of her drink. "Couldn't say. By the time I woke up, he was gone."

"So, that's all I got," Tommy relayed to Dani over the phone the next morning. "Bingham could have easily left her house before sunrise and started the fire at Becky's. Whether out of anger at her rejection or wanting to play the hero, I can't say. But he was in Glen Brook without anyone seeing him during the key time period."

"But how would he have gotten into her house? The fire investigator's report said an accelerant was poured on the floor in the children's bedrooms, the hallway, and by the front door. He'd need to have gotten inside to do that."

"You sure she even locked her front door? From the trial transcript, it sounded like she was pretty soused by the time Marci left, and she went back inside."

"I suppose that's possible."

"So, is it helpful? What I got?"

"It could be. If we can get her a new trial. Then, between her and Susan Granger and Oscar White, it's evidence we can bring in to create reasonable doubt."

"Good."

"Except it's a long shot that we'll get her a new trial."

Three weeks later, Dani drove in her rental car to the Texas Court of Criminal Appeals, in Austin, Texas. All appeals in death penalty cases bypassed the regional courts of appeal and went directly to the highest criminal court in Texas. She parked, went through the usual identification and security process now routine throughout the country, then made her way up to the courtroom. All nine judges would hear Becky's appeal of the lower court's denial of a new trial. Dani was happy that two of the judges were female jurists. She realized she was once again doing her own version of gender stereotyping, but in her experience, or maybe it was just her wishful thinking, women judges seemed more sympathetic, especially when a woman had been sentenced to die.

Dani had flown to Austin last night for a morning calendar call. Becky's case was third on the calendar, so Dani would have to sit through two other oral arguments. She crossed her fingers that the cases before hers were quick. Tonight was Keith's school talent show, where he'd be playing a classical guitar piece that Jonah had composed, and she'd promised Jonah she'd be there for it. This was one of those times when guilt gnawed at her for working such a demanding job. One that took her away from home so often.

Dani entered the courtroom and took a seat near the back. Jeremy Wilson was already seated a few rows ahead, on the other side of the aisle, impatiently tapping his foot. Given his youth, and the obvious blunder he'd made during his cross-examination of Susan Granger during the hearing, Dani wondered if appearing before an appellate panel was still a relatively new experience for him. Newly minted assistant DA's tried a lot of cases—one reason many chose that job straight out of law school—but less often argued appeals. A patina of prestige often surrounded appellate courts, making trial courtrooms seem dimmer. And appellate ones more intimidating.

Ten minutes later, the justices entered the courtroom and took their seats on the bench. The court clerk called the first case, and two sets of attorneys walked up to the front, taking their seats on either side of the lectern. The first case was a civil matter, a dispute over property lines, and the arguments both straightforward and dry. The second case involved a drug bust, and the issue on appeal was the chain of command of the heroin confiscated during the arrest.

Finally, the clerk called, "State of Texas v. Rebecca Whitlaw." Dani and Wilson both stood, and Dani nodded to him as she walked to the front, then took her seat at the table on the left.

Judge Bertram Carter, the presiding judge, nodded to Dani. "You may begin. You have ten minutes."

Dani walked to the lectern with her notes, noted the green light on the side that, when it turned yellow, would tell her she had two minutes remaining. "May it please the court, my name is Dani Trumball, and I represent Rebecca Whitlaw in her bid for a new trial, based on a Brady violation and upon newly discovered evidence. Ms. Whitlaw was sentenced to death after her conviction of the arson death of her three children. At the trial . . ."

"Aren't both those issues," interrupted Judge Sienna Melnick, one of the women on the bench, "based on the credibility of one witness, a convicted felon? And aren't credibility issues the purview of the trier of fact, in this case the judge below?"

Oh boy, Dani thought. *I didn't even get past my second sentence.* "I don't believe that's the case. With respect to the Brady violation, namely, that the prosecutor solicited the confession witness, and knew once that witness testified that she'd committed perjury, the fact that the charge against her for possession of cocaine was subsequently dropped supports her testimony."

"Wasn't that because the evidence was lost?" Judge Melnick asked.

"There was also testimony that lost evidence is a rare occurrence. That it should occur in a case where the witness testified she'd get favorable treatment if she testified her cellmate confessed to setting the fire seems like too much of a coincidence. When there is cumulative evidence, there are factors beyond merely the credibility of the witness."

Dani looked down at her notes, then continued. "With respect to the newly discovered evidence, namely, that the witness lied when she said Ms. Whitlaw had confessed to setting the fire, the issue is not whether the witness is credible. For newly discovered evidence to justify a new trial, the defendant must show that the new evidence was learned of after the trial and couldn't have been discovered earlier with due diligence, the evidence is not cumulative, and had it been known, it probably would have produced a different result at trial."

"That last factor is the issue," Judge Melnick said. "Didn't the hearing judge rule that there was enough other evidence that it wouldn't have made a difference? And isn't that judgment more appropriately made by the hearing judge? Particularly in this case, where he also presided over the trial?"

So much for female judges being a softer touch, Dani thought. "Not when that determination is a manifest abuse of judicial discretion, which I believe was the case here. There is abundant research on the impact of purported confessions on jurors.

Ignoring that research was a manifest abuse and, when coupled with a Brady violation, requires his decision to be overturned and a new trial granted."

Dani glanced over at the timer light and saw it had already turned yellow. "I'd like to reserve one minute for rebuttal. Thank you."

As she sat down, Wilson stood and walked to the lectern.

"Good morning, Your Honors. My name is Jeremy Wilson, and I represent the State of Texas. Ms. Trumball is grasping at straws to say this appeal is not predicated on the credibility of one witness. Each of the claims goes to whether Ms. Granger is believable. Judge Gertner decided that she was not, and appellate courts do not interfere with those determinations."

As Wilson continued to speak, Dani watched the nine judges. None of them interrupted Wilson with questions, and one seemed to nod as he ticked off his points. Dani had known her chances were slim. As she sat and listened to her opponent, she realized the needle had moved from slim chance to none.

The only good thing about Dani's trip to the appellate court was that she had reached the Austin airport early enough to make her flight and return home in time for tonight's school concert. Although Jonah knew how to eke out tunes on a piano keyboard, his true talent was in composing music. She often marveled at how he could hear the different instruments in his head, then translate those sounds onto a piece of paper. But until one of his compositions was performed, Dani and Doug couldn't truly hear it. The first time had been when the Westchester Philharmonic performed his symphony. As Dani had sat in the audience, tears streaming down her cheeks, she'd realized for the first time that, despite Jonah's deficiencies in other areas, he was a musical genius.

It was only when they heard an orchestra, or a musician, perform Jonah's music that they could truly appreciate his accomplishments. That's why it had been so important for Dani to attend another school's talent show. Although the New York Philharmonic had recorded one of Jonah's pieces as part of an album, and of course Dani played it constantly, it wasn't the same as hearing his music performed live.

Ruth was already asleep in her crib when Dani popped her head into the living room, where Elsa had settled in with a book. "We're leaving now. Here's the baby monitor. I don't think she'll wake up."

"Don't worry about it, Miss Dani. She'll be fine."

"Thanks, Elsa."

"Hurry, Mom," Jonah called from the front hallway. "It's getting late."

Dani gathered her coat and purse, and the family poured into their Honda CR-V. She couldn't understand why so many people in Stanford and nearby Palo Alto drove SUV's, where snow or even icy rain were rare. Yet, it seemed every other vehicle on the road was one. Usually a Mercedes, a BMW, or even a Porsche. An SUV was hardly a glamorous sports car, but all still had prestigious names.

They pulled up to Henry M. Gunn High School and parked, then found their way to the auditorium. Although Dani had seen the high school previously, it still struck her how different it was from those in New York. Bronxville High School, like most in the New York City suburbs, was a traditional brick three-story building. Students and teachers entered through the front doors, and indoor corridors and stairs led to individual classrooms. Here, there were multiple buildings, most one-story, with doors from the outside leading directly to each classroom. It was another reminder to Dani that she was living in a place where she no longer had to worry about frigid temperatures and snowy winters.

As soon as they entered the auditorium, they spotted Keith's parents and took seats next to them. Stu and Christine Goldman were older than Dani and Doug and had two daughters already in college. Although they didn't socialize as couples, Dani and Christine had often chatted when they'd run into each other.

"Keith has been practicing so hard, he really wants to do justice to Jonah's music. It's incredibly beautiful," Christine said. "You must love listening to it."

"We've never heard it, actually," Dani answered. "Jonah doesn't play the guitar. In fact, I never even knew classical music could be played on that instrument."

"Oh, my, you must listen to Andrés Segovia. His playing is brilliant. Keith's instructor studied with someone who'd learned directly from Segovia himself."

Dani smiled. "I'll download one of his CD's."

The lights dimmed, and a short, bespectacled man with floppy, curly hair took the stage. "Welcome, everyone, to Henry M. Gunn's annual talent show. For those who don't know me, I'm Mr. Klein, the music teacher. I have to say to all the parents here tonight, we've never had such a talented group of students grace our stage. To our students, please refrain from calling out to anyone on the stage, and to everyone, turn off your cell phones." There was a rustle in the audience as parents and students alike took out their phones and silenced them. "Now, let's begin."

The first performance was a five-member rock band, playing a cover of "Thunder" by Imagine Dragons, followed by a female trio, a violinist, a magic act, an Ed Sheeran look-alike, complete with a mop of red hair, singing one of his songs, and a stand-up comic. Finally, Keith took the stage. He sat on a chair, the microphone in front of him, and began to play. The piece started slow and melancholy, then gradually became livelier, finishing with a burst of speed that sounded like pure joy.

Dani had never heard a guitar sound that way, so rich and melodic. She turned to Jonah, whose face was lit up with a beaming smile, and hugged him. "Just beautiful," she whispered in his ear. At that moment, the dread that had tightened her chest ever since leaving the courthouse washed away, replaced with a deep sense of happiness. She knew how lucky she was, with a husband who loved her, children who inspired her, and incomes that meant they never had to worry about paying their bills. She knew, too, how that luck could change on a dime, with a fatal accident, a terminal illness, or an uncontrolled fire that wiped out your family and landed you on death row.

Two weeks later, with Doug on his break between semesters and Jonah's school closed for the Christmas holiday, the family drove to Lake Tahoe. Elsa had come along to watch Ruth when the others were skiing. Not for the first time, Dani appreciated how lucky she'd been to find Elsa. She'd been widowed four years earlier, and her children and seven grandchildren were scattered across the United States. She smothered Ruth with affection—Jonah, too, when he allowed her to—and always welcomed the extra hours when Dani needed her outside of the normal workday. Not for the money, she'd told Dani—although Dani knew she needed it—but because it dampened her loneliness when she returned from Dani's home to her quiet apartment.

The weather in Lake Tahoe was glorious, the snow deep and powdery, and the time spent with the family nourishing. They returned home on December 30, feeling both rested and invigorated at the same time. After getting the children settled, Dani went through the mail that had accumulated during their absence.

Courts must have been trying to clear their backlog before the holiday break, because waiting for Dani were letters on two of her outstanding cases. The DNA analysis on Patton Swinton, who'd been convicted of rape and burglary, had come back, and it was not a match for him. Dani smiled, then the smile instantly turned to a frown. The district attorney nevertheless felt he had enough other evidence and would not join Dani in a motion to free her client: *You, of course, are free to make a motion for a new trial based on this new evidence, which we will oppose. In the event it is granted, we will retry the defendant,* the letter said.

Dani seethed. Patton Swinton was black. She had no proof, but statistics told her that if he were white, the district attorney might have made a different determination.

With the DNA results failing to identify Swinton as the perpetrator, it was a virtual guarantee that her motion for a new trial would be granted. And based upon what she'd read in Patton's trial transcript, Dani felt confident that she'd prevail in a new trial. Meanwhile, Dani had no doubt that Swinton would remain in prison on bail that he had no hope of posting. It would be her job to hold the prosecutor's feet to the fire and get him a new trial quickly.

The second letter was from the court on her motion to compel ADA Samuel Xavier to run the DNA found in Dominic Webster's case through CODIS, the FBI's Combined DNA Index System. The court ruled in her favor. It didn't mean CODIS would identify another perpetrator of the murder of Webster's girlfriend, but if it did, then the prosecutor would have to drop his stance on retrying Webster. If not, Dani would prepare for his new trial.

With both cases, along with her lawsuit seeking compensation for Rick Turner, Dani had plenty of other work to keep her busy until she heard back from the court on Becky's appeal.

Back in New York, Dani and Doug usually spent New Year's Eve quietly at home, playing games with Jonah as he struggled to stay awake until midnight, then turning in themselves soon after the Times Square ball dropped. But for the first time, Jonah had been invited to a party—at Keith's house, with his parents supervising, they'd reassured Dani—and Elsa was free to babysit Ruth. Dani made sure Jonah knew to call them if he felt uncomfortable with Keith's friends and wanted to come home early, and after sending him off, they left for a party at Lauren and Gregory's house.

Although Dani had been meeting Lauren regularly for lunch, she'd never been to her house. It was a bit out of the way for Stanford but convenient to the tech company that Gregory, a computer scientist with more than a dozen patents to his name, had helped found. It had struck gold, making him an instant billionaire. They drove up to the Mediterranean estate—it was so big and so lavish that it only could be considered an estate—in Saratoga, in Santa Clara County, and found a spot to park in the oversize circular driveway. Dani had previously asked Lauren what she could bring, and Lauren had said their presence was enough. She briefly wondered if she should be embarrassed by the thirty-five-dollar champagne bottle in her hands, then just as quickly dismissed the notion. No matter how opulent the house, Lauren herself was down-to-earth.

They rang the doorbell. Moments later, a young woman dressed in black pants and a black T-shirt, with the name *Elegant Catering* emblazoned on the front, opened it. She took their light jackets as they stepped inside. The foyer, with its marble flooring and dramatic curved staircase, looked like it had been pirated from a Hollywood movie set. Crowds of people were already inside, and Dani and Doug wove their way through them to find Lauren and Gregory. Some of those present were colleagues from

Stanford, and as Doug passed them, he stopped to shake their hands and introduce Dani. They found their hosts in the family room.

"My God, this place is magnificent," Dani said.

Lauren eyes dipped downward as she smoothed out the designer fitted black jersey dress she wore, with just a simple long strand of pearls hanging around her neck. She leaned in close to Dani's ear and whispered, "Oh, you know how it is in Silicon Valley. We have to entertain investors often, and nothing makes them feel more comfortable than seeing tangible signs of wealth. It makes them believe the company's doing as well as the books say it is."

Dani laughed. "Well, don't be embarrassed by it. It's gorgeous. Can I get a tour?"

"Sure."

Dani followed her through the almost eight-thousand-square-foot house. From every room were views of the surrounding hills and the lights of the town below. The living room and family room had soaring ceilings, with a wet bar in the latter room. The kitchen had a large center island, Thermador appliances, a built-in refrigerator, two ovens, and two dishwashers. In addition to a master bedroom suite, with two walk-in closets the size of Jonah's bedroom and a bathroom Dani thought she could live in, the main floor also had a library, an office, a maid's room, and a dining room with a table that could seat twenty people. Upstairs were four additional bedrooms, each with its own bathroom. Down from the main floor was another office, a fully equipped gym, and a home theater with a 150-inch screen and a dozen leather recliners facing it. The home sat on two acres, and the grounds were just as impressive as the home. An infinity pool shaped like a river curved around lush landscaping, and a tennis court and full-court basketball court were off to the side.

When Dani commented on Lauren's exquisite taste in the contemporary furnishings, Lauren chuckled. "Don't give us any credit for it. We hired a decorator and gave her free rein. Neither of us knows anything about décor."

"I've never been in a home like this," Dani said. "It's just incredible. I think I'd get lost in it if I lived here."

"Yeah, it took getting used to. I grew up in a solidly middle-class family in a suburb of Boston. Gregory did, too. He never thought about 'hitting it big.' He just enjoyed tinkering around with new ideas." She shrugged. "Frankly, I'd be happy with a lot less. And I feel guilty sometimes that we have so much and so many don't have enough to buy food. But we give away a lot also."

Dani thought about suggesting a donation to HIPP. They always struggled to raise money. But this wasn't the time or place. She tucked away the thought. It was something she could bring up at one of their lunches.

The tour over, Dani followed Lauren into the family room, now filled with dozens more people than when she'd arrived. As she headed to the bar for a glass of wine, she spotted Chuck Stanger.

"I didn't know you'd be here," she said as she walked up to him.

"Last-minute decision. Another doctor asked me to switch our on-call schedule, and I suddenly found myself free. I had no plans since I expected to be working, and I haven't seen Lauren and Gregory for a while, so—here I am."

"Well, it's lovely to see you. And I'm sure Lauren's thrilled."

"Yes. It gives her the opportunity to remind me in person that I need to have a life outside of work."

"Sounds like a reasonable reminder."

"I suppose."

He followed Dani over to the bar and poured her a glass of chardonnay. "I realize that you probably don't want to think about work tonight, but anything new with Becky?"

Dani shook her head. "I'm still waiting for a decision on my last appeal."

"It just seems so unfair."

Dani placed her hand on Chuck's arm. "You of all people must understand how unfair life can be. You have little children whose hearts are failing them. I'm sure some of them don't survive."

"Yes, but—and I know it sounds crass, because nothing makes up for the loss of a child—those parents can over time go on with their lives. Maybe they have other children to love. Maybe the woman will become pregnant again. Maybe they'll devote themselves to their careers. They will continue to live—with a hole in their hearts, yes—but they'll live. Becky lost all three of her children, and on top of that devastating loss, she faces death herself. I know she didn't start that fire. I'm convinced. You need to convince the courts."

Chuck's face had reddened during his discourse. Maybe Lauren was right—he had a crush on Becky. She longed to reassure him that all would work out. It was New Year's Eve. A time for optimism, for wishes of peace and harmony over the coming year. She couldn't, though. It would just give him false hope.

⁓

On his flight back to Dallas, Chuck couldn't stop thinking about Becky. Dani hadn't sounded very encouraging. He'd contributed to Citizens Against State Imposed Death as he'd given money to other organizations. Doctors Without Borders, the Red Cross, the Global Alliance for Improved Nutrition, and Americares all were on his regular list. Occasionally, he'd attend a benefit given by a local chapter. Although he cared deeply about each of their missions, it was from a distance, as an onlooker, removed from the dirty realities the people working for these organizations faced daily. That began to change when he received his first letter from Becky. Suddenly, it wasn't an abstract desire to help make a difference in the world but a real person, facing a real execution. Her intelligence and kindness shone through in those letters and was reinforced when he finally visited her in person.

He was opposed to the death penalty. Even if Becky had been guilty of doing something so horrendously cruel as to kill her children by fire, even then, he didn't believe the state should execute her. Nor anyone else. That's what prisons were for. Take away evildoers' freedom forever. Never let them roam the streets to harm more people. That's what he believed. He'd say to friends supportive of the death penalty, "But, what if they get it wrong? What if they kill an innocent person? The death penalty is final." Even as he'd say that, he knew it was an intellectual argument, made by someone who would never be in that position himself, never have a loved one, innocent of any crime, face that. Never be the person to feel the gut-wrenching pain of that irreversible loss and injustice.

Now, he was that person. He didn't love Becky, not in a romantic way. That's what he told himself, at least, when at night he'd let himself think about her being free. He cared about her, though, deeply—that much he would admit. As a surgeon, he sympathized with his patients' families but didn't emotionally invest himself in their lives. He needed to remain objective to do his job well. His love life had taken a back seat to his career, and so there wasn't a woman to whom he opened himself up emotionally.

Until Becky. She bared her soul to him in her letters, and soon he began opening up to her. In doing so, he found himself invested in righting the wrong that was done to her. He'd been so hopeful Dani could accomplish that. Now, he didn't know.

On January 5, 2019, an envelope with a return address of the appellate court in Austin, Texas, arrived. Dani ripped open the envelope and took out the two-page decision, then quickly scanned to the end.

For the above-stated reasons, the lower court's decision is upheld. Appellant has not shown sufficient grounds to find a Brady violation, or to demonstrate newly discovered evidence warranting a new trial.

Becky's hands trembled as she reread the letter in her hands. Nine words, that's all it was. *Your execution has been scheduled for March 11, 2019.* She'd known her time would run out eventually. Before Dani had appeared in her life, she'd lost hope long ago that she would ever be free. But Dani had given her hope. Hope that she would walk away from the prison. Hope that she would once again be able to wrap her arms around her mother. Hope that her name would be cleared, and she wouldn't return to Glen Brook with her head hung down, afraid to look anyone in the eyes. Yes, she'd dared to hope that not only would she be released, but it would not be on some technicality that reversed her conviction while a cloud of doubt followed her around. How foolish she'd been.

She pulled out a notepad and pencil and began writing down the names of those she'd need to notify. Her mother, of course, although that would be the hardest letter to write. Tim Willoughby, the attorney who'd represented her at the trial. Even though he hadn't handled her later appeals, she knew he'd want to know. She thought back to his entreaties, so many years ago, begging her to accept a plea bargain. How could she have known then that she'd one day emerge from the dark fog that had filled her soul? Back then, it was impossible to believe that life without her children would be worth living, and so it was easy to say no to a plea. That changed when Chuck Stanger entered her life.

Chuck. Of course, she'd have to tell him. The sweet, selfless man who'd allowed her to think about a life beyond prison. He would be devastated, she knew. He had such an innocent belief in the fairness of life, that errors would be corrected, that justice always prevailed. Maybe this was justice for her. Maybe she'd done what the jurors had said she'd done but had no memory of it. She shook her head. No. It was not possible.

Marci? Should she tell her, too? Her pencil was poised over her notebook when she heard a booming voice. "Whitlaw. Phone call. It's your lawyer."

Becky stood up and walked to the front of her cell, stuck her hands through the opening in the bars, and waited for the handcuffs to be slapped on. When that was done, the bars slid open, and she walked to the one phone on the death row block.

"You've heard?" Becky said when she picked up the phone.

"I have. They faxed me a letter just a few moments ago."

"I want to thank you for all you did. Even though it didn't matter."

"It's not over yet. We have another appeal. I'm not giving up."

Chuck had told Becky that this lawyer had a reputation for fighting hard, for persevering until the very end. Becky supposed that was good. But, deep in her gut, she knew it wouldn't change anything. She was going to die. Soon.

Dani hung up the phone, frustrated. Not with Becky. With the judicial system. She'd heard the despondency in Becky's voice and wished she could reach through the wire and give her a hug, tell her that it was okay to hope, that until she was strapped into the gurney and intravenous needles stuck in her veins, there was still a chance. She'd had that with a client before—well, maybe not the needles already inserted, but close enough—and the governor had come through, stopping an innocent man from execution. If she had to, she'd petition the Texas governor for clemency in Becky's case, but they weren't there yet. She'd already filed a writ of certiorari with the US Supreme Court, appealing the decision of the Texas Court of Criminal Appeals. It wasn't over. Not yet.

Still, Dani had to admit reluctantly that if the Supreme Court upheld the lower courts' decisions, and they didn't get a new trial for Becky, nothing Tommy found out about Billy Bingham would matter. And the likelihood of a governor from Texas, the state with the highest number of prisoners executed, granting clemency and staying the execution was so small as to be a fantasy. Now, she started to feel the same despair she'd detected in Becky's voice.

Dani needed to clear her head. There was nothing more she could do for Becky now, other than wait. She headed to her bedroom and changed into jogging shorts and a T-shirt, then put on her running shoes. She let Elsa know she was going out for a run. A five-mile jog always helped put her at ease, think of new avenues to pursue with her clients, fashion arguments to make before a judge. She started out her street and headed toward Applewood Park.

As she drew closer, lost in her thoughts, it took a while before she realized she smelled smoke. She looked up, saw black plumes in the direction of the park, and stopped. In the distance, she heard sirens. She stared into the sky for a few moments, then turned and headed back to her house. She needed to be with Ruthie. She needed to make sure her children were safe.

By the time Doug returned that evening, the fire in Applewood Park was the lead story on the local news. This time of year, it should have been a routine fire, easy to extinguish. Although the Santa Ana wildfire season ran from September through May, the most difficult fires to control usually occurred in the autumn months. But Northern California had been experiencing a drought for many months, the winds were high, and the temperatures had remained warmer than usual. Nearby fire departments had joined the efforts of the Palo Alto firefighters to contain the blaze, but the fire was spreading.

"Do we need to leave?" Dani asked. It was "honeymoon hour;" Ruth was asleep, and Jonah was in bed, reading.

"I don't think so. The news reports haven't indicated any mandatory evacuations."

"Even so, is it safe to stay?"

"We'd be told if it wasn't."

Dani lay in Doug's arms. He always made her feel secure. She brought him up to date on the cases she was handling, and he filled her in on the politics rampant in his new position. They waited until 11:00 p.m., then turned on the evening news. The lead story was about the fire. After video of the firefighters fighting the blaze, Rachel Gottlieb, the anchorwoman, turned to Joshua Jacobs, a technical expert with a state forestry agency.

"The problem here," Jacobs said, "is that much of the trees in Applewood Park are on a hill, at some places as much as a twenty percent gradient. That quadruples the speed of the fire, because it's preheating the trees and the underbrush above it. The greater the slope that's heavily treed, the more violently a fire will burn. Add to that how dry it's been in California, and it makes the fire much harder to control."

"Are the surrounding homes in danger?" the anchor asked.

"Those within a mile of Applewood Park have been evacuated. Hopefully, more won't be affected."

"What about the smoke in the air?"

"Yes, that's a concern, too. When wildfires burn vegetation, it lets off toxins and gases that can sting your eyes and irritate your skin and lungs. It's especially dangerous for people with heart or lung conditions and expectant women. If you have any of these health concerns, stay indoors until the fire is out."

"You've heard it folks. Stay indoors, and stay safe."

When the anchorwoman started in on another story, Dani turned off the TV. They'd only evacuated homes within a mile radius. Their home was two miles away, so Doug was right. There was no need to worry.

A pounding on the front door awakened Dani. She opened her eyes, saw the large digital numbers on her clock read 3:16, and shook Doug awake.

"Wait here," he said, his voice groggy.

As soon as he ran down the stairs, Dani jumped out of bed, then waited by the top railing, giving her a clear view of the front hallway. When Doug opened the door, she saw two police officers standing outside.

"Sir, you and your family need to evacuate immediately. Embers from the fire have spread to this neighborhood, and the fire is close."

Doug rubbed his eyes. "How much time do we have?"

"None. Who else is in this house?"

"My wife and two children."

"You need to wake them up now. Take five minutes to throw some essentials together. Then leave. The Holiday Inn on West El Camino Real has set aside a block of rooms."

Dani felt her heart race. She rushed back into her bedroom and quickly changed into jeans and a T-shirt, then grabbed her cell phone. She took two tote bags from her closet and went into Jonah's room. She gently shook him awake.

"What? What time is it?" he asked, his voice thick with sleep.

"We have to leave. Put on some clothes, then put in this bag your schoolbooks and a few things you'll need for the next day or two."

Jonah continued to lie in bed.

"Now, Jonah!" Her voice was harsher than she intended. She knew she needed to remain calm for the kids but running through her head were images of the pictures she'd seen of Becky Whitlaw's burned house, the bodies of her three children.

Just as Jonah swung his feet onto the floor and began to move slowly, Doug popped his head into the room.

"You heard?"

Dani nodded. "Go pack us a few things." She headed into Ruth's room and quietly opened the drawers of her dresser. She took out some clothes and placed them in the second tote, then added several diapers. She moved over to the crib and retrieved Ruth's favorite stuffed animal, Fuzzy, a small bear that Ruth deemed essential for falling asleep. She wouldn't wake Ruth yet, not until she knew everyone was set. She headed back into the hallway. Jonah was standing there, his bag filled, his eyes half-closed.

"Doug?"

"Ready," he said as he stepped out of the master bedroom, dressed in sweatpants and a T-shirt, a gym bag in his hand. "Where's Ruth?"

Dani handed him the tote with Ruth's belongings. "I'll get her now. Go start the car."

"Come on, Buddy," Doug said to Jonah, who followed him down the stairs.

She went back into Ruth's room and reached into the crib to pick her up. Ruth stirred but quickly settled into Dani's arms, her head on Dani's chest. Dani grabbed her crib blanket and wrapped it over Ruth's body, then headed out the front door. As soon as she stepped outside, she was hit with the musky odor of burning wood. Orange and red embers floated in the air, and behind the house across from her street, flames shot up into the black sky. She lifted Ruth's blanket over her mouth and nose, then rushed to the car. Jonah, already inside, sat slumped against the door, his eyes closed. Dani placed a still sleeping Ruth into her car seat, then got into the front passenger seat.

"All set?" Doug asked.

"Ready."

Just as they started to move, Jonah sat bolt upright. "Where's Gracie?"

"Shit," Doug murmured under his breath. Gracie, their cat, now old and fat, usually slept at the foot of Jonah's bed, but the tumult must have frightened her off. In their frenzied rush to leave, they'd all forgotten her. "I'll get her."

Dani put her arm out to stop Doug, then slowly withdrew it. They all needed to get to safety quickly. The fire was already too close to their home. But—Gracie had been with them since before Jonah was born. She couldn't bear the thought of her dying, alone, engulfed by smoke and flames.

Doug put the car in park, then ran into the house. Seven anxious minutes later, he returned with the cat carrier, Gracie inside. By then, the smoke had thickened, and when Doug returned to the driver's seat, he had a dry, hacking cough.

"You okay?"

Doug nodded but continued to cough. He headed the car away from the fire. Within a few blocks, he was on Page Mill Road, and a mass of cars in front of him had slowed to a crawl, then stopped completely. Dani looked ahead and spotted flames shooting up from trees lining the roadway, thick gray smoke coming toward them.

"We've got to turn around," she said.

"We can't. There are cars behind us." ·

Dani turned and saw a row of cars filled with families. As she faced front, a man and woman ran toward them, waving their hands, the man shouting as he ran past each car, "Get out, the fire's coming this way. There's smoke behind us, too." Dani spun backward again, and now noted the smoke coming down the street behind them.

"We have to leave," Doug said.

Dani could tell he was trying to keep his voice calm, but she still felt a rising sense of panic. They were trapped. If they left the car, the advancing smoke could kill them before any flames reached them. If they stayed locked in their cars, fire would consume them.

Doug had opened his door. "Hurry up!" he shouted at Dani, who sat frozen in her seat. "Come on, get Ruthie."

Dani slowly opened her door. People ran all around her, screaming, their children crying. The air felt heavy. A bitter odor pinched her nose, and smoke stung her eyes. She opened the back door and unbuckled Ruth from the car seat. As she picked up her daughter, Ruth awoke and added her own cries to the mix of noise all around them. Dani bundled Ruth in her arms, grabbed the bag with Ruth's essentials, then joined Doug and Jonah, who held on tightly to Gracie's carrier. "Where do we go?"

Doug pointed ahead. "The fire's coming from the east. There are some commercial buildings a little way up. We can cut through their parking lots and reach El Camino Real. Then head west."

Dani nodded, and they began to run in that direction. When they reached the open space of the parking lots, the only light was from the orange flames cutting through the starless night. They made their way carefully. Soon, the lot was filled with people, and their cries and shouts jumbled together in one cacophonous swell. As Dani rushed forward, she felt her heart racing. Smoke-filled air burned her lungs and stung her eyes. She struggled to keep Doug and Jonah in her sights but gradually fell behind.

"Doug!" she called out to him, but he must not have heard, because he didn't turn around. She called again, then a third time. Finally, he stopped.

"Do you need me to take Ruthie?" he asked.

Dani felt like she wanted to drop to her knees from exhaustion. A moment later, Doug was by her side. He lifted Ruth from Dani's arms and motioned for her to take one of the tote bags.

"We'll be okay. I think a road is just up ahead," he said. Dani nodded, unable to speak.

Ten minutes later, they reached El Camino Real. Parked in front of a strip of stores were several police cars, herding people into vans.

"This way, folks, we'll get you out of here," one said through a megaphone.

Dani almost collapsed with relief. She ushered her children into a van and settled into a seat, Ruth on her lap.

When Doug sat down behind her with Jonah, she asked him, "Our car?"

"After the fire is under control, they'll send a tow truck out to bring the abandoned cars to a police lot. Assuming there's something left to bring there."

Dani nodded, then leaned back in her seat. How could their escape have been so close? Back at the car, with people running every which way, she'd been afraid they would die. Or be horribly burned. She felt furious at the officials who waited so late to evacuate them, then at the police for failing to direct them to a safe street when they finally drove away from home. The fury burned in her for minutes before she realized she was angry at herself, angry at Doug. They shouldn't have waited for the knock on their door. They shouldn't have taken a chance with their children's lives when the fire was only two miles away.

She understood now how Becky Whitlaw could have been consumed with guilt even if she hadn't set the fire that killed her children. Her job was to protect them. And she'd failed.

It was nearly 5:00 a.m. by the time they were settled in their room at the Holiday Inn. The serviceable room, with two double beds and a crib, was fine for the remainder of the night but not something that would work long-term. Jonah and Ruth quickly dropped off to sleep, both exhausted by the events of the night, but Dani lay shivering in Doug's arms. Gracie, barely bothered by the change in her environment, lay curled up, gently snoring, by Jonah's legs. In the hallway outside, Dani could hear more families moving into their rooms, the security of their lives disrupted by flaming embers traveling from tree to tree. She wondered if they felt the same tightness in their chests, the same fluttering in their hearts, the same beads of perspiration on their foreheads. *We're safe.* She had to keep reminding herself. *We're all safe.*

"What are we going to do?" Dani asked.

"We don't even know if the fire reached our house."

"But if it did?"

Doug squeezed Dani's shoulders. "We have insurance. And none of us was hurt."

"But all our things? Our furniture? Our clothes?"

"Everything is replaceable."

Dani thought for a moment. All her work was stored on her laptop, sitting on the desk in her office. Everything she worked on was backed up to HIPP's main computer system, though. If necessary, she could replicate her current documents. She started to relax, until she remembered the photo albums tucked away on a shelf in her closet. All of Ruth's pictures were digital, stored on the cloud, but Jonah's baby pictures, although digital, were taken before it had become automatic to save pictures in that way. Back then, she'd printed out the best photos and made books of them, then reused the disks for new pictures. She started to remind Doug of that, then stopped. Even if the fire had reached their house, even if everything inside had burned, she still had Jonah. She still had Ruthie. She still had Doug. Nothing else mattered.

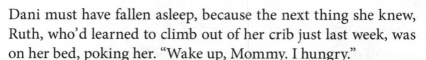

Dani must have fallen asleep, because the next thing she knew, Ruth, who'd learned to climb out of her crib just last week, was on her bed, poking her. "Wake up, Mommy. I hungry."

Dani glanced over at the clock on the night table: 7:45 a.m., a full hour after Ruth normally awakened. Jonah and Doug still slept soundly. "Okay, Ruth," she whispered. "Let's let Daddy and Jonah sleep." She slipped out of bed, reached for Ruth's tote, pulled out a new diaper, then lay Ruth down where moments ago Dani had been sound asleep. She quickly changed Ruth's diaper, then dressed her in a pair of leggings and a dress. It had been the first things she'd grabbed from Ruth's dresser last night as she'd scurried to leave. Next, Dani threw on the same jeans and T-shirt she'd worn last night, quickly wrote a note for Doug that she placed on her pillow, then took Ruth's hand and led her out of the room. As soon as she was in the hallway, she called Elsa. She caught her just as she was leaving for Dani's house to babysit.

"Don't come. We were evacuated last night."

"The fire?"

"Yes."

"Is everyone safe?"

"Thankfully. We're in a hotel, and I don't know if we'll get back home today or later. I don't even know if our house was affected. I'll call you when I know more."

"I can come to the hotel to take care of Ruth."

"No, stay home. I'll call you when I need you."

Dani hung up, and she and Ruth took the elevator to the lobby. The hotel offered a complimentary breakfast buffet, and when Dani arrived there, the room was already filled with families, most looking as haggard as Dani felt. She found a table for two, placed Ruth on a chair, then joined the line holding a plate for herself and a bowl for Ruth. She scooped Cheerios into Ruth's bowl, added milk, then served herself a helping of scrambled eggs, bacon, and hashed browns. She never ate like that at home. Breakfast was an English muffin with cottage cheese on top, a glass of orange juice, and a cup of coffee. But now she felt frazzled from last night and needed comfort food.

She returned to her table and placed Ruth's bowl and a spoon in front of her. She wished she had a bib, but there had been no time to pack more than essentials. Instead, she tucked a napkin into the neckline of Ruth's dress.

"You escape the fire?" the woman seated at the next table asked when Dani sat down herself.

Dani nodded.

"Have you heard anything more about it?"

"No. We just got up and came for breakfast."

"Someone earlier told me more than a hundred homes were affected. Some worse than others."

"Is it out—the fire?"

The woman shook her head. "I don't think so."

Dani looked around the small room for a television screen mounted on a wall, but there was none. She wished she could be back in her room, able to turn on the television to get the latest developments. But Doug and Jonah needed as much sleep as they could get.

"What street are you on?" the woman asked.

"Prescott."

The woman frowned. "I live one street over. I heard we got hit pretty bad."

Dani took her iPhone from her pocket and looked for the latest update on the fire. She'd been so focused on getting Ruth out of the room quietly before she woke the others that she hadn't had a chance to check this morning. From what she found, the woman was correct. More than two hundred homes had been evacuated throughout the night, the families placed in hotels throughout the Palo Alto area. Firefighters from Palo Alto and four surrounding towns were still working on putting out the fire, but it looked like they were close to succeeding. She couldn't find anything about the damage the flames caused.

What will we do if we don't have a home? If they were back in New York, they'd stay with Doug's parents. But they had no family here in California.

"All done, Mommy."

Dani looked up from her phone. Half of Ruth's cereal was on the napkin tucked into her dress, or on the table. She looked down at her own plate. She'd barely eaten two bites of the eggs, but she suddenly had no appetite. She pushed back from the table, then stood and picked up Ruth. "Let's go see Daddy."

When Dani opened the door to the room, Doug was sitting up in bed, looking at his iPhone, while Jonah still slept. Ruth scurried over to him and climbed on the bed.

"Morning, princess," he said as he scooped her onto his lap. "How was breakfast?"

"Yummy."

He looked up at Dani. "Have you heard anything?"

She shook her head.

"I couldn't find out anything specific about our street online. I was just looking up the phone number for the fire department. I figured that's the best way to find out if it's safe to return."

"I think they're still putting out the fire. At least, that's what someone at breakfast told me."

A frown appeared on Doug's face. "I'd like to get our car back, assuming it's drivable. I was able to find online that abandoned cars were towed to various lots, but I don't know which one has ours. And phone numbers for the lots weren't listed."

"Maybe the front desk knows. There are a lot of families here who've been evacuated."

He picked up the phone on the night table and pressed the button designated for the front desk. Dani heard it ring three times before someone picked up. "Good morning. This is Mr. Trumball, in Room 305. I was wondering if the fire department, or maybe the police, have given you any information about our homes and cars."

Dani saw Doug's head nodding as the person on the other end spoke, his frown still in place. After a minute, he reached for the pencil and notepad next to the phone and wrote down a number. When he finished, he said, "Thank you," then hung up and turned to Dani. "Your informant was right. The fire is still burning, but it doesn't appear to be a danger any longer. I have a phone number to call to find out about both the house and the car."

Dani reached for the piece of paper. "I'll call them." She took out her cell phone, put it on speaker, then dialed the number. When her call was answered, she said, "This is Dani Trumball. My family was evacuated from our home at 4236 Prescott Avenue, in Stanford, last night, and our car was abandoned on Page Mill Road. We were wondering if you have any information for us about our house and our car."

"Hold on a sec."

Dani heard some papers rustling, then the woman was back on the line. "The fire reached your block, but I can't say how much damage was done to your house. It'll be at least a day before you'll be able to get back there to check."

"And our car?"

"All the cars abandoned on Page Mill Road were taken to the police impound lot on Farley."

"Thanks." Dani hung up.

"Why don't you stay here with the kids, and I'll take an Uber to the car?" Doug said.

Dani nodded.

"And then I need to go in to work. I teach a class at two and need to take care of some administrative work. But I'll get back here as soon as I'm finished. That's okay, isn't it?"

It really wasn't a question. Dani had pressing work as well, but it would need to wait. Without her car, she couldn't drive Jonah to school. His school wouldn't have been affected by the fire—it was in another town. And it wasn't practical for Elsa to come to the hotel to care for Ruth.

She'd occasionally had friends, both working and stay-at-home moms, who said that nothing was more important than being a mother. Dani would always nod along and agree—she would put her children's needs above anything else—even knowing that the work she did sometimes saved the life of an innocent person. Yet right now, she wondered why she'd never heard a man say there was nothing more important than being a father. They had just gone through a traumatic experience together, but Doug, by any measure a wonderful father, was comfortable moving on with his responsibilities to his job, leaving the nurturing to Dani. Women had come a long way in the world, and gender barriers were slowly being erased. Still, she would prefer that, in that one respect, it was men who changed, not women. She'd like a world in which it was acceptable for men to put their children's needs before their job's demands, as women had been doing for eons.

"Sure, Doug. Just don't stay too late."

"I have some good news," Doug said when he returned to the hotel. It was close to six, and the children had been clamoring for dinner, but Dani had wanted to wait for Doug. Fortunately, the hotel had a swimming pool, which kept both Ruth and Jonah happy, although he'd groused at the only bathing suit available in the gift shop. ("It looks like Dad's," he'd complained.)

"We can go back to our house?" Dani asked hopefully.

"No. But Lauren and Gregory have invited us to stay with them until we can."

Dani knew that there was plenty of room in their home. Even though they had no children to fill their many bedrooms, Dani hated imposing on them. For a childless couple, having the noise of boisterous children around could be jarring.

"But we don't know how long that will be. We don't even know when we can get back to check out the house."

"Look, even if it's for a day or two, it'll be more comfortable than this one room."

That was true. After just one day at the hotel, she felt claustrophobic. Still, she was always uncomfortable sleeping in another's home, feeling like she was being waited on, knowing she was disrupting her hosts' routines.

"Let's get some dinner. We can talk about it then."

Doug nodded. They piled into the car, which was charred but fortunately still drivable, and headed to an Italian restaurant in Palo Alto they'd dined at before with the children. Over a bowl of pasta, it somehow seemed easier to accept their friends' offer. Scarfing down comfort food made everything seem workable. She wished she'd thought to grab her laptop before leaving the house—then, she'd be able to do some work while there—but in the moment, her only thought was getting them all to safety.

"Let's call Lauren," Dani said as they waited for dessert. "Maybe we can check out of the hotel and sleep at their house tonight."

———

Dani had worried needlessly. Although Lauren and Gregory were new friends, they made Dani feel like family. Each of the children had their own bedrooms, with a rented crib in Ruth's. Dani and Doug were given a guest room bigger than the master bedroom in their own home. Lauren had even picked up a coloring book, crayons, and three books for Ruth. Once the children were fast asleep in their beds, Dani joined Doug, Lauren, and Gregory in the living room.

Lauren had a welcoming laugh. It invited people in and made her one of the more popular professors at Stanford Law School. She exuded both warmth and intelligence. She was on the short side and overweight, and next to Gregory, they looked like the mismatched comics pair Mutt and Jeff. He was tall and thin, with thick glasses and long hair tied back in a ponytail.

"I know a guy on the city council," Gregory said. "He told me the fire's all but out now, and they'll start opening the streets to homeowners in the morning."

"That's a relief," Dani said. "I keep imagining nightmare scenarios."

Doug leaned forward in his chair. "Dani always does that. She convinces herself with every case that it's hopeless, and then manages to pull off a miracle."

"Not every time."

"Well, if it were one hundred percent, I'd have to suspect you were a high priestess, performing some black magic. Instead of the super-competent lawyer you are."

Dani blushed. Doug was her biggest advocate, often praising her in front of their friends. His intentions were good, but she wished he wouldn't. She was naturally introverted; his accolades embarrassed her.

"Say, how's it going with my brother's friend?" Lauren asked.

"Not good. The Supreme Court should hand down its decision any day now on whether it will take the case. Frankly, I don't think they will."

"So, what will happen?"

Dani hated to say it, because admitting that there were no other options seemed to put a stamp of finality on the matter. As long as Becky was alive, anything could happen, she kept telling herself. "I don't know. Hope for black magic."

⌒

Dani awoke early the next morning, even before Ruth. She tiptoed through the quiet house to the kitchen and picked out a coffee pod to place in the Keurig. While it brewed, she looked through her emails on her smartphone, her eyes peeled for the all-important decision from the Supreme Court. Nothing yet. She needed to take her mind off waiting by working her other cases but had to retrieve her laptop first. She hoped Gregory was right, that they'd be let back in this morning.

Dani didn't know what she'd find when they got there. It seemed unlikely that the house was untouched, given that they hadn't been allowed back earlier. Maybe it just needed some heavy cleaning to remove smoke damage, perhaps a paint touch-up. Or maybe everything was destroyed. Whatever she found, she and Doug needed to bring normality back into their lives. Jonah had to return to school. Dani and Doug needed to return to work, which meant Elsa needed to care for Ruth again. As much as Lauren had invited them to stay as long as necessary, that wouldn't work for them. Their home was almost an hour's drive, with the ever-present traffic, from Stanford, and it would be too difficult for Elsa to reach. Perhaps she could arrange for Jonah's school to pick him up from this location, but he would spend too much time on the school bus.

As she was working through these issues, Gregory joined her in the kitchen, filled his own cup with coffee, then sat down with her. "I just spoke to Mayor Martello. The fire's completely out, but the fire marshal hasn't given permission yet for residents to return. I think there's still noxious gases in the air. Maybe tomorrow."

Dani sighed deeply. She wished she could crawl back into bed and pretend this was all a dream. Wake up in her own home to the smell of Doug brewing fresh coffee in the kitchen. Get the kids dressed, and send Ruth into Elsa's arms and Jonah onto the school bus. Enter her office and get to work.

She shook her head. She had to toughen up and stop feeling sorry for herself. Hundreds of families were dealing with the aftereffects of the fire. She needed to buy some essentials until they could get back into their house. Changes of underwear, more diapers, toiletries.

Gregory's voice broke into her thoughts. "Tomorrow's Saturday. If you're cleared to check out your house then, Lauren can watch the kids, and I could go with you, help assess the damage."

Dani knew Gregory, among his many skills, had an undergraduate degree in engineering before he went on to earn his PhD in computer science. "Thanks. I appreciate that." She felt antsy to get back home but understood it was necessary to wait until it was safe. Hopefully, she'd have to wait just one more day before learning what was left of their house, their belongings, their life.

By early afternoon, Dani had managed to get in a few hours of work using the computer in Lauren's home office. Doug had gone out early to rent a car for her, and she'd used it to drop Jonah off at his school, then swing by Elsa's apartment to leave Ruth with her. She was deep into her research for a brief when her smartphone rang. She answered it quickly when she saw it was the telltale 202 area code for Washington, DC.

"Ms. Trumball, this is Herb Kaplan. I'm in the clerk's office at the US Supreme Court. We've been trying to fax you the court's decision on your writ of certiorari in the matter of Becky Whitlaw but haven't been able to."

"There's been a fire at my house. The telephone lines are probably destroyed. Can you tell me what they decided?"

There was a pause before he answered. "I'm sorry. It was denied."

Dani's shoulders slumped as she sighed deeply. She had to do the one task she always dreaded—telling a client that they'd reached the end. She picked up the phone, dialed the Mountain View prison, and asked for Becky Whitlaw.

Becky dragged herself back to her cell and, when she reached it, lay down on her narrow bed. She thought she'd accepted her fate when the letter had arrived setting her date of execution, but the weight in her chest now felt worse, much worse, than she'd felt then. *Will it hurt?* she thought. Everyone on death row knew of the botched executions around the country. She'd read once that 7 percent of all executions were botched, the prisoner subjected to excruciating pain. Sometimes people with no medical training attempted to insert the needle into a vein, continuing to jab at the arm without success. But most of the issues arose because pharmaceutical manufacturers who'd previously made the three-drug cocktail traditionally used in executions had refused to continue making their drugs available to kill people. That made sense to Becky. Drugs were supposed to heal.

Some states turned to midazolam, a sedative that didn't always keep the inmate unconscious. She'd heard of one guy who'd struggled breathing for almost two hours before he was pronounced dead. Becky supposed some people would think that's fine. Anyone who'd done something so horrible to be sentenced to death deserved to suffer. Maybe they were right. Becky probably would have felt that way before she'd been sent to prison, before she'd met some of the women on death row with her. Sure, there were a few who were just plain evil, but most were women with sorry lives. She wasn't excusing what they'd done—those that admitted to it; there were some, like her, who clung to claims of innocence—but she didn't think any of them deserved to be tortured.

Texas used pentobarbital, and although they supposedly had enough left to take care of everyone on death row—both men and women, and that was a lot—the rumor along the grapevine was that the state kept extending the expiration date on its supply. She wondered what that might mean when they inserted the needle in her vein and pumped in the drug. Would it still work the same way if it was old? Would it knock her unconscious, so she didn't feel her heart stopping? Or would she wake up and writhe in agony until death became a welcome relief?

She spent more than an hour lying on her back, worrying about how she would die. Before the fire, before Grady died so suddenly in a car crash, she'd thought it would be lovely to go in her sleep. She'd never been afraid of death, only of a prolonged and painful dance toward it. When she lost Grady, she'd realized that her vision of dying always had her as an old woman, surrounded by her children and grandchildren. It was how her own grandmother had died, felled by a brief illness at the age of ninety, her pain dulled by morphine.

Finally, Becky stopped thinking about the needle. It was out of her hands and so pointless to dwell on it. Instead, she turned her thoughts, as she so often did, to her children. Would she be reunited with them? Was there a heaven where they waited for her with their father? She wanted to believe that would happen.

She needed to believe it would. That was only thing that made getting through the next weeks bearable.

The next morning, after Doug turned onto their street, all Dani could see was devastation. Blackened houses, burned trees, lawns bleached yellow. When a minute later, he pulled into the driveway of their home, her heart sank. The structure stood, but the roof was charred, the windows all cracked or broken. As she got out of the car, the smell hit her like a punch in the face. Doug began coughing, a hacking cough that worried her.

"Maybe you should stay in the car?" she told him.

He shook his head. "I'll be okay."

Gregory had accompanied them, and the three entered the house. Smoke damage seemed to cover every surface of the rooms. Glass littered the floors, and the paint on the walls had blistered. Pools of water remained in spots, the smell of already formed mildew mixing with the odor of burned wood. Carefully, they made their way through each of the rooms, opening closets, pulling out drawers. Some things were salvageable, others lost for good. Her grandmother's antique vases, hand-painted in a floral design, were destroyed. The living room couch and two cushioned armchairs, all bought for their new house, her first purchases of new furniture in twenty years, soiled beyond repair. Photo albums that held pictures of Jonah from birth on, ruined. An oriental rug in the master bedroom that had once belonged to Dani's parents was badly singed. Dani wanted to cry. She knew she should be grateful that no one had been hurt, and she was, yet she still felt overwhelmed by what they'd lost.

As they returned to the front door, Gregory said, "It looks like the house is still structurally sound. It'll need a lot of work to bring it back, but it's probably worth it. It has good bones."

Dani nodded wordlessly. She didn't feel an attachment to this house. They'd been living in it too briefly. But so many of the items within, collected over years, had meaning for her and were irreplaceable.

"How long do you think it'll take?" Doug asked.

"At least six months."

Doug grimaced. "So, we'll have to find something in the meantime."

"Really, there's no rush. You can stay with us as long as you need."

~

Dani spent the next ten days searching for a home to rent for the six months it would take to make their own house habitable again, a task that seemed more insurmountable each day. It needed to be within a reasonable distance of both Stanford and Jonah's school, as well as commutable for Elsa. It needed to have at least two bedrooms—she figured Ruth and Jonah could double up temporarily. It needed to be affordable, which right away eliminated so many homes in Silicon Valley; and it needed to be available on a month-to-month basis. So far, she'd come up empty.

As long as Lauren and Gregory had opened their home to them, Dani wanted to make herself useful. When she got back from the day's house-hunting and had picked up Jonah from school and Ruth from Elsa's home, she began to prepare dinner for both families. As she chopped vegetables for a salad, she heard Doug's hacking cough even before he entered the house.

"You've got to see a doctor about that," she called out to him once he stepped inside.

"It's nothing," he said as he came into the kitchen and planted a kiss on Dani's cheek.

"Don't assume that. The smoke from the fire could have damaged your lungs."

"I just need to give it time."

Dani stopped her chopping and turned to Doug. "You need to see a doctor."

"Well, we don't really have one, do we?"

Dani knew that was a jab at her. As soon as they'd moved to Stanford, she'd searched for, and found, a pediatrician for the children but had put off finding someone for themselves. Doug, of course, could have done so, but Dani had promised she'd handle it, then got distracted by work. They were both healthy, and it hadn't seemed a priority.

"There's an urgent-care office near the campus. Go there tomorrow."

"Tomorrow's a busy day. Maybe—" Another coughing fit overtook him before he could finish.

"Tomorrow is Friday," Dani said. "If you don't go then, you'll have to wait 'til Monday. You're going—even if I have to come to your office and drag you out."

At 1:00 p.m. the next afternoon, Dani showed up at Doug's office. "Let's go. I checked with your assistant, and you don't have anything scheduled until three p.m."

Doug stood up from his chair. "You're overreacting. It's just a cough. It's not uncommon for it to take a few weeks to clear up."

"It's been almost two weeks, and it's getting worse, not better." She opened the closet in Doug's office and took out his jacket, then handed it over to him. "Come on."

Doug shrugged, then took his jacket from Dani and followed her out of the office. "I'll be back before three," he told Janice, his assistant.

Ten minutes later, he had checked in with the urgent-care receptionist, then sat, checking his watch every few minutes, for almost an hour. When they finally were ushered into Dr. Noah Delman's office, he once again muttered to Dani, "This is such a waste of time."

Delman's nurse took Doug's vitals and typed into the computer a list of his medications, then left. A minute later, Dr. Delman entered the room and introduced himself. "What's bothering you?" he asked, as he sat down by the computer.

Before Doug could answer, Dani piped in. "We were evacuated from our home two weeks ago because of the forest fire, and Doug's been coughing ever since."

"Any difficulty breathing?"

"No," Doug answered.

"Tightness in your chest?"

"No."

"History of asthma or COPD?"

"No."

"Any heart disease or diabetes?"

"No. I'm really very healthy."

"Okay." Delman stood up and approached Doug with his stethoscope. He placed it on Doug's back. "Deep breath." Doug complied, and Delman repeated it as he listened to several other spots, then came around in front of Doug and listened to his heart. He checked his eyes and then his ears, then sat back down again.

"It's not uncommon to have a lingering cough after inhaling smoke from a forest fire, but I don't like that you say it's getting worse."

"Dani thinks it is. I think it's about the same."

"Well, it should be getting better by now. I'd like to send you for a chest CT scan."

Dani held back her "I told you so" smirk.

The following Monday, Dani was buried deep in her writing when the door to her office opened. Doug stood in the doorway, his face ashen.

"What's wrong? Why are you home so early?"

He walked over to her desk and sat down on a corner. "Dr. Delman called my office this morning. He got back the test results and asked me to come in. I just came from there."

Dani's heart was throbbing. "The fire? It caused some damage?"

Doug picked up Dani's hand, as he shook his head slowly. "Not the fire. He saw a mass on my lungs that looks suspicious. He's referred me to a pulmonologist."

Dani felt tears spring to her eyes and forced them back. It couldn't be cancer. Doug hadn't smoked since Jonah was born. Dani had insisted that she didn't want their baby to inhale cigarette smoke, and Doug had quit cold turkey. It had to be something else. A cyst, maybe? She looked up at Doug's eyes and read his concern. She would be strong for him, just as she was strong for her clients. She'd get him through this.

"When are you seeing him?"

"Thursday."

Dani took a deep breath. "You're going to be fine. You'll see."

He smiled wanly. "Yes. I'm sure I will be."

The three days seemed to take forever to arrive. When they finally did, Dani accompanied Doug to Dr. Ephraim Garvey's office. She had checked him out beforehand—a graduate of Harvard Medical School, with his internship and residency at Stanford School of Medicine. He now headed up the pulmonology department at Stanford Hospital. Although he also had a private office in Palo Alto, where Dani suspected the office was swankier, they saw him at his purely functional office at the hospital.

"I agree with Dr. Delman," Garvey said after he'd looked at the CT scan, and they were seated in front of his desk. "The mass is of concern. You need to have it biopsied."

"But it's not necessarily cancer, is it?" Dani asked.

"Of course not. That's why we need the biopsy. To rule it out. I'll make a small incision in your skin to insert a thin needle, guided by a CT scan, and remove some tissue. You'll be anesthetized and won't feel anything."

"And if it is cancer?" Doug asked. "Then what?"

"Let's not get ahead of ourselves." He buzzed his assistant, and when she answered, asked, "What's my schedule for tomorrow? Can I fit in a biopsy?"

He listened, thanked her, then hung up and looked over at Doug. "Does four o'clock tomorrow work for you?"

Before Doug could answer, Dani said, "He'll make it work."

Dani could barely concentrate on any work Friday, and once again, the hours seemed to drag on. After bringing Jonah to school and Ruth to Elsa's home, she filed a motion for DNA testing for a client, then half-heartedly thumbed through the letters from inmates seeking representation. Thoughts of lung cancer kept filling her head, try as she might to push them away.

She couldn't imagine losing Doug. They'd been together for over twenty years, and during all that time, he'd been her rock. When it became apparent that Jonah had developmental difficulties, it was Doug that kept her from falling apart. When those difficulties were diagnosed as Williams syndrome, again it was Doug who helped her keep it in perspective. It was Doug who'd pushed her to go back to work, and Doug who rallied her when she was unsuccessful in freeing a client. When she was stymied, bouncing ideas off Doug always helped her find the right path. And, if she shared her fears with him over his biopsy, he would no doubt calm her. But she wouldn't burden him with her worry over this. It wouldn't be fair.

At 3:45 p.m., she met Doug at Stanford Hospital and waited with him as he was prepped for the biopsy. When it was time to wheel him away, she was directed to the waiting room.

Forty-five minutes later, Dr. Garvey, dressed in scrubs, joined her there. "It went fine," he said. "Doug is still foggy from the anesthetic, but you can join him now."

"How long for the results?"

"We should know something by Wednesday of next week. Thursday at the outside."

Five more days. Dani didn't know how she'd make it.

The following Monday, Dani met with an insurance adjuster at their house, an unsmiling man with a pasty complexion and horn-rimmed glasses around his narrow eyes. She walked through the rooms with him as he wrote notes into a small book. "Is it as bad as it seems?" she asked when he finished.

"It needs a lot of work."

"My friend says it'll take six months. Does that seem right to you?"

"You'll have to ask your contractor that."

"Any recommendations for one?"

"Sorry, we're not permitted to suggest anyone. But you should get started on finding someone right away. There are a lot of homes damaged from the fire, and you're going to have competition getting a good firm. May even have to wait several months before they can start."

Dani groaned inwardly, then stopped. *Maybe this is just what I need to keep my mind off Doug's health.*

Back at Gregory and Lauren's house, she called Gregory and asked if he could recommend a contractor. Thirty minutes later, he called back with four names. Dani called each one, was told by two that their schedules were filled for the next year, then made an appointment with two others for the next day.

On Tuesday morning, she dropped Jonah off at school, Ruth at Elsa's, then headed to meet the first contractor at her home. He didn't look like Dani's image of a builder, with his expensive suit, shiny leather loafers, and neatly manicured nails. She'd expected to meet someone with dirt under his nails and a sunburned complexion from days working outdoors.

"So, you just do estimates?"

He smiled. "Nope. I work on homes, too. I just clean up when I'm meeting potential customers."

He walked with her through the house, pointing out each of the things that needed to be replaced as they went along. "You're going to need new flooring here," he said in the living room, and "Oh, my," when they entered the kitchen. "This room needs to be gutted." Like the insurance adjuster, he took notes as he went along.

Finished with the inside, they stepped out the front door. He pointed up to the roof and said, "The whole roof will need to be replaced. You can stick with asphalt shingles, like you have now, or upgrade to architectural shingles, or even slate."

"Can you give me estimates for all three?"

"Sure."

They walked over to the living room window. "Most of the windows need replacing. I recommend doing all of them, even those not cracked, and putting in energy-efficient windows. They'll pay for themselves over time with lower heat and electric bills."

As he talked, Dani stared at the window. She'd hadn't really looked closely at any window on her previous walk-throughs of the house. Now, she stood rooted in her spot.

"You okay, Mrs. Trumball?"

"This window. The way it's cracked. It looks just like crazed glass."

"So?"

"I thought glass only breaks this way when an accelerant is used with a fire."

"I don't know about that. We've worked on plenty of houses affected by wildfires, and many of them have windows that cracked just like this."

⸺

By the time Dani returned to Lauren and Gregory's home after meeting with the second contractor, then picking up Jonah and Ruth, Gregory was back from work and ensconced in his home office. She got the children snacks, settled Ruth in front of the television, then knocked on the open door of Gregory's office. "Can I interrupt you for a minute?"

He spun around in his chair. "Sure. What's up?"

Dani showed him the pictures she'd taken of her windows. "I don't understand. The cracks in the windows? They look like the pictures of Becky Whitlaw's house. The fire investigator said it was crazed glass."

"It is."

"But this fire wasn't started with an accelerant."

Gregory looked at her quizzically. "Of course not. It's not rapid heating that causes crazed glass. It's rapid cooling. The firefighters must have gotten to your home when the fire was fresh and used their hoses on it."

"But . . . but . . ." Dani could hardly speak. Crazed glass was one of the indications of arson. Miner, the fire investigator who testified at Becky's trial, had been very clear about that. Even Hamburg, the expert hired by Becky's attorney, had agreed that the rapid heat that resulted from the use of an accelerant caused crazed glass. "Are you certain about that?"

"I am. It's been well established for more than twenty years."

"That's not what the fire investigator said."

Gregory shook his head. "It's disgraceful how hard some investigators hold on to old myths."

"What about puddle configurations? Soot marks forming a V? Are those proof an accelerant was used?"

"Again, myths, passed down from investigator to investigator, not science."

Was it possible? Could it be that no one started the fire in Becky's house? Dani could feel the stirring of excitement throughout her body. "How do you know this?"

"A colleague of mine from back in grad school has studied fires for decades. Over the years, he's sent me some of his published articles. I'd be glad to put you in touch with him." He opened a drawer in his desk and rumbled through some papers, finally pulling out a business card. He handed it to Dani. "Stuart Halstein. That's who you should speak to about Becky's case."

Dani leaned over and gave Gregory a hug. All thoughts of the damage to her own home, of the problems they'd face getting resettled, of the headaches they'd endure restoring their house, even of Doug's health, disappeared. All she could think of was the possibility of freeing Becky Whitlaw before the State of Texas inserted a lethal injection into her veins.

Dani took the card and headed into her bedroom. She placed a call to Halstein, left a message when she got his voice mail, then plopped down on the bed. *How could I have missed this?* She prided herself on being thorough, on catching the little details that others missed. But this wasn't a little detail—it was the essence of the case. She'd gone over the file meticulously, especially keying on the testimony of Becky's fire expert. He, too, had no doubt that the fire that killed Becky's children had been deliberately set. Why hadn't she verified that he still felt that way? Why hadn't she spoken to an independent fire expert? Instead, she'd focused her energy on finding another suspect, perhaps rushing into court too soon.

Dani wrapped her arms around her body and began rocking back and forth. Was it too late? Had she failed Becky? *This never would have happened if we'd stayed in New York*, she thought. There, she'd always pop into Melanie's or Bruce's offices and bounce ideas off them. They'd offer suggestions. Here, she was alone. It didn't matter that they were a phone call away. It wasn't the same.

Fat tears rolled down her cheeks as she feared that her lapse of judgment would be fatal for Becky Whitlaw. *Stop it*, Dani thought after a few moments. *It's not about you. It's about Becky.* She grabbed a tissue and wiped her cheeks dry, then opened her laptop, which thankfully had survived the fire, and began a search on Lexis. Ten minutes later, she was able to breathe again. Five years ago, Texas had enacted a law known unofficially as the "junk science writ." It permitted a prisoner to apply for a writ of habeas corpus – a legal procedure demanding that the court prove a prisoner's detention is lawful -if scientific evidence used at their trial had been subsequently debunked. If Gregory was right, if his friend, Halstein, could confirm it, then it wasn't over yet for Becky. Dani would have one more string to yank.

J ust as Lauren announced dinner was ready, Stuart Halstein returned Dani's call. "Do you mind if I take it?" Dani asked Lauren.

"Go ahead."

Dani headed back into her bedroom, grabbed a notepad, then sat down on the bed. "Thanks for getting back to me."

"No problem. How can I help you?"

"My client is in a Texas prison with a date set for execution that's only six weeks away. She was convicted twenty years ago of setting a fire that killed her three children. Fire investigators on both sides agreed it was arson, but now I'm wondering if that was the case. I just learned that crazed glass and certain other things the investigators relied on for their conclusions don't always mean an accelerant was used."

Dani heard Halstein take a deep breath. "The only thing crazed glass indicates is that the glass got hot and the fire department sprayed water on it. That's all. What's criminal is what passed for truth back then."

"My client's own investigator didn't challenge the finding."

"You have to understand - fire investigators weren't scientists. In fact, some only had a high school education, and very few had advanced degrees. They had a set of assumptions that were handed down from one generation to the next and accepted as true. Those beliefs were false."

"And yet courts routinely accept them as experts."

"Changes first started back in 1992, when the National Fire Protection Association issued guidelines for conducting fire investigations. Unfortunately, they weren't well received by fire investigators."

"Why not?"

"Because then they'd have to admit that thousands of fires they claimed were arson were in fact accidental. And that their testimony may have sent innocent people to prison."

Dani thought about Becky. "Or to their deaths."

"I'd like to think that never happened, but I suppose it's possible."

"You said changes first started in '92. What about now?"

"By 2000, the NFPA guidelines were more generally accepted, but even today, there are fire investigators who approach investigations as an art rather than the application of scientific principles."

"So, when my client was on trial, it's possible that the fire investigators were relying on old assumptions?"

"Yes. I'd check their education as well. In 2009, the NFPA listed subjects that investigators should have demonstrated competency in beyond a high school level. Especially fire chemistry, thermodynamics, hazardous materials, and failure analysis."

"Can I retain you to look at my client's case?"

"I'm swamped right now. And you mentioned her date of execution's been set. I don't know that I'd get to it in time for you.

There are several others in the field who are trustworthy. I can give you their numbers."

"But it's precisely because her execution date is coming up so quickly that I don't have time to look for someone else. Please, the State is getting ready to kill someone for a fire that may have been an accident. Couldn't you possibly push someone else back?"

Once again, Dani heard a deep sigh. "Do you have the investigator's report?"

"I do. I also have a video they took of the scene, and pictures of the house both before and after the fire."

"Overnight them to me. I'll take a look."

~

Dani was still obsessing over cracked windows the next day when she and Doug sat in the office of Dr. Garvey. She tapped her fingers nervously on the arm of the chair, waiting for the doctor to enter, and when he did, scanned his face to see if his expression revealed anything about the results. It didn't.

"Mr. Trumball, Mrs. Trumball." He nodded at each of them as he sat down behind his large, uncluttered desk, so unlike Dani's messy one at home. "I'm afraid it's bad news."

Dani quickly looked over at Doug. His face remained still.

"You have small-cell lung cancer."

Dani clasped her hands, which had begun to tremble. She'd pored over the internet the past few days, trying to quell her fears, and in the process learning everything she could about lung cancer. Foolishly, she'd thought if she worried about the worst outcome, it wouldn't occur. And small-cell lung cancer was the worst outcome. Rarer, but much more aggressive, than non-small-cell lung cancer. It had a dire prognosis, unless it was caught early.

"What type?" she asked. There were only two stages, she'd learned from her search.

"Extensive. It's spread."

Dani grabbed Doug's hand. The color had drained from his face, and his lips quivered.

"But I don't really feel bad," he said. "Just this damn cough."

"That's not unusual," Garvey said. "Unfortunately, symptoms often don't occur until later in the disease. I suspect, in your case, the irritation of your lungs from the fire's smoke hastened one of the symptoms—your cough. I'd hoped that meant it was still at an early stage, but that's not the case."

"So, what now?" Doug asked. "What's the treatment?"

"The tumor is too big to operate. I'm going to recommend an oncologist, who will walk you through the nonsurgical options. But you should expect it will be a course of chemotherapy, at least."

"And the prognosis?"

"I'm not going to sugarcoat this. You have a rough road ahead."

Dani knew what that meant. Extensive small-cell lung cancer was rarely curable. It was only a question of how much time was left. Dani felt the walls of the room close in on her, and her breathing became labored. *It can't be. This can't be.* She felt a pain in the back of her throat, and when she tried to speak, she couldn't. She looked over at Doug and saw tears in the corners of his eyes. Just as quickly as it had come on, her panic dissipated. Doug needed her to stay strong, and that's what she would be for him.

"We have to tell Jonah," Doug said as they drove back to Lauren and Gregory's house.

"Not yet."

"He's going to know something is wrong."

Dani knew Doug was right. Despite his disability, Jonah was very observant. Telling him, though, would make it real, and she wasn't ready to accept that.

Doug glanced over at Dani. "I'm going to fight this. I need you to fight with me."

She fought for her clients every day. Fought for their freedom. Fought for their lives. Of course, she would fight for Doug. But, as much as she wrapped herself in her clients' struggles, despite Bruce's admonition that she maintain an emotional distance, she recognized this was different. She despaired when she lost a client's fight. But, if Doug lost his fight, her world would crumble. She didn't want to face that possibility. She didn't want her son to face that possibility. Doug was right, though. Avoiding it wouldn't change the results.

"Okay, Doug. We'll tell him when he gets home."

Dani picked Jonah up from his school, and when they returned, he made a beeline for the kitchen—as always, ravenous for a snack. Dani took hummus, cut-up carrots, and cucumbers from the refrigerator, and Jonah devoured them. When he finished, she took him into Gregory's office, where Doug was waiting.

He looked at his father with a puzzled expression, then said, "I wasn't anticipating you home."

Doug patted the sofa. "Come, sit down. I need to tell you something."

Jonah's expression immediately changed to one of worry.

"I have cancer, and I'm going to be very sick for a while from the medicines the doctor gives me."

Jonah's eyes teared up. "Are you going to expire?"

"I'm going to do everything the doctor tells me to do, and I hope when the treatment is finished, the cancer will be gone."

Jonah rushed over to Doug, sat down on his lap, and wrapped his arms around his father. Dani looked at her almost-grown son, curled into his father like he'd done as a toddler, and understood his anguish. They'd never lied to Jonah and wouldn't do it now. They wouldn't promise him that his father would survive, only convey their honest hope for that outcome. That's all they could do.

⁓

Later that evening, after the children were asleep, Doug broke the news to Lauren and Gregory. Dani knew by the look in Gregory's eyes that he immediately grasped the severity of the diagnosis.

"You have to stop looking for another place and just settle in here," Lauren said. "We can set aside another room for Elsa so she can live here during the week—I know how hard it's been for you to have to bring Ruth over to her house every day. And I'm sure Gregory's company can spare a driver to bring Jonah to and from school each day."

"Thank you," Dani said. "That's more than generous of you. But we've talked about it, and we really want to go through this privately. I'd looked at a house close to Stanford that was out of our price range, but we're going to go ahead with it. It'll just be until the repairs on our house are finished, and we'll dip into our savings."

"Are you absolutely certain? We really enjoy having you here."

Dani nodded. "We're certain."

~

Two days later, Halstein called back. "I've spent the better part of the afternoon pacing back and forth and screaming at the incompetence of those men."

"So, you think it might not have been arson?"

"Might not? You're the lawyer. Shouldn't they have to prove it was? Because nothing in their findings pointed to arson as the only explanation."

"I know you explained about crazed glass, but what about the other indicia?"

"I'll go over each of them, but first, I want to give you a little history about arson science. I already told you that before 1992, there were no real scientific guidelines for arson investigations. What were thought to be telltale signs of arson were passed down from so-called experts to those they trained, and when those trainees became experts, they passed down the same erroneous assumptions."

"How did that change?"

"In 1990, a private fire investigator was hired to investigate the case of a man accused of setting a fire that killed his wife, his sister-in-law, and four children. He insisted that his son had accidently set the living room couch on fire while playing with a cigarette lighter. All the indicators said a liquid accelerant was used. As luck would have it, there was an identical home next door that was scheduled for demolition. The fire investigator placed the same kind of furnishings in the house next door, then set fire to the couch. To everyone's surprise, the buildup of smoke and gas caused the entire space to burst into flames in under five minutes. It had reached a point called 'flashover.' They found in the second house the same indicators of the use of an accelerant as in the first house—only none was used. That was the beginning of changes in the field of arson investigation.

"The next year, the same investigator examined fifty homes destroyed by a brush fire, and once again, found numerous things that had traditionally been attributed to arson."

"But Becky wasn't convicted until 1999. The investigators must have known about those findings a decade later."

"In a survey taken not too long ago, almost forty percent of investigators still didn't know that crazed glass is caused by rapid cooling, not rapid heating. Twenty-three percent thought puddle-shaped burns indicated arson. Eight percent held on to the belief that alligator blistering meant that a fire burned fast and hot, which only happened with an accelerant. And that study was undertaken almost twenty years after the investigators in your client's case testified. So, am I surprised that the Whitlaw fire was ruled arson? Sadly, no."

Dani wanted to run into someone's office and shout, "Becky's going to be freed!" But she wasn't in New York, where she was just across a hallway from her colleagues. At Lauren's house, all was quiet, with Doug and Lauren both at Stanford, and Gregory at his office. As quickly as the elation rushed through her, Dani's practical mind took over.

"They testified to more than crazed glass at the trial. Can we go over each item?"

"Sure. I mentioned flashover. That's when the heat from a fire rises so high that the whole room explodes with fire. In other words, it goes from being a fire in a room to a room on fire. If there's furniture in the room, when that ignites, the fire goes into 'post-flashover,' and the path of the fire depends on new sources of oxygen. The fire report said that Becky had thrown a rock through her children's bedroom window. That gave the fire more oxygen, which would propel it out their door and down into the hallway toward the front door. That would explain the burn trail the investigators found.

"It's the same thing with the V-shaped patterns," Halstein continued. "During post-flashover, those patterns occur in multiple spots, not just where the fire originated. Also with puddle configurations. Miner testified that they occur only if an accelerant is used. Not true. Studies of fires known to be natural have shown time and again that puddle configurations also appear after flashover. It's impossible to tell just by looking whether an accelerant was used or whether it was the result of post-flashover. The only way to confirm an accelerant is to take samples and test them in a laboratory. The investigators did that, and it showed something by the front door. But the file you sent me included pictures of Becky's house before the fire, and on the front porch was a small grill with a can of lighter fluid next to it. It's likely that when firefighters sprayed water on the porch, they spread lighter fluid into the opened front door, and that's what the lab found. That would be consistent with the lab finding no evidence of mineral spirits anywhere else in the house."

As Dani listened, she began to feel a growing pit of anger. It was the twenty-first century, and still so-called experts were coming into court and, often solely on their testimony, sending people to prison because of junk science.

"Can you tell from the pictures and the reports what caused the fire?"

"It's impossible to be precise without having visited the post-blaze site. Most likely faulty electrical wiring. It looks like the origin was in the children's bedroom, and post-flashover happened quickly. But it certainly wasn't arson. Your client shouldn't be in prison. You have to stop her execution."

"Telephone call, Whitlaw."

The guard's voice took her by surprise. Only her attorney's call would be put through to her, and Dani never called her past five o'clock. It was now closing in on 7:00 p.m. The guard approached her cell, and Becky followed the routine—hands through the opening in the metal slats, handcuffs snap on, then door opens. She walked over to the phone on the wall and picked it up. "Dani?"

"Hi, Becky."

"Is something wrong?" *Really, how much more wrong could it be?* Becky thought. The Supreme Court had turned down her appeal, and her execution date was set.

"No. Something very good."

Becky could hear excitement in Dani's voice, and her own heart started to race.

"It wasn't arson. The fire in your house—it was an accident."

An accident? Not arson? The fast beats of her heart now turned to a pounding in her chest. She could barely get words out. "How? How do you know?"

"The experts were wrong, all of them. Everything they said was proof of an accelerant wasn't proof at all."

Becky couldn't talk. Deep sobs rose from her chest, and she sunk to the floor. Her body shook from her cries, so loud that they brought the guard to her side.

"You okay?" the woman asked, concern in her voice.

For two decades, she'd wondered if she had blacked out the events of that night, not wanting to believe she could have done what a jury said she had, *almost* convinced that she never would have harmed her children, yet still—there always remained a kernel of doubt. Was it possible? She still harbored blame, rightful blame. If she hadn't drunk so much the night before, maybe she would have awakened earlier. Maybe she would have been able to rescue her children. But that blame was different from the blame that came with the speck of fear that she'd set the fire herself. For the first time in two decades, she felt a glimmer of happiness. She knew, if she somehow escaped this hell, she'd never again feel untarnished happiness, for no one who lost a child, much less three, could ever be the same. But it was there—a lightness throughout her body, and as her sobs subsided, a smile on her face.

"Becky, are you still there?" she heard through the phone.

She stood up, her legs shaky, and wiped the splotches of tears from her cheeks. "I'm here, Dani."

"One other thing. The fire happened very quickly. I don't think there's anything you could have done to save your children."

Becky took a deep breath and let that sink in. "What happens now? Will I go free?"

"Not yet. But you're one step closer."

February 2, 2019

Dear Chuck,

Ever since I arrived in prison, I've felt like with every step I took, I was pulling a Mack truck behind me. It was filled with the voices of my children, my husband, even my mother, with the accusing stares of the twelve men and women who sent me here, blaming me for the fire. Now, for the first time in more than twenty years, that truck is gone. Dani has told me the most amazing thing! The fire that burned down my house, the one that killed my children—it wasn't deliberately set! It wasn't arson!

Dani found someone who knows all about the science of arson. All the things that the state's expert said showed someone—me—had poured turpentine throughout the house just weren't true. Everything he found occurs naturally when a fire gets very hot very quickly. He even said the fire probably started in the kids' room, and even if I hadn't drunk so much the night before, I probably wouldn't have been able to get into the room to save them.

I can't tell you how much this has changed me. Dani thinks that I'll be set free. She has to file some papers with the court, but she really thinks it will happen. Before, when I thought about the possibility of leaving Mountain View, it was just the idea of getting out. I didn't think about what I would do— not seriously, at least. Now, I'm thinking about it. I don't want to go back to Glen Brook—there are too many bad memories there. Do you think I'd like Dallas? I've never even been to a big city.

Can you do me a favor and check to see if there are any companies that transcribe braille in Dallas? Or even Houston. I'd like to get a job doing that and take college classes at night. Maybe it's not too late for me to become a nurse.

Your friend,

Becky

February 5, 2019

Dear Becky,

I'm ecstatic to learn of your wonderful news. I hope this bring you the peace of mind you've searched for. From the time I first began corresponding with you, and especially once I'd met you in person, it never seemed possible to me that you'd deliberately killed your children. Now you know that wasn't the case.

I've investigated jobs for certified braille transcribers, and it seems most of them are in schools with programs for the visually impaired. Once you are released, I'm sure you could find a place that could use your skills, as there seems to be a shortage of qualified braille transcribers. If you can't find an opening when you're ready, I suspect I could get you a job at my hospital. I think you would love Dallas. It's probably a good idea to stay away from Glen Brook, although I suppose your mother would not be happy about your decision.

If you'd like, when it gets closer to your release, I can look for a small place for you to rent. Let me know.

Yours,

Chuck

Halstein's report came in on Tuesday, two days earlier than expected. Dani skimmed through it, then read it more thoroughly, making notes as she went along. Everything they'd discussed was in it, fleshed out with more detail, and for each so-called proof of the use of an accelerant, he demonstrated why the facts showed the investigators were incorrect. *The fact, as indicated in the investigators' reports, that the windows in the children's room had blown out shows that the fire had reached flashover,* the report read. *The path the fire then took was, contrary to the investigators' conclusion, not the result of an accelerant but the expected path that would occur during post-flashover.*

Later, he wrote, *The burn patterns and puddle configurations noted by the investigators also are routinely found post-flashover. As testing of the samples performed by a laboratory did not identify an accelerant, it is incorrect to conclude that they could only occur from the use of an accelerant.*

He finished by saying, *In my opinion, based upon hundreds of fires examined post-flashover, this fire was not the result of arson, but rather an accident, most likely due to faulty wiring in the children's room.*

Halstein's report was solid. In any other state, it was a slam dunk. This was Texas, though, notorious for the number of prisoners who were executed. She hung up, then got to work finishing up her application for a new trial. When she was finally satisfied with it, she put it aside and phoned ADA Jeremy Wilson.

"Hello, Mrs. Trumball," he said upon answering. "How can I help you?"

"The Applewood Fire a few weeks ago, in California, reached my home. It was extensively damaged."

"Oh? I'm sorry to hear that."

Dani could picture him wondering why this virtual stranger was telling him about her house fire.

"The thing is, when I went back to assess the damage, I saw the windows had crazed glass."

There was silence on the other end of the phone.

"That's one of the things that led the fire investigators to believe the fire in Becky Whitlaw's house was arson."

"There were a number of things in that house that led them to conclude it was arson."

"Yes, that's true. But the crazed glass really bothered me. So, I reached out to someone who's now considered a national expert on the source of fires. And he told me that arson science has evolved to better understand when an accelerant is used, and the things noted in Becky's house were just the result of the way the fire behaves. I sent him the reports of the state's fire investigators, including their pictures, and he's quite certain Becky's fire wasn't the result of arson."

Again, Wilson was silent.

"Becky Whitlaw is about to be executed for a crime that didn't occur."

More silence. Then, "What do you want from me?"

"I'd like to send you the expert's report, as well as my draft of an application for a writ of habeas corpus under Texas's junk science statute. Then I'd like you to join in on the application."

Dani heard him sigh. "Send it. I'll look it over. But no promises."

Dani felt a rush of relief. She'd run across prosecutors occasionally who were obstructionist, despite overwhelming evidence of innocence. It didn't seem Jeremy Wilson would be that way. It was one less thing for her to worry about.

The next afternoon, Wilson called. "I'm afraid I'm not going to be able to help you."

"Why not? You can't seriously believe it was arson."

"Doesn't matter what I believe. My boss nixed it."

The Tarrant County DA was up for reelection next November, Dani realized. *That's what he's worried about.* "You know the judge is going to agree with me."

"Make your application. But, Dani—don't get too confident."

Dani had spent a few days struggling with a decision over Dominic Webster and Patton Swinton. She'd never walked away from representing a client before. Finally, she called Melanie. "Can you do me a favor?" she asked.

"Sure. What's up?"

Dani filled her in on Doug's condition. "I'm not taking on any new cases. While Doug's undergoing treatment, other than Becky's case, I'll only work on DNA cases. Webster was convicted on bite-mark evidence, and Swinton on hair analysis. DNA has disproven both, but their prosecutors are fighting back. I need someone to take over their cases. They're each going to trial."

"Oh, Dani, I wish I could, but my obstetrician has given me a no-fly order. I'm sure I can get someone else in the office to handle them."

Dani knew every attorney in the office was good. But she'd trained Melanie herself and had high confidence in her.

"I'll work from the office with whomever takes over," Melanie continued.

That would have to be good enough. Dani would do almost anything for her clients, but family came first. Always.

⌐◦⌐

The next week was spent in a whirlwind. First, meeting with Dr. Andrea Fishbein, the oncologist Dr. Garvey recommended, then signing a month-to-month lease for a furnished, three-bedroom house just two miles from Stanford and moving into it.

"I prefer Lauren's house," Jonah grumbled when he first saw the basic ranch home, with a small yard and dated kitchen. But after being reminded it was only nine blocks from Keith's home, and he could walk there by himself, he perked up.

Doug was to start chemotherapy the following week, with three days of chemo followed by three weeks of rest, and then again, for three cycles. If that didn't work, three more cycles would be added. *Almost six months,* Dani thought when the doctor described the treatment. *Time for the repairs on our house to be completed. We'll move back in with Doug in remission.*

At the end of the week, she picked up her mail from the post office, which had been holding it each day ever since the fire, and saw a letter from Samuel Xavier, the prosecutor who wanted to retry Dominic Webster despite DNA excluding him as the perpetrator.

Dear Ms. Trumball:

This is to inform you that the DNA found on Ms. Susan Cordon, whom your client, Dominic Webster was convicted of raping, was run through CODIS, as ordered by the court. A match was found, and it

> *identified the DNA as belonging to Orson Binder,*
> *a man currently serving a life sentence for another*
> *rape and murder of a woman two years after Ms.*
> *Cordon's. Accordingly, I will notify the court and*
> *move that your client be released forthwith.*

No apology. No regrets. No recognition that this man's life had wrongly been taken away from him. Dani would make a motion for compensation on his behalf. Colorado, where Webster was convicted, provided $70,000 for each year Webster had been wrongfully incarcerated, plus an additional $50,000 for each of those years spent on death row. Webster would be a millionaire, yet Dani was certain he would gladly be a pauper rather than have spent those years facing death for a crime he knew he hadn't committed.

⁓

The following Monday, Doug, with Dani by his side, reported to Dr. Fishbein's office for his first day of chemo. He'd started on a regimen of antinausea and steroid medications the day before. A nurse brought him into a large room with eight leather recliners, next to each a folding chair. Five of the chairs were already filled with others already hooked up to the intravenous drips by their sides. Doug nodded to them as he took his place in one of the empty recliners.

The nurse worked efficiently in inserting the catheter into Doug's vein, and he settled back in the chair, ready for the eight-hour day. Tomorrow would be five hours, then Wednesday, three hours. As Doug retrieved his iPad from the tote bag he'd brought with him, Dani glanced at the other patients. Only one woman among the five others, and she also appeared to be the youngest. She looked like she was in her twenties, and a middle-aged woman—Dani guessed she was her mother—sat by her side, knitting. One of the other men looked to be around Doug's age, and the other two seemed elderly. None of the men had someone keeping them company.

The middle-aged man caught Dani's eye and said, "First day?"

She nodded.

"My wife stayed the first day, too. Becomes a bit of a bore, and there were things she could accomplish at home. Same is true for the other fellas here."

The other men murmured in agreement.

"Dani, I don't mind if you leave," Doug said. "I've got my laptop and my iPad. There's enough here to keep me distracted."

"No. I want to stay."

And she did, that first day. For the next two days, she accompanied him there, then left. She returned at lunchtime with food for him, then left again until it was time to bring him home.

That man was right. Doug was fine without her by his side, and working at home kept her mind off the unthinkable.

At the end of the first three days of chemo, Doug was weak but able to work from home. He felt strong enough to return to Stanford the following Monday, the first day of his three-week hiatus before returning for his second round of chemo.

On Wednesday, she received notice that Judge Gertner had scheduled oral arguments on her motion for a new trial in Becky's case, based upon the junk science statute, for the following Wednesday. Doug told Dani to go. "I'm fine by myself," he said. "Maybe just ask Elsa to stay late the night you're away. Just until Ruth is in bed."

And so, the following Wednesday, Dani once again sat in the Tarrant County, Texas, courtroom of Judge Gertner. Unlike the last time—indeed, unlike every time she'd appeared in a court on Becky's behalf—she felt confident of her position. When her case was called, she moved to the front of the courtroom. After ADA Jeremy Wilson took his seat up front, Dani stood.

"Your Honor, Article 11.073 of the Texas Code of Criminal Procedure recognized that scientific advancements may demonstrate that previously held beliefs by experts in different fields were, in fact, incorrect. The Texas legislature expressly recognized that arson science was one of those areas in which scientific investigations have led to new understanding of fires, both how they occur and how they react. As a result of that understanding, prior testimony of arson investigators was often flawed, and thus led to wrongful convictions. That is exactly what happened in Becky Whitlaw's trial. As you can see in the affidavit of Stuart Halstein, the conclusion reached by Sam Miner, the arson investigator who testified on behalf of the prosecution at Ms. Whitlaw's trial, was based on incorrect assumptions on the dynamics of a fire. There was, based on current scientific knowledge of fires, no basis to conclude that it was arson. It was likely faulty wiring—a hazard unbeknownst to Ms. Whitlaw. She has been on death row for twenty years for a nonexistent crime. This court should recognize the tragic mistake that has been made and order her release immediately. Based on this new scientific evidence, she should not be subjected to a new trial, but if the DA chooses to go ahead with one, she should be released on her own recognizance, without bail. Thank you, Your Honor."

Dani sat down and took a deep breath.

Wilson stood slowly. He glanced over at Dani, and she saw a look of sadness in his eyes. "Your Honor, Ms. Trumball is correct about the purpose of Article 11.073, but she failed to point out the defendant's obligation under the statute. Before a court may grant relief under this statute, the defendant must show that the relevant scientific evidence she now relies upon was not ascertainable through reasonable due diligence. As stated in the affidavit of Morris Holcolm, a noted fire investigator and provided with the State's response to the defendant's application, the dynamics of fire that Ms. Trumball referred to were discovered by fire scientists well before the defendant's trial.

"As early as 1977, a study showed that the telltale signs fire investigators relied upon to indicate arson were not scientifically valid. In 1991, a team of fire investigators discovered that crazed glass was not solely caused by use of an accelerant. In 1992, the National Fire Protection Association published scientifically based guidelines for arson investigations. All these facts could have been discovered by the defendant for her trial in 1999 with the exercise of due diligence. She failed to do so and cannot now come before this court and ask for a second chance. The statute simply does not permit that. For this reason—"

Dani couldn't remain seated any longer. She jumped up. "Your Honor, the statute very clearly states it applies. First, if it wasn't available to be offered at trial, or—not *and*, but *or*— if it contradicts scientific evidence used by the state at the trial. Mr. Wilson can't possibly deny that the State's own expert witness offered so-called scientific evidence that has now been discredited."

"That may be so," admitted Wilson. "But the statute still requires the exercise of due diligence. The evidence was there to be discovered."

"It required more than due diligence to discover it. Even today, more than twenty years later, many arson investigators are unaware of the new advances."

"Still," Judge Gertner broke in, "it was out there. The defendant could have brought it up back then."

Dani's mouth dropped open. "You can't—" She'd started to say, *You can't be serious,* then caught herself. It wouldn't help Becky to antagonize the judge. She stopped, then began again. "Ms. Whitlaw is about to be executed for the arson murder of her three children. Whether or not her lawyer could have discovered back in 1999 what were then almost universally overlooked studies should take a back seat to the grave injustice that would occur if, at the least, she was not given another trial in which scientific evidence could be introduced that clearly refutes a conclusion of arson. This court cannot condone killing an innocent person."

"I remind the court that the defendant confessed to setting the fire," Wilson said.

"To a jailhouse snitch, who's since recanted," Dani shot back.

"I admit the law isn't the most artfully worded," said Judge Gertner. "But I must decide based upon what is clear about it, and I have to agree with Mr. Wilson here. The defendant hasn't met the requirement for relief to be granted. Application is denied."

Dani had never cried in court. She'd cried in her office. She'd cried in execution chambers. She'd cried out in the field with Tommy. Never in court. Until now, as she sat rooted in her seat, and tears flowed down her cheeks. She just wasn't certain whether they were for Becky, or for Doug.

Dani was still numb when she arrived back home. Although Doug had gone into Stanford for a few hours, he was home when she stepped through the front door, and he wrapped his strong arms around her.

"Are you going to appeal?" he asked once she'd settled in.

"Of course. It's just so crazy. I don't understand this judge."

"It's not just him. Remember the Supreme Court decision, where Justice Scalia took the position that the Constitution doesn't prohibit the execution of a convicted defendant who's had a full and fair trial? Even if a habeas court finds evidence of actual innocence."

Dani shuddered. She remembered it well. It placed the importance of finality above justice. Of course, Scalia assumed that the lengthy process of appeals in capital cases prevented the execution of innocent defendants, but Dani had seen enough to harbor doubts that such was the case. Times like this made her wonder about her chosen profession. Not just the area of law she practiced—representing the wrongfully convicted—but the law itself.

Before starting college, she'd thought she wanted to pursue a degree in literature, perhaps a doctorate, followed by a position teaching at a university. The thought of spending her life on a college campus, surrounded by students eager to learn, had been enticing. Once she entered college, she realized such jobs were hard to find and hard to keep. Her goals switched to becoming a psychologist, thinking it would be a way to help people, to give back to others. Her focus turned to law only after she learned of the unjust conviction of her childhood nanny's nephew. It was then that she realized she might have more of an impact as an attorney.

Doug had managed to combine his love of law with the joy of imparting his knowledge to others. After eight years as a federal prosecutor, he'd switched to teaching at Columbia Law School. Every time Dani thought about making a similar move herself— and the idea of working on a college campus still appealed to her—she realized she couldn't. She would feel selfish abandoning HIPP.

She took a long look at Doug. "How are you feeling?"

"I'm managing."

Doug had always been stalwart, refusing to buckle when he had a bad cold, only staying home from work if he had a fever. Before this, that was the extent of any illness he'd had. But now, his skin had a grayish pallor, and dark circles were below his eyes.

"Any nausea yet?"

"Some."

"Is that why you came home early?"

He nodded.

Dani leaned back into his arms. Ruth was at the playground with Elsa; Jonah's bus would arrive in an hour. She breathed in the scent she'd always associated with her husband—an earthy odor that reminded her of outdoors, deep in a forest. Early in their marriage, they'd spent many weekends hiking somewhere—Bear Mountain, the Catskills, or, if a long weekend, in the Adirondack Mountains far west of Albany. That stopped when Jonah was born. Once, when he was around five, they took him for a picnic at Bear Mountain and followed it with a short hike. He'd hated it; cried every few steps that he wanted to return to their blanket and play with the keyboard that he'd never gone anywhere without. Even then, he'd shown musical talent.

When he's older, they'd promised themselves. Then, after Ruth was born: *When they're off on their own, we'll travel. Do hikes all over the world.* It was so easy to push into the future wishes for the present. Now, Dani wondered if they'd have a future together.

Becky felt like she was on a roller coaster, the extreme kind, where the cars on a track went upside down on a big loop, making your stomach do flip-flops and your head feel like explosions were going off inside. She wanted the coaster to stop. Wherever it stopped. With the prison doors opening, or with her strapped onto a gurney. She couldn't take the ups and downs anymore. Dani told her the next court would see the truth, but Becky no longer believed that. The truth didn't matter to anyone but her. She held the truth inside her like a precious gift. She hadn't set the fire that killed her children. That was the truth that counted. Nothing else did.

She sat in front of her computer screen and robotically typed out the braille. She could do her job without thinking, without feeling. That's what she needed. To block out all feeling.

"Why you looking so sad?" Amy, sitting next to her, whispered. "I thought your lawyer was getting you out?"

Becky just shook her head. She couldn't bring herself to talk, even though Amy was a sweet woman who often helped the time pass quickly. She was working on a history textbook, filled with battles and dates. Maybe all of life was a battle, a struggle to survive. Sometimes those in the thick of it just gave up. Walked into the fire and let whatever happened happen. That's what she wanted for herself now. To just give up.

She had lost track of time when the bell sounded. She marked the page she was up to in the history textbook and walked, alone, back to her cell. The other inmates in the computer room weren't on death row. They would head to the prison mess hall, eat their dinner in a communal room, then mingle before mandatory bedtime. Becky went, as required, straight to her cell. The guard locked her inside, then twenty minutes later brought her a meal on a tray. Becky ate it listlessly, then lay down on her bed. She knew she should write her mother, write Chuck, let them know of the newest setback, but she couldn't bring herself to do it. She couldn't bring herself to write down in black and white that, once again, a judge had decided her life wasn't worth saving.

Dani hunkered down to work on an appeal and a stay of execution while the appeal was pending. This single judge's opinion would go to a panel of nine judges on the Texas Court of Criminal Appeals, and if she lost again, she'd ask once more for the US Supreme Court to intervene. It was the same pattern she'd just gone through with Becky's case, only this time on more solid footing. Repeated appeals were par for the course with death penalty cases. It was why prisoners usually languished on death row for so many years—oftentimes decades.

Two weeks later, Dani was back before the Texas Court of Criminal Appeals. Once again, ADA Jeremy Wilson had an apologetic look in his eyes. Once again, Dani stood before the nine justices, draped in their black robes, neutral expressions on their faces. She'd barely spoken when Judge Melnick, the same female jurist who'd peppered her with questions during her last appearance on this case, asked, "Isn't it true that the National Fire Protection Association issued standards for fire investigations in 1992, well before the defendant's trial?"

"That's correct," Dani answered. "But the State Fire Marshal's office only kept one copy of that report at each regional office. It took a long time before it became widely accepted."

"Still, it was there to be discovered with diligence."

"*Black's Law Dictionary* defines due diligence as, 'such a measure of prudence, activity, or assiduity, as is properly to be expected from, and ordinarily exercised by, a reasonable and prudent man under the particular circumstances; not measured by any absolute standard but depending on the relative facts of the special case.' With respect to arson investigations, there has been an enormous difference in the understanding of what indicates arson between scientists and engineers studying fires, and those in the field investigating fires. This gap still exists today, although it's narrowing. Even with a thorough investigation, it would have been extremely difficult to discover that the indicia relied upon for generations to pinpoint arson were without scientific validity."

"Difficult, but not impossible, right?"

Dani took a deep breath. She hoped that Judge Melnick was in the minority on the bench; that the eight other jurists were not so rigid. "No, not impossible, but the reasonable man standard should be measured not by what a scientist would know and therefore pursue, but what a typical fire investigator during that time period would know, and therefore pursue."

She continued with the remainder of her argument—that the clear language of the statute mandated a new trial if expert testimony relied upon by the prosecution turned out to be flawed. When it was Wilson's turn, he built on the questions raised by Judge Melnick and hammered away at the defendant's lack of due diligence in discovering the new advances in fire science. When it was over, the confidence she'd felt when she filed her appeal had dimmed. As strong as the evidence was that no one had purposefully set the fire in Becky's house, this was Texas. One study had shown that between 1995 and 2000, the Texas Court of Criminal Appeals had granted a new trial in a capital case only eight times, while affirming the death penalty two hundred twenty times. She suspected those odds hadn't changed much in the intervening years.

When the decision arrived ten days later, Dani's fear was confirmed. The short written opinion stated, *Although we are sympathetic with defendant's plight, the statute is clear that for relief to be granted, due diligence in uncovering the flawed science at the time of the initial trial is required. Defendant failed to exercise due diligence, and for that reason her appeal is denied. The appropriate path for her now is to seek clemency.*

Dani's fear turned to anger. How was it possible for the court to be so callous? She picked up the phone and called Bruce Kantor, then railed over the phone to him about the injustice.

"You still have another chance at the Supreme Court," he said.

"Hah! They've been great, so far, haven't they?"

"Then you'll seek clemency. They can prevent her execution. Make as strong a pitch as you can."

"Can I hire another fire expert? Pile it on?" Dani knew that HIPP's budget was tight. They always found money for one expert, but hiring multiple ones was usually nixed.

"Do you have someone in mind?"

"Halstein mentioned someone to me. He's supposed to be the preeminent expert in the field."

Bruce hesitated before answering. "How much?"

"Probably double Halstein's fee."

Another hesitation, then she heard him sigh. "Go ahead. Anything we can do to stop this travesty."

Dani thanked him, then switched over to Tommy. "See what you can find out about the clemency board in Texas. Who they are, the cases where they granted clemency, what factors are most important to them. That kind of thing."

"Sure. But it sounds like a sure thing to me. It wasn't even arson."

"I just want to make certain the board sees it that way."

Promptly at 9:00 a.m. the next morning, Tommy called. "It wasn't too early, was it?" he asked. "I know you're three hours earlier there. I wasn't sure when you actually got down to work."

When she lived in New York, she usually didn't arrive in the office until 9:30, partly so she'd send Jonah off on the school bus, and partly to avoid the rush-hour traffic. When she just had to walk down the hallway to her office, she was usually at her desk by 8:30.

"It's fine. What do you have for me?"

"Nothing good, I'm afraid."

"Tell me."

"There are seven members on the board. Six men and one woman. All but one was appointed by the current governor, and all but one come from a background of law enforcement."

"That doesn't sound promising."

"The governor has to have a recommendation for clemency from the Board of Pardons and Paroles to issue a pardon. He can choose to deny clemency despite a recommendation in favor, but he can't grant it without a recommendation. Since 1976, the board has only recommended clemency in a capital case three times."

"Damn."

"It gets worse. I tracked down someone who was a prior board member. He told me that although the rules permit a hearing to consider important new evidence, in his tenure, they'd never held one."

It couldn't be as bad as Tommy said. Surely, with evidence of such a glaring error before them, they'd have to act to prevent Becky's execution. But Tommy's findings made it clear: she needed as much reinforcement as possible. As soon as she hung up, she called Stuart Halstein. She filled him in on the court losses. "I want to get a second report to the clemency board; really lock it up that this wasn't arson. You mentioned you knew a big gun in this field."

Halstein didn't hesitate. "You need Greg Berman. He's the top guy in the country. Want me to call him for you?"

"That would be helpful. There's one wrinkle.'

"What's that?"

"If the Supreme Court denies *cert*, which is likely, a new execution date will be set. The application for clemency must be received at least twenty-one days before that date. So, time is of the essence here."

"I understand. I'll let him know."

Two hours later, Halstein called back. "We're all set. He'll do it."

Doug was back on his second round of chemo and now considerably weaker. This time, Dani stayed with him. He was too fatigued to work on his laptop, even too fatigued for conversation. His once-strong body seemed caved in now. He'd lost his appetite, and when he struggled to eat despite that, he often couldn't keep the food down. There wasn't much Dani could do for him, but it made her feel better to be by his side.

She still hadn't heard from the Supreme Court, but as she checked her emails, she saw one from Greg Berman. She quickly clicked on it. Just one line: *Here's my report.* She opened the attachment and began reading.

> *I have investigated more than three hundred fires over the past twenty years, including ones whose cause was unknown and those where the cause was known, such as fires deliberately set, or from a gas leak causing an explosion, or from a wildfire. I lecture about fire dynamics internationally and have assisted federal, state, and local governments with respect to fires.*
>
> *I have reviewed the report written, and pictures taken, by Sam Miner, the fire investigator who examined the premises of Rebecca Whitlaw's home after it was consumed by fire, resulting in the deaths of three children. In addition, I've reviewed the report of Donald Hamburg, Ms. Whitlaw's so-called 'expert.' Rarely have I seen such gross incompetence and ignorance of the standards for determining arson.*

> *There is absolutely no scientific basis for conclud-*
> *ing that the Whitlaw fire was arson. The investiga-*
> *tors ignored evidence that was contrary to the use*
> *of an accelerant, seemingly had no understanding*
> *of fire dynamics or the concept of flashover, and*
> *instead based their conclusions on discredited*
> *myths. Their approach led to conclusions that were*
> *no more reliable than that of a self-proclaimed*
> *psychic.*
>
> *The investigators either willfully, or through igno-*
> *rance, violated not only the standards of today for*
> *determining arson, but those of 1998 as well.*
>
> *In my opinion, this fire was accidental.*

It was a strong letter. Coupled with Halstein's report, it would be hard for the clemency board to ignore. She pulled out her laptop and began typing an application for clemency.

Just before the end of this round of Doug's chemo, the Supreme Court decision arrived. *Cert denied.* Dani had enough experience to know that her chances were slim, yet still had held out hope. She put the finishing touches on the application for clemency and filed it. There was nothing more she could do. She'd asked for a hearing but doubted the board would grant it. Becky's life was now in the hands of six men and one woman.

The notice was waiting on Becky's bed when she returned from her work. A slim, letter-size envelope. As soon as she spotted it, she knew what it meant. A new execution date had been set. She almost considered not opening it, but then thought that her mother would want to know. She'd want to prepare herself for it. She slipped her finger under the flap and lifted it open, took out the single sheet of paper, and saw the date: April 22. That was the day she was scheduled to die unless the Board of Pardons and Paroles recommended clemency, and the governor granted it. She no longer held out hope for that reprieve.

She pulled out the box under her bed and withdrew her writing pad and a pen. Her first letter was to her mother, the second to Chuck. Those were the people she wanted to bear witness to her murder by the state. For that's what it was when an innocent person was killed—murder. And thanks to Dani, she knew she was innocent.

She was interrupted by a clanging on her cell, followed by the call of dinner. She stood up to retrieve her tray from the guard.

The woman, Stella, normally just passed it through then moved on to the next cell. Now, she lingered. "I'm sorry," she whispered to Becky.

D ani hadn't heard yet from the clemency board, and April 22 was just two weeks away. Although she'd handed off most of her caseload, she felt too jittery to not work. Poring through letters from inmates, sending out requests for DNA testing, helped calm her nerves, and so she spent a few hours each day on those tasks. When she wasn't working, she attended to Doug, whose condition had weakened considerably during his third round of chemo. Her once-robust husband looked gaunt most days. He had difficulty keeping food down and so ate very little. Every hour Dani stood over him while he drank a bottle of Boost, to make sure he got some nutrition.

Ruth was too young to understand what was happening, but not Jonah. Much as Dani and Doug tried to reassure him that this weakness and nausea was common following chemotherapy, Jonah began to retreat into himself. He stopped going over to Keith's after school, preferring instead to remain in his room.

Although Doug's parents both still worked, they took a week off and flew out to California the day after his third round of chemo was finished. Dani liked her in-laws; her own parents were both gone, and Doug's mother, Beth, had welcomed her warmly from the first time Doug took her home to meet them. His father, Ben, was more reserved, but over the years, Dani had come to appreciate that was just his nature, not a reflection of his feelings toward her.

For the first few days, they hovered over Doug, refusing to leave his side until, exhausted from their attention, Doug suggested they spend the day in San Francisco, touring. They demurred until he finally told them he needed to just curl up in his bed for the day and rest. Dani sympathized with them. Once they returned to New York, unable to see their son up close, they'd no doubt agonize daily over his condition. By the day after their outing, they'd returned to more normal interaction with the family, spending time with Jonah and Ruthie instead of jumping at every wince from Doug. They'd no doubt talked during their day's excursion and realized how enervating constant attention could be.

By the time the week was up, both Dani and Doug were sorry to see them go. "I'll FaceTime you," Dani said to Beth as she hugged her goodbye.

"Take care of him," she whispered back to Dani.

Dani just nodded.

Five days later, Dani and Doug were back at the hospital. It was time for the PET scan, the test that would tell them whether the chemotherapy had killed all the cells of the tumor. By now, they were well familiar with the hospital, its long corridors and antiseptic smell, its gift shop filled with balloons and stuffed animals, the harried look on the faces of the nurses, who never-theless always had a smile for them.

Dani had barely slept the night before. She'd tossed and turned most of the night, unable to turn off her fears over the results from today's test. If cancerous cells were still present, then his prognosis was poor, and Dani couldn't fathom that possibility.

She sat in the waiting room as Doug was led to the radiology department, where he'd undergo the scan. As she waited, eyes drooping from her lack of sleep, her thoughts drifted to her first days with Doug. They'd met over the copy machine at the US Attorney's Office for the Southern District of New York, she a fresh-out-of-law school new attorney and Doug, three years her senior. Both worked in the criminal division, but she'd been as-signed to cases of drug-trafficking organizations as well as street gangs, and he, financial and securities fraud, and so their paths hadn't crossed before.

She'd immediately been drawn into his serious, brown eyes, wavy chestnut hair, and tall, trim body. He wasn't handsome in a traditional way. His ears were a little too big, and his nose too sharp, but his chiseled features made him look distinguished, even though he wasn't yet thirty. They began dating, slowly at first—the long hours in the US Attorney's Office made it difficult to find time when they both were free. But from the beginning, their connection was strong. Dani never looked at another man once she and Doug had their first "sort of" date—a quick bite at an all-night diner when they both discovered they were leaving the office at the same time, just before midnight. He made her laugh, gave her confidence in herself, and made her feel loved. Then, and always. She couldn't bear the thought of life without him.

Ninety minutes later, Doug walked into the waiting room. "How did it go?" Dani asked.

"Fine, I suppose. We'll know more tomorrow. Day after at the latest."

The dye they'd injected into his veins for the test made him mildly radioactive for twenty-four hours; harmless for most people except pregnant or nursing women, or young children. They'd arranged for Elsa to keep Ruth overnight, and even though Jonah wasn't at risk, he was going over to Keith's after school and then, despite it being a school night, sleeping there. It had been a long time since Dani and Doug had been alone together without the children.

Each day since the end of chemo, Doug had begun to regain some strength. They left the hospital, then went to a bistro for lunch. Although Doug still couldn't eat much, he enjoyed the restaurant's soups. After they'd settled in and the waiter had taken their order, Doug said, "I want to talk to you about my life insurance."

"Stop it. I don't want to hear that."

Doug picked up her hand and began to stroke it. "You need to. In case."

Dani felt tears well up, then struggled to push them back. She refused to cry, to put that burden on her husband. "I know where our policies are."

"Those are our personal policies. A million for each of us. But I'm covered under a group policy for Stanford. It was one of the perks of being dean. Three million. It should be more than enough for you to take care of the family. Pay for colleges for the kids. Maybe even take a break from HIPP."

Before Dani could say anything, their food arrived, and a surge of relief rushed through her. She didn't want to think about money, about what she would do if Doug were gone. She glanced around the small restaurant, just ten tables, each covered with a different patterned gingham tablecloth. Most were filled with what appeared to be work colleagues, taking a break for lunch from their pressured day. A young couple held hands at one table, the woman looking longingly into the man's eyes. Were they just starting out—the beginning of a relationship, the heady rush of early passion? Or were they newlyweds, already having promised to love each other for the rest of their lives?

Thoughts of Becky popped into Dani's head. She'd expected to love Grady forever, only to have him taken from her life much too early. Then, had her children ripped away from her, unjustly imprisoned for their deaths. Dani always understood the loneliness that had torn Becky apart after Grady's death, but now she *felt* what Becky must have endured. Dani had long been deeply angered by the injustices she'd witnessed. But now, sitting across from Doug, fighting her own fears for his health, something inside her raged. She was helpless to control the course of Doug's disease, but not so with Becky. She'd make sure Becky didn't die in prison. She had to.

After lunch, she took Doug back to their house to rest, and she returned to her work. When it was close to dinnertime, she packed a picnic dinner, and they drove to Gray Whale Cove State Beach on the Pacific Coast. When they'd first arrived in California, each weekend the family had explored their new environs, traveling to San Francisco, visiting the different state parks, walking in the hills. Gray Whale Cove was Doug's favorite, with its high cliffs overlooking the pounding surf. Especially at sundown.

After they arrived, Dani set up a blanket on top of the cliff—Doug was too weak to walk down to the sandy beach—then took out the tarragon chicken she'd prepared, along with a bottle of wine. Before they ate, she nestled her body in Doug's arms, and together they watched the orange sun deepen in color as it slowly sank below the horizon. She felt at peace for the first time in months. Everything would be all right, she felt at that moment.

Two days later, the PET scan results were back. Cancer cells were still present in Doug's body.

Scott Harness took his seat at the head of the table and announced in a loud voice, "Time to get started. We've got a lot of files to get through." The five other men and one woman, all members of the Texas Board of Pardons and Paroles, had been milling about by the coffee urn and platter of cookies, chatting among themselves. They took their cups and walked over to their seats around the conference table. In front of each was a list of names on two sheets of paper and a stack of folders. Most parole requests were processed by a parole panel, consisting of one board member and two parole commissioners. They reviewed the convicts' offenses, their history, and their adjustment and behavior in prison. Sometimes they interviewed victims or their families, sometimes the offenders or others supportive of parole. For a panel to grant parole, two of the three members had to vote affirmatively.

The Board of Pardons and Paroles worked differently for certain offenses. Certain sex trafficking offenses and sexual abuse of a child required a two-thirds majority of board members to grant parole. The same was true for a recommendation for clemency to the governor. Today, the board had convened to discuss those cases. They would go through a guidelines system to assign numbers to various risk factors. These numbers would add up to a single score. The higher the score, the higher the likelihood the offender would handle parole successfully.

Once they were all seated, Harness cleared his throat. "Okay, let's start with the potential paroles first."

Six of the seven board members sitting at the table had come from law enforcement in Texas, a state revered for its tough stance on crime. They brought that background into their deliberations. A lawbreaker was always that. Someone who'd flouted the law and gotten caught and was more than likely to do so again. They went through their checklist and ticked off the boxes to see if people met the criteria for parole, but they were prison numbers, not flesh and blood human beings.

The seventh board member, Jed Olsen, had been career military, working his way up to the rank of colonel in the marines. He, too, considered himself tough on crime but with a worldlier view of human nature. He'd seen too many young punks join the marines, not to serve their country with dignity but with the sole thought of escaping a dim future. He'd watched them turn into the finest recruits he'd ever seen, noble and self-sacrificing. So, when he came across an inmate who'd accepted responsibility for his crime, who'd spent his years in prison learning to be a better person, he believed in second chances.

"Okay," said Harness. "First up is Tom Hampton." He waited as the others opened the top folder in front of them. "Next-door neighbor to then-twelve-year-old Tracy Powell; he was twenty-two. Sexually abused her over a six-month period; threatened to kill her if she ever told her parents. Convicted of Texas Penal Code Section 21.02, for which he received a sentence of twenty-five to life. This is the first time he's come up for parole."

No one spoke for a few minutes as the board members leafed through the pages in the first folder. When they all looked up, Harness continued. "No prior incarcerations, and no prior history of parole revocations. Age at first admission, twenty-two. Unemployed prior to arrest." After each statement, the board members marked a number on the top sheet in the folder. "Currently aged forty-two, no gang affiliation, took some college classes during incarceration. Disciplined three times since incarcerated, but none in past twelve years." Again, after each statement, the members marked a number. When they'd all finished, Harness said, "I've got a score of nine. Anyone have anything different?"

Each board member shook their head.

"He has an Offense Severity Ranking of High. That, with a Risk Level of High, gives him a three out of seven." A score of one meant the inmate had the greatest probability of success on the outside; a score of seven, the lowest. "Let's vote. I'll begin. Denied."

"Denied."

"Denied."

"Denied."

"Denied."

"Denied."

"Denied."

Board members weren't required to follow the guidelines matrix. Nevertheless, barring unusual circumstances, they usually did. Over the past fifteen years, only about one-third of parole applications were approved. They went through the same process with seven other inmates eligible for parole, granting it to two and denying it to the others.

When they were done, Harness said, "Just two requests for clemency today. The first is Rebecca Whitlaw." He stopped as the members opened the next folder. "Convicted twenty years ago for the arson death of her three children, all under five years old. Sentenced to death. Scheduled for execution in eight days."

"I remember that," murmured one of the board members.

"The top documents are letters from a guard on death row and several inmates," Harness said. Again, he waited for the members to read through them.

"She seems to have adjusted well in prison," Amy Seldon said. "The guard describes her as a calming influence on the other prisoners. Never any discipline issues, and one of the best workers in the braille transcription room."

"Still," John Garofano piped in. "Three toddlers were murdered. So what if she's well behaved now?"

They argued back and forth while Jed Olsen remained quiet, reading through the rest of the documents in the folder. Finally, he spoke up. "There are two reports in here from fire experts saying the fire was an accident, not arson. Both say she's actually innocent of murdering her children."

"There were two experts at her trial that were certain it was arson, one of them her own expert," Harness said.

"Yes," Olsen said. "But that was two decades ago. According to these reports, arson science has changed. They understand fire and how it acts better now."

"It's not our job to relitigate the case," Harness said. "We have to look at the nature of the crime, whether the offender is remorseful and has evolved, whether there are compelling circumstances to override a jury's decision, especially in a capital case. You know that."

"Isn't new fire science compelling enough?" Olsen rubbed the back of his neck as he made eye contact with each of the others around the table. "How can we allow someone to be killed if she's innocent?"

"She's not innocent," Garofano said. "A jury found her guilty. Multiple appeals courts agreed with their decision. So, she paid someone now to say she's not. That doesn't mean it's true. I'm not a scientist. I can't say whether these new reports deserve any more respect than the experts at her trial. There sure as heck isn't a report in here from the state's fire expert. If it was so clear-cut, why hasn't the State asked her charges to be dropped? I agree with Scott. It's not our job to go back over the evidence."

"There was a big outcry when this happened," Mike Arnoff, another board member, said. "Her trial was carried on the news channels all over the state. Three beautiful babies dead. A lot of folks remember that. They wouldn't be happy to see her get off."

"If we're not sure about these reports, then we can recommend a reprieve of execution," Olsen countered. "A life sentence instead. Isn't there enough doubt raised by these reports for that, at least?"

"Okay, enough discussion," Harness said. "Time for a vote. First question, 'Do we recommend commutation of sentence?' If the answer is no, then we'll vote on whether we recommend a reprieve of execution. We'll start with you, this time, Mike, then continue around the table. Yes or no on question one."

"No."

"No."

"Yes."

"No."

"No."

"No."

"And my answer is no." Harness said. "Second question. Reprieve of execution. Mike?"

"No."

"No."

Olsen straightened his spine. An emphatic "Yes!"

"No."

"Yes."

"Yes."

It was back to Harness. "I vote no." Two-thirds of board members had to vote affirmative for a reprieve from execution. He picked up one of the two black stampers next to him, then pressed it down on Whitlaw's file. In large red letters, it read, *Denied.*

Dani felt like a steamroller had passed over her and pressed out all the air in her body. She stared at the paper in her hand, still unbelieving the words on the page. *Application for clemency denied.* Tears streamed down her cheeks. She was usually good at maintaining professionalism, but her emotions had been running high, and so she cried at the smallest trigger. This news wasn't a small trigger.

She slumped into her chair, then dropped her head to her knees. *It can't be. It can't be.* How was it possible for six men and one woman to ignore her experts' reports? How was it possible for them to send a woman to her death even if there was just the *possibility* of actual innocence? She'd had clients before whose appeals she'd lost. Clients she'd believed were innocent, even though she'd been unable to convince the courts. Clients who were executed after she'd failed to free them.

Becky Whitlaw was different. It wasn't just Dani's belief in her innocence. Two experts had confirmed there was no crime committed. Instead, a tragic but accidental fire had sent the grieving mother to await her death.

In Texas, the governor couldn't grant clemency without a favorable recommendation from the Board of Pardons and Paroles. He could deny clemency when it was recommended, but not the reverse. The only course open to the governor was a thirty-day reprieve. She would have to push for that, then hope to get the media interested in Becky's case, maybe put pressure on the board to reconsider.

She picked herself up. It wasn't time to feel sorry for herself. She had to make some calls. First, to Becky. Then, to Tommy. Finally, to Texas Governor Connor Wilson.

Thirty minutes later, she hung up the phone with the governor's office, frustrated by their lack of urgency.

"Governor Wilson is in Washington, DC, this week, meeting with the president. He's part of a consortium of governors there," Wilson's personal assistant had explained.

"Ms. Whitlaw is scheduled to be executed in five days," Dani had said. "It's imperative that I speak to the governor before then."

"He's away, I told you. And anyway, clemency decisions are made by the Board of Pardons and Paroles. Governor Wilson can't grant one if the board doesn't recommend it."

"But he can issue a thirty-day reprieve. If this goes through, it will be a gross miscarriage of justice."

They went back and forth like that for five minutes, Dani urging the assistant to reach out to the governor in DC, and the assistant repeatedly saying Wilson was helpless to stop it. Finally, the assistant agreed to include Dani's phone number in the messages she gave the governor the next time he called in.

Next, Dani turned to her computer and did a Nexis search for every news article on Becky's case. There were hundreds— from every paper throughout the state. A mother charged with murdering her children by fire was a gold mine for reporters and newscasters. One reporter out of Fort Worth, though, seemed to have written stories about the fire, her trial, and the outcome of each appeal with a more sympathetic slant. Her name was Alison Randolph. Dani did a quick Google search and discovered that Ms. Randolph was still with the newspaper. She jotted down the phone number, then called.

After she introduced herself, Dani said, "I represent Rebecca Whitlaw."

"She's getting the needle in five days, isn't she?"

"That's what's scheduled. But she's innocent."

"You have proof?"

"It wasn't arson. The fire was an accident."

There was silence on the other end of the phone. Finally, Randolph spoke. "Talk to me."

Dani did. She told her about the new understanding of fire science, about her quest for a new trial, about the denial of clemency.

"You want me to drum up interest to put pressure on the governor, is that it?"

"Yes."

"There's not a lot of time left."

"No."

"Send me the reports. If I think they're solid, I'll push for a story on tomorrow's front page."

Dani let out her breath. It was a long shot, but at this point, she needed to try everything.

Alison Randolph had come through. The next day's *Fort Worth Star-Telegram* carried a front-page story.

REBECCA WHITLAW INNOCENT?

New reports claim that the fire that destroyed Rebecca Whitlaw's home in 1998 and killed her three children was likely the result of faulty electrical wiring and not arson. Two experts have debunked the conclusions reached by original arson investigators Sam Miner and Donald Hamburg. These reports state that new research since Whitlaw's conviction demonstrates that the factors Miner and Hamburg cited as definitive evidence of arson are merely myths handed down from generations of fire investigators. Puddle configurations, crazed glass, and "V" marks, cited at Whitlaw's trial as proof an accelerant was present at the fire, have since been proven to be present in fires where no accelerant was used.

Whitlaw was convicted of murder by arson in 1999 and sentenced to death. Her request for a new trial based on these reports was denied, and she applied for clemency. On Wednesday, the Board of Pardons and Paroles voted to deny clemency. Her execution is scheduled for 6:00 p.m. Monday, at the Texas State Penitentiary at Huntsville.

Is the State of Texas about to execute an innocent woman?

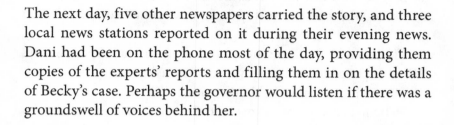

The next day, five other newspapers carried the story, and three local news stations reported on it during their evening news. Dani had been on the phone most of the day, providing them copies of the experts' reports and filling them in on the details of Becky's case. Perhaps the governor would listen if there was a groundswell of voices behind her.

Chuck Stanger called Dani as soon as he saw the article in *The Dallas Morning News*. Every morning, before heading into his office, he sat down at his kitchen table with a bran muffin and a steaming cup of black coffee and perused the paper. Many times, he'd thought about giving up his subscription—it was so easy to get the news online nowadays—but he worried about newspapers going out of business. Articles online seemed so ephemeral, there to be glanced at and then gone. It lacked the permanency of print. His father still had stored away a copy of the Dallas paper the morning after President John F. Kennedy was shot.

His heart nearly stopped when he saw the story on the third page. He immediately called Dani. "Please tell me it's not so."

She could hear the pleading in his voice.

"I'm afraid it is. The governor won't return my calls."

"And if he doesn't before Monday?"

"Then Becky will be executed."

Doug held the phone in one hand and buried his head in the other. He'd spent his career working to save lives, often against difficult odds. It was unfathomable to him how the clemency board, the governor, wouldn't do everything in their power to try to save the life of an innocent woman. He'd come to care for her, not as a lost soul, as someone who'd lost so much, but as a woman who had so much potential, who had so much left to give.

He thought for a moment, and then his head popped up. "What if I tried to call the governor?" he asked.

"Why do you think he'd take your call?"

Patient privacy laws prevented Stanger from explaining to Dani his reason. He'd operated on the governor's nephew three years ago. The boy, then five, had been born with a rare congenital heart defect, and two previous surgeries had failed to correct it. Stanger was the family's last hope, and he'd been successful. The governor had paced the waiting room with the boy's parents for the full five hours of the operation and had been effusive with his thanks when Stanger entered the room and told the parents it had gone well. "You ever need anything, if I'm still in office, just call me," he'd said at the time.

"I've met him before. I believe he'll remember me."

"Go ahead and try. I'll take any help at this point."

⁓

As soon as Stanger hung up, he dialed Amy Hunter, Governor Wilson's sister, the mother of the child whose life he'd saved, and asked for her brother's cell phone number.

"Why do you need it?" Amy asked.

"It's a personal matter. Your brother offered to help me if I ever needed something. I'd rather go into it with him, if you don't mind."

Amy hesitated, then rattled off the number. "This is just for your use. Don't give it to anyone else."

"Of course not. And thank you."

Governor Wilson answered on the fourth ring.

"This is Dr. Stanger. I operated on your nephew, Joseph. Do you remember me?"

"Of course, I do. None of us will ever forget you. Are you calling because you need something from me?"

Right to the point, Stanger thought. "There's a report on your desk from the clemency board. On Rebecca Whitlaw. They denied her petition."

"The woman who killed her children in a fire, right?"

"She didn't kill them. The fire was an accident. Arson science has improved over the last decades. The investigators back then were wrong."

"What's your connection to her?"

"She was a stranger to me until I became involved in an organization that encouraged people to write to inmates on death row. I chose her. At first, it was just letters, but then I met her and came away convinced she was innocent. Now, two renowned fire investigators have confirmed that."

"Then why did the clemency board deny her petition?"

"I don't know. It makes no sense to me."

"So, you're asking me to look into it." It was a statement, not a question.

"Yes."

"No promises, but I'll make a call."

Stanger let out the breath he was holding. "Thank you, Governor. Thank you."

"Who was that?" Wilson's wife asked when he hung up.

"Remember that surgeon who saved Joey?"

"Of course. What did he want?"

"Wants me to intervene with the clemency board's decision on Rebecca Whitlaw, the woman whose kids died in a fire."

"You going to?"

He picked up his coffee and took a sip. They were sitting in the coffee shop of the Four Seasons Hotel, in Washington, DC. His wife had joined him for the governors' junket and done some shopping while he and the others had their official meetings. "I don't know. I want to get briefed on what's gone on with her and the courts before I decide. I'll ask Justin to look into it."

"You have an election coming up in November. Freeing a woman who killed her children won't make you very popular."

"Even if she's innocent?"

"If she's innocent, why haven't the courts freed her?"

Wilson patted his wife's hand. "Don't worry dear. I won't do anything foolish."

By Saturday, Becky's story had blown up on social media, with comments running ten to one in support of her. Yet Dani still hadn't heard back from Governor Wilson. She knew he was back from the nation's capital, but every phone call to his office was met with apologies from his assistant.

"Yes, he got your message."

"No, he isn't available right now."

"I'm sorry, but the governor is tied up. He certainly understands the urgency."

And, finally, "The governor has asked me to inform you that he will abide by the decision of the Board of Pardons and Paroles."

Becky was awakened at 4:00 a.m., the same as every other day. A tray of breakfast food was shoved through the slot in her prison door, the same as every other day. Later, the same as every other day, a tray of lunch food was brought to her cell.

But today, she did not head off to the braille room after breakfast, then again after lunch. Instead, she waited for the two guards to order her to slip her hands through the opening so that handcuffs could be placed around her wrists. When they were snapped in place, the door opened, and a chain was run down the handcuffs to ankle cuffs, which a guard placed around her feet, then snapped closed. She was escorted by two guards down the prison hallways, then out a side door, where three prison trucks waited. She walked up the steps and into the opened back door of the middle vehicle, then took a seat.

She was alone, the only prisoner on death row being transported by a three-vehicle caravan to the Huntsville Unit where, at approximately 6:00 p.m., she would be given a lethal injection.

When she arrived, she was processed and led to a small cell, steps away from the execution chamber. She settled onto the small chair and waited. There were no more tears left; she'd cried them out over the past two days. Chuck had visited when he'd heard the news, and they'd cried together. Then, yesterday, her mother came to see her for the last time before she would watch her daughter die. They, too, cried together. Now her eyes were dry, but she couldn't stop the shaking of her hands, the tapping of her foot, up and down, up and down. She wrapped her hands around her body, trying to still them, but it just made her whole body shiver.

She didn't know how long she'd been sitting there when the door opened and a chaplain stepped inside, a bible in his hands.

"My name is Jonas Weldon," he said. "I'm the prison chaplain. Is it okay if I sit and talk to you?"

Becky nodded silently. She stood up and moved over to the small cot, so that Reverend Weldon could have the chair. He was an older man, perhaps in his sixties, dressed casually in beige chinos and a short-sleeved, navy-striped shirt, open at the collar. He had fine lines around his eyes, and a serious expression on his face.

"Is there anything you'd like to tell me?"

Becky looked at him. "If it's a confession you're looking for, I can't give you that. I didn't start a fire. I didn't kill my children."

He was silent for a moment before saying, his voice barely a whisper, "I know."

The tears Becky thought had been gone suddenly sprang up, and she wiped them away from her cheeks.

"I've read the newspapers. I've seen the new fire reports."

A plaintive wail arose from deep in Becky's chest. "Why? Why are they doing this to me?"

"I don't know. I only know that God must have a plan for you."

Becky turned away from him. She wished she shared his belief in the Almighty, but she'd given up after her husband had died so senselessly, after her three children had perished so painfully, after she'd spent decades punished for a crime she didn't commit.

"We can't always understand God's plan. But, when this is over, you will be reunited with your husband and your children. Hold on to that."

Once, that thought would have been enough. Now, the injustice of what was coming filled her with rage.

When Dani arrived at the Huntsville Unit, hordes of protestors were assembled outside the gates, most carrying signs protesting the upcoming execution of Rebecca Whitlaw. Pursuant to the rules of the Texas Department of Criminal Justice, only five relatives or friends of Becky were permitted to view her execution. She would have just three—her mother, Chuck Stanger, and Dani. Up to six family and close friends of the victims were permitted, seated in a room separated from the prisoner's family. There would be no one there. Five members of the media were allowed inside. The Associated Press, United Press International, and *The Huntsville Item* were guaranteed spots. Dani knew that Alison Randolph from the *Fort Worth-Star Telegram* had gotten a seat.

Dani had called the governor's office once again before leaving her home that morning. Normally, she would have gone the night before and spent as much of the day as permitted with Becky, but she hadn't wanted to leave Doug alone. Elsa had agreed to stay late, and Dani would return on an evening flight.

Once again, the governor had dodged her call. Last night, she'd arranged for copies of the fire experts' reports to be hand delivered to the governor's mansion today, and she continued to hold out the slimmest of hope that he would read those reports and grant a thirty-day reprieve. Anything could happen in thirty days.

After being processed at the prison, Dani was led to a small room where she awaited Becky. Ten minutes later, Becky was led in. Her prison clothes hung from her gaunt frame—she looked like she'd lost at least ten pounds since Dani had last seen her. Puffy pouches were under her eyes, and her nails were bitten down. Dani placed her hands over Becky's. "I'm so sorry."

"I know."

"Is there anything you'd like me to do for you? Anyone you'd like me to give a message to?"

Becky shook her head, then after a few moments, said, "I don't understand. I didn't set the fire. Nobody did. Why are they doing this to me?"

Dani wished she had the answer. Although the court had ruled that the new reports didn't justify a new trial for Becky, the ruling hadn't been on the merits of her case but on a technicality in the law. When the clemency board reviewed the case, all they would know is that Becky's petition—with the evidence that it wasn't arson before the judge—had been denied. Without a court's ruling of actual innocence, the board was powerless to find Becky innocent. Not that they would have. The board rarely recommended clemency to a capital defendant, and the one time it did in the past decade was when the victim pleaded for it. The governor, up for reelection in November, had run on a tough-on-crime platform. Without the backing of the board, he was unlikely to go out on a limb for a high-profile prisoner. It was the domino effect—once the judge had denied a new trial, the pieces of justice for Becky kept falling away.

The guard standing outside knocked once on the door, then opened it. "Time to go," he said.

Becky stood. Dani hugged her. "The world knows you're innocent," Dani whispered in her ear.

If only that were enough.

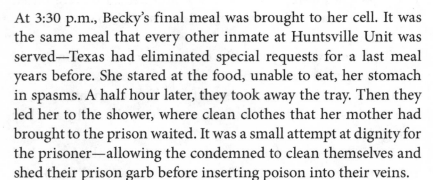

At 3:30 p.m., Becky's final meal was brought to her cell. It was the same meal that every other inmate at Huntsville Unit was served—Texas had eliminated special requests for a last meal years before. She stared at the food, unable to eat, her stomach in spasms. A half hour later, they took away the tray. Then they led her to the shower, where clean clothes that her mother had brought to the prison waited. It was a small attempt at dignity for the prisoner—allowing the condemned to clean themselves and shed their prison garb before inserting poison into their veins.

When she was back in her holding cell, the chaplain returned. "Would you like me to wait with you?" he asked.

Becky nodded. She didn't want to be alone with her fears. He asked if she'd like to pray, and she said no. He asked if she'd like to talk, and she said no. And so, together they sat in silence, waiting for six o'clock.

At 5:53 p.m., Becky was led into the execution chamber, her head hung low. She was brought to the gurney and lay down. Two guards secured her in the gurney, and then a third person inserted a catheter into a vein in her arm, with a tube that was fed through the wall to a separate room. A saline solution started into the vein. She was now ready for the lethal injection.

At 5:59 p.m., Dani, Becky's mother, Sarabeth, and Chuck Stanger, along with the media representatives, assembled in the lounge next to the viewing room. A few minutes after six, the door to that room unlocked, and they moved inside. Although a familiar sight to Dani, it nevertheless unnerved her each time she stepped inside such a room. Sarabeth clung to Dani's arms, and when she saw Becky lying on the gurney through the glass window, broke out in sobs.

"My baby, my baby," she wailed.

Dani led her to a seat in the back row. She'd learned from experience not to sit in the closest row to the execution chamber. She kept glancing at the large clock on the wall inside the chamber and the phone just below it, hoping against hope that it would ring; that Governor Wilson would stop this perversion of justice. It remained silent.

The prison warden stood over Becky and asked if she'd like to make a last statement.

Becky nodded and began to speak, her voice amplified by the microphone that carried her words into the glassed-in viewing room. "For many years, I blamed myself for the death of my children, and I wanted to die. I believed that I deserved to die. And maybe part of me is responsible. If I hadn't had so much to drink the night before, maybe I would have awakened earlier. Maybe I would have been able to reach my children's room before it was too late. Even now, I don't know the answer to that. But Chuck, you allowed me to forgive myself, and for that I am so grateful. You made me want to live, although I had no hope I would. Until you found Dani Trumball. Dani, your fight for me gave me hope. More than hope, you proved to me, if not to the courts or to the clemency board, that I wasn't responsible for the fire that killed my children. That no one had set that fire. For that, there aren't enough words to express how thankful I am. And finally, Mom, you always believed in me, even when I didn't believe in myself. You always loved me, even when I didn't love myself. And, because I know the excruciating pain a mother feels when her child dies, especially when that death is senseless beyond words, I know how much pain you are in right now. So, these, my very last words, are to you, my dear mother. I hope they will provide some comfort for you. I am at peace. I accept what is about to happen. And I love you so very, very much."

When she finished, the warden nodded. A man on the other side of the wall, invisible to the viewing gallery, picked up a syringe from a nearby tray, inserted the syringe into the catheter, and squeezed. Dani watched as Becky's eyes slowly closed. Five minutes later, she was pronounced dead.

THREE MONTHS LATER

Dani stood on top of the cliff at Gray Whale Cove State Park, Ruth's hand held tightly in hers, Jonah standing by her side. "Over here," she said, walking to a spot where the sand beach had disappeared, and the foaming waves crashed up against the gray rocks.

A taxi waited for them in the parking lot. Gracie, ensconced in a cat carrier, was settled in the back seat. They were headed back to New York. It had taken months, but the renovations on their Stanford home had been finished, and a buyer found. A woman who'd accepted the position of dean of Stanford Law, and her fiancé, starting a new job at one of the tech giants in the valley, had purchased it. They hoped to start a family in the next year or two, and that made Dani happy. The house was too big for just two people. It needed the sound of children's laughter.

Dani's furniture and possessions had been packed up over the past week and this morning loaded onto a truck that would drive it back to New York. Another truck had taken her car. Their old home had been sold, so they couldn't return to it, but Dani had found another one in Bronxville, just a few blocks away.

Before heading to the airport, she had to stop here first to say goodbye. It had been Doug's favorite spot on the West Coast.

"You ready?" she asked Jonah.

"Are you certain we should do this?"

"Yes."

"But then Daddy will be in California, and we'll be in New York."

"It's what Daddy wants. And besides, Daddy will always be with us. He's in our hearts."

Jonah nodded, then twisted open the lid of the urn he held in his hands. "Do it with me," he said to Dani.

She let go of Ruth's hand and placed hers on the jar, and together, she and Jonah tossed Doug's ashes into the surf below, both with tears running down their cheeks as Ruth looked on with the innocence of a child who didn't yet understand how drastically her world had changed.

They walked back to the taxi in silence and took their seats. Dani had grown to like Stanford, and she would miss Lauren and Gregory, but New York was home. HIPP was her family. It was where she belonged.

AUTHOR'S NOTE

Although *Burning Justice* is fiction, it was inspired by the real case of Cameron Todd Willingham. In 1991, Willingham's Texas house went up in flames, killing his three children—one-year-old twins and a two-year-old daughter. His wife had been at work at the time. Fire investigators ruled arson, based on evidence of crazed glass, burn trails, puddle configurations, and the like, which they said could occur only from the use of an accelerant, and Willingham was arrested, convicted, and sentenced to death.

In 2004, a renowned scientist and fire investigator looked into his case and concluded that there was little doubt the fire that killed Willingham's children was accidental. Despite his report, which described the advances in fire investigation since 1991, the Texas Board of Pardons and Paroles denied his application for clemency, and he was executed.

For an excellent article on the Willingham case, read, "Trial by Fire: Did Texas Execute an Innocent Man?" by David Grann, published in *The New Yorker* on September 9, 2007. Also, read "Former Texas Prosecutor Probably Sent Innocent Man to His Death. Now He's On Trial for Misconduct," by Jordan Smith, published in *The Intercept* on May 2, 2017.

In April 2011, the *Report of The Texas Forensic Science Commission, Willingham/Willis Investigation,* was issued. The commissioners were especially disturbed by the perceived gap in the understanding of fire dynamics between scientists and fire investigators. They recommended numerous steps be undertaken to improve training of fire investigators and in the creation of reports.

I have taken liberties with the timeline for *Burning Justice*. Because the Texas Forensic Science Commission report was published in 2011, I'd like to think that by 2019, both courts and clemency boards would have been more sensitive to Becky's situation. (However, that may be wishful thinking on my part.)

Finally, although the Mountain View Unit does train and certify its inmates to transcribe braille, and death row women are permitted to work, they cannot work in the braille unit. They do crochet blankets.

ACKNOWLEDGEMENTS

Typing 'The End' at the completion of a manuscript is just the first step in getting a book ready for readers. I'm enormously grateful to David Downing, my developmental editor, and Valerie Kufrin, my copy editor, for their insights that helped me deliver a more polished story.

Thanks also to Robert Hurst, Communications Officer at the Texas Department of Criminal Justice, for his information on the details of life on death row at the Mountain View Unit. Any mistakes in the story about those details are purely my own.

Finally, I thank my family – my strongest advocate and always amazing husband, Lenny, my sons Jason and Andy; their wives, Amanda and Jackie; and my beautiful grandchildren, Rachel, Joshua, Jacob, Sienna and Noah – for their love and support.

ABOUT THE AUTHOR

Marti Green is the award-winning and Amazon best-selling author of the Innocent Prisoners Project series and the stand-alone psychological thriller *The Good Twin*.

Although she initially received a Master of Science degree in school psychology, she quickly realized her true passion was the law. After obtaining a law degree from Hofstra University, Green worked for twenty-three years as in-house counsel for a major cable television network.

A lifelong New Yorker, she now lives in Florida with her husband, Lenny, and cat, Misha. Her family includes two sons, two daughters-in-law, and five grandchildren. When she's not writing, Green enjoys hiking, traveling, and reading.

CPSIA information can be obtained
at www.ICGtesting.com
Printed in the USA
LVHW091517280420
654675LV00002B/591